FIND HIM WHERE
YOU LEFT HIM DEAD

FIND HIM WHERE YOU LEFT HIM DEAD

KRISTEN SIMMONS

TOR PUBLISHING GROUP

NEW YORK

FIND HIM WHERE YOU LEFT HIM DEAD

Copyright © 2023 by Kristen Simmons

A Tor Teen Book
Published by Tom Doherty Associates / Tor Publishing Group
120 Broadway
New York, NY 10271

www.tor-forge.com

Tor® is a registered trademark of Macmillan Publishing Group, LLC.

The Library of Congress Cataloging-in-Publication Data is available upon request.

ISBN 978-1-250-85112-3 (hardcover)
ISBN 978-1-250-85115-4 (ebook)

Our books may be purchased in bulk for promotional, educational, or business use. Please contact your local bookseller or the Macmillan Corporate and Premium Sales Department at 1-800-221-7945, extension 5442, or by email at MacmillanSpecialMarkets@macmillan.com.

First Edition: 2023

Printed in the United States of America

0 9 8 7 6 5 4 3 2 1

AUTHOR'S NOTE

This story takes place in a world of monsters. Please be aware that there is blood, gore, death, abandonment, and grief in these pages. It's a book about finding courage, trusting, healing, and fighting to make your way home, together.

FIND HIM WHERE
YOU LEFT HIM DEAD

MADELINE

Madeline swam toward the light like her life depended on it.

She tucked her knees to her chest and rolled through the final turn of her 100-meter butterfly sprint. A hard kick off the wall and she was flying, both arms cutting through the cool water in tandem. One stroke, one breath. One stroke, one breath. The pattern was grueling. Comforting. A structured dance of strength and coordination.

One stroke, one breath.

She pulled her chin to her chest as she stretched her body, eyes dropping to the straight black line on the bottom of the pool marking her lane.

With a blink, the line softened. Spread. Black bled across the bottom of the pool, forming the shape of a cave. Its jagged entrance widened, the water shifting to pull her down.

She flinched out of position. Her right hand scraped against the plastic ring of a floating lane line, snapping her attention to the surface. When she looked back down the cave was gone and only a clean, dark stripe remained.

Focus.

She pushed her muscles to the brink of failure, and with one last burst of effort she jammed her fingers against a touchpad. Her time froze in bright red: 1.02 minutes.

Pathetic.

Gulping breaths, she pulled off her goggles and threw them onto the cement deck next to her keys and the pool entry card Coach K had given her after she'd won regionals sophomore year. She'd been fifteen then, two years younger and weaker than she was now, but pulling faster times.

Her legs pedaled slowly through the water as she gasped for breath. The blue surface of the pool glowed against her brown skin, the only light coming from the locker room behind the starting blocks above her. Sweat and chlorine brought a familiar sting to her eyes. She prodded her braids beneath her cap. Then, tilting her head back to stare up at the white backstroke flags, she floated until her pulse slowed.

The sickness inside her didn't settle.

One more. One more 100-meter, and she'd be too worn out to feel it. Then she'd be able to drag herself home, to lie in bed without seeing the cave behind her eyelids, and sleep.

Movement on the opposite side of the pool caught her eye. She twisted toward it, but the light from the nearby locker room only reached halfway across the water. The pool seemed to go on endlessly into a long, dark night.

"Hello?" she called. It was after nine. No one else should have been here. Even the janitors had left hours ago.

She squinted, but saw nothing.

Another shift in the shadows, and a boy stood at the far end of the pool.

Madeline bit back a scream.

"Who's there?"

No answer.

The paleness of the boy's skin was bright against his dark shorts. He was soaked, dripping, his face obscured by wet, black hair. The dim light made him look grainy, like an old photograph.

"The pool's closed," Madeline tried. "You shouldn't be here." Certain privileges came with being the best, and they weren't extended to everyone.

"You shouldn't be here," the boy repeated.

"This isn't funny." She hated the rising pitch of her voice. Her teammates were just trying to scare her. This was just a prank, like how they'd replaced her racing suit in her bag with a pink string bikini at the holiday invitational and she'd nearly missed the first heat, or the time they'd written "blow Coach K" on her weekly training schedule.

But it didn't feel like a prank. Adrenaline poured through her veins.

The boy stared at the water, frozen. Statue still. The steam from the pool rose around his sharply cut shins and calves. His chest was so pale it took on a reflection of the water, glowing a light blue.

"Fine," Madeline said, her voice hollow. She twisted and placed her hands on the side of the pool, ready to push herself out.

"Maddy."

Madeline's stomach filled with lead. She turned back slowly, squinting through the steam, to see the boy step to the edge of the pool. His gait was strange—his legs and arms bent like he had too many joints.

Cold filled her. Even in the dim light she registered his concave chest and rib lines. He was too skinny to be a swimmer. Skin and bone.

"Maddy," the boy said, louder now. "Maddy."

Her fingers gripped the gritty cement of the deck.

"Mad—"

"Stop!" She needed to get out—to run. Instead, she sank deeper into the water, as if it might protect her.

"Why'd you do it?" he asked. "Why'd you leave me in the dark?"

Her lips parted on a sharp inhale. "Ian?"

Impossible. Ian was dead.

But when she looked at the boy on the edge of the pool, she saw him. His long limbs, his mess of dark hair. His memory took shape before her. Wild-eyed. Forever thirteen.

"Ian," he repeated, and then he gave a shrill laugh that cut off as quickly as it had started. "By dawn, there will be no more Ian."

"No." She shook her head. Ian was dead. This was a prank. A hallucination. Maybe she was dreaming. Another nightmare.

Dizziness had her hand slipping off the side of the pool. She fixed her grip.

This wasn't real.

"Finish the game," the boy who couldn't be Ian said.

She shook her head, water sluicing from her cap as she tried to push the images he'd conjured back into the locked box in her brain. Cards, painted with symbols they'd acted out like charades. The cave, punched into the riverside. The moments before the end, when everything had felt right.

"You're not real," she whispered. She knew what today was. She'd felt it coming all week, a storm on the horizon. The brain did strange things in response to the anniversary of trauma. A coping mechanism—that's what this was.

A splash. The boy went under, the water flattening instantly over him. Not a ripple moved the glassy surface.

Terror jolted through Madeline. She pushed out of the pool and spun, peering down into the water. No one swam beneath the surface. No dark shapes. No waves or bubbles.

Ian wasn't in the pool. Ian wasn't there at all.

A breath huffed from her lips. She didn't notice that the humid air had begun to cool until goose bumps covered her arms and legs, and her shuddering breath made a puff of steam.

At the far end of the pool, the water began churning in a spiral motion, as if it were being drained. Then something at the bottom bolted toward her, its wake rippling the surface like an accusing arrow.

She scrambled back, just barely grabbing her keys, and ran.

EMERSON

Emerson was going to beat level twenty-one if it killed her.

She was on hour thirteen in the shadowlands of *Assassin 0*, her favorite metal album playing on a loop through her computer's speakers. She'd finally beaten the fire sorcerer and narrowly avoided the Choke—a poisonous cloud that grew with every player it consumed—and was now in a race against a three-legged orc called N00bki11er87 (Had they made up that handle themselves? Must have taken hours . . .) to get the final poison stone at the top of the twisted tower.

A clatter erupted in her right earpiece and she flinched reactively. Spinning the viewfinder, she caught a flash of a smooth snakeskin head ducking behind the crumbled brick of an arrow slit.

"Nice try." Emerson activated her weapon wheel and swapped her wrench for her flamethrower. Her loadout had a throwing knife that worked well against orcs, but she liked to watch things burn. Before she could use it, N00bki11er87 leapt out, peppering the room with arrows from their crossbow.

"Shit!" Emerson dropped her soldier to the floor and sent a spray of fire across the room. The orc went up in flames.

And that was why you didn't bring a crossbow to a flame-thrower fight.

She hardly had a moment to celebrate. Within seconds, the mossy avatar started decomposing into the Choke's green mist. Urgency pumped through Emerson's blood in time with the bass straining through her shitty speakers. Her player climbed the spiral stone stairs two at a time. At the top floor she flung the door open, but the dark room before her was overrun by a wave of thick, emerald fog, and with a gasp she pedaled backward.

"Are you seriously going to let her stay in there?" Her mom's voice cut through the music and the heavy sigh of the Choke, drawing Emerson's shoulder blades together. Their two-story condo was narrow and, with the original wood flooring, sound travelled. She was probably in the kitchen, just below Emerson's bedroom.

"What do you want me to do, Hannah?" Her dad sounded tired. He was always tired.

She reached toward her keyboard, covered with greasy fingerprints and chip crumbs, and tried to crank up the album's volume, but it was already maxed out.

"She won't eat any real food. She won't even look at me," her mom railed on as a second moan came from behind Emerson. She spun her viewfinder, focusing on the fog creeping around the turn in the steps.

"No no no no no." Emerson pounded the controller as she twisted past it, leaping down the stairs to the landing. This was her last chance to get the poison stone.

"Is this how it is now?" her mom asked. "She comes and goes as she pleases. Doesn't even go to school?"

"She said she'd take the GED."

"She said that *last year*."

Emerson gritted her teeth.

The distraction cost her. The mist shifted, surrounding her on a rugged exhale. She couldn't jump free—her avatar began to writhe and screech, and her health on the bottom corner of the screen plummeted.

Before Emerson could take another breath, the bloodred letters FARE THEE WELL, ASSASSIN splattered across the screen.

"Dammit!" She hurled the controller onto her desk, where it collided with a half-empty box of Corn Pops. Her head fell against the back of the chair, neck aching from staring at the screen. Her fingers had locked more than a dozen times in the last hour alone.

She ran a hand over her freshly buzzed hair, the soft prickle tickling her palm. The clock in the corner of her monitor read 10:43 PM.

Maybe she should restart.

Maybe she should eat something first.

She stood and stretched, the reflection of her white skin ghostly as her tired eyes stared back from the window over her desk. She peered through her own image, to the drawn curtains of the apartments across Foxtail Avenue, then two blocks down to the left, where, at Washington Park, heavily armed cops were trying to intimidate another wave of peaceful protesters. People like her dad, who actually thought their speeches and marching made a difference in a good old boys' town like Cincinnati. To the left, a yellow glow came from the late-night coffee shop on the corner. It had been good once, before gentrification had priced out the old owners. Now it was filled with hipsters, drinking eight dollars' worth of coffee-flavored milk.

"Don't you have anything better to do?" she muttered as if they could hear.

The monitor blinked RESTART?

A headache brewed at the base of her skull. She leaned over her desk to close the blinds.

With a sigh she looked around her room. It was bad, even by her standards. Empty bottles of energy shots littered the floor around her trash can. A half-eaten candy bar sat on her nightstand beside a stack of gaming magazines and her phone.

As she sat back down, something caught her eye on the monitor screen. A reflection from behind her.

She spun her chair, and her stomach dropped.

Across the room, a person stood in the full-length mirror. A boy so thin his gray skin looked like it had been painted on. His ankles and wrists were sharp, his fingers skeletal. He wore tattered, dripping clothes, like a shipwreck survivor, and his dark hair was tangled and missing chunks.

Emerson froze in her chair, her heart punching her ribs in a crashing, panicked rhythm as she forced herself to look him in the face.

His teeth were pointed, filed down to small gleaming spears that punctured his lips. Blood wept from his mouth.

His eyes were blank, pupilless and gray.

Panic surged through her. She shoved back in her chair. The arm caught the corner of her desk and tipped to dump her onto the floor. The drum solo on track nine of the metal album slammed in her temples. She opened her mouth to scream, but no sound came out.

The boy in the mirror craned his head toward her, watching her with his unseeing eyes.

This wasn't real.

It couldn't be real.

"Ian?" she whispered.

The mirror cracked. Emerson flinched as the boy started clawing at the surface, as if he were trapped behind the glass. His jagged nails broke as he scraped the backside of the mirror. He bit at it like an animal, smearing blood across his chin.

She shoved sideways across the floor, her socks sliding on the wood. She collided with the nightstand, knocking her phone and the magazines to the ground.

"No way," she whispered.

Ian scratched harder, faster. Rabid and caged. He kicked at the glass until his feet began to bleed like his mouth. His fingers broke, sticking out at odd angles.

She was delirious. She'd been playing *Assassin 0* too long. She wasn't hydrated. She hadn't eaten enough.

None of the explanations made Ian stop.

She pressed herself against the nightstand, curling into a ball. Her arms squeezed around her knees. Fear unfurled in her chest, cold and sharp. She squeezed her eyes shut.

Then the music stopped.

Her ears rang in the sudden silence. Her skin prickled.

When she opened her eyes, her own reflection stared back from the mirror. Her chest was rising fast with hard breaths, her pale skin damp with sweat. Her bottom lip was white on the side where she'd bitten her lip ring.

"Hello?"

Silence.

Seconds turned into minutes.

Slowly, she rose on weak knees, snatching her phone off the floor. Holding it like a shield. She stepped closer to the mirror, but there was nothing out of the ordinary about it. No crack, no blood. Only smeared lines, made by a dirty finger: "dawn."

She shook her head.

Just random prints and smears. Not letters. Not a word.

She scrubbed the marks away quickly with her sleeve, but they turned red under the pressure, spreading like blood.

She jerked back but her sleeves were clean.

Her breath came out in a shudder.

With shaking hands, she dialed a number she hadn't called in four years.

DAX

Dax strummed his guitar, calloused fingers on worn metal strings. Laughter accented the chatter around him. The scent of dark roast permeated the air. As he switched chords, the barista—a scruffy lumberjack with poetry tattooed on his forearms—passed a wide-brimmed mug to the woman across the counter, a heart drawn in the foam.

"I wanna dance with somebody," Dax sang, playing an intricate run over the hiss of the steamer. "I wanna feel the heat with somebody."

The customer looked up at the barista and blushed. Romance at the goddamn coffee shop. That's why he loved this place. That, and the mismatched chandeliers.

On her way back to her table, the customer glanced back at the counter, and nearly stepped in Dax's guitar case.

"Free falling," he sang, switching to a familiar chorus. "Now I'm free . . ."

She was too smitten to notice.

"I'm a bad boy for breaking her heart."

The words cooled inside of him.

He flattened his scarred palm over the strings, feeling the familiar vibrations echo inside his chest. With a gentle hand, he cupped the neck of the instrument, and laid it into the case at his feet. Then he went to the counter.

"Can I get some water?" he asked the barista. Despite the warmth of the room, a blast of cold air from the door clawed under his leather jacket. He shrugged deeper into it with a shiver. The barista set a fingerprinted glass on the counter, but his focus was too consumed by the woman across the room to fill it in the small metal sink.

With a sigh, Dax reached over the bar, and did it himself. Who was he to interrupt the start of their beautiful rom-com? *A Whole Latte of Love*, it'd be called. Or *The Perfect Blend*.

Dax downed the water in one gulp, but it barely soothed his dry throat. Grabbing his guitar, he made for a swinging door marked by a tin sign that said TOILET. The case seemed heavier than usual, but maybe he was just tired. He'd been playing for hours.

He locked the bathroom door behind him and set his guitar case against the wall. At the sink, he splashed cold water on his face. Maybe girls would notice him if he had scruff and tattoos. Muscles, instead of his angular frame. At least he had a tan, though that was more from his dad's unknown roots than the sun.

He grabbed the toothbrush in a ratty bag from his guitar case.

Forget the handshake, his mom whispered from the past. *First impressions are made with a smile.*

He didn't even know where she lived now.

A creaking sound came from behind him, and he paused mid-brushing. He turned to see the tarnished pipes over the toilet lurch, peppering the air with a spray of drywall dust as something big passed through them.

His pulse kicked up.

A hand emerged from the toilet bowl, black as tar and glistening wet. It gripped the faded yellow seat, then rolled outward, a wrist and a rubbery, boneless forearm following. Another hand, grasping blindly upward, then winding its spindly grip around the silver flushing rod.

Dax brushed faster.

"Aka ka, ao ka, dochira ni shimasu ka?" a terrible, crackling voice whispered as a head of matted hair rose from the water. The face was wet and glistening, eyes and lips and cheeks painted ink black. Shoulders, folded in on themselves, unfurled as the creature pulled itself from the toilet, inch by dreadful inch.

"Aka ka, ao ka, dochira ni shimasu ka?" it groaned again.

Dax spit out his toothpaste and rinsed his mouth. "Let me guess, Aka Manto. Red or blue?"

Behind him, one sopping leg extended to the tile floor. The rest of the body stretched like a dead spider coming back to life, and soon was human in shape. A man draped in midnight.

Dax was tall, but Aka Manto towered over him.

"Red . . ." Aka Manto hissed. "Or blue."

Dax carefully tucked his toothbrush into the bag, then tossed it into his guitar case. "What is it with you and bathrooms? Find yourself a nice park fountain to haunt. Or a waterfall. Wouldn't that be nice?"

Aka Manto stepped forward, quick enough that Dax spun and cracked his thigh against the porcelain sink.

"Easy, pal," Dax cautioned, wincing.

A tiny cut, a strange voice buzzed in Dax's head, pressured, and high like a mosquito. *That's all it would take. The right artery and it all comes out like a fountain. Red, red, red.*

Dax grimaced. Adrenaline readied his muscles. He reached into his pocket, hand curling around the small folding knife he kept there.

No more air, the same small, greedy voice whispered. *One cell dies, and then another, and then another, and you are blue and dead and gone.*

"Aka ka, ao ka, dochira ni shimasu ka?" Aka Manto said aloud.

"That's all we talk about anymore." Dax continued as Aka Manto tilted its greasy, faceless head. "You never ask how I'm doing. How the set went. I've got new songs, you know. You might like one or two of them."

This was the longest conversation he'd had in a week.

Aka Manto lunged for Dax, but Dax leapt out of the way, ripping the knife from his pocket and flicking it up in a practiced move. His throat tightened as Aka Manto's dark mouth opened, revealing a glimmering row of sharp, onyx teeth.

"That's right," Dax said in a warning tone. "You can turn around and go back where you came from, or we can do this the hard way."

Aka Manto laughed, a sound that filled the room like a flood of frigid water.

"It's time to come with me. There is only one way. Red . . ."

"Or blue, right, right." Dax snorted. "Thanks, but I'll pass."

"It is not a request." Before him, Aka Manto grew, his arms unfolding into another joint. His neck dripping oil like candlewax down his body. "The others already gather."

"I'm sure they do."

"The Foxtail Five." Aka Manto gagged on the words.

Dax went still. "What did you say?"

Aka Manto smiled, a curving black hole. He slid closer, until Dax was pressed into the sink. "The Foxtail—"

Flipping the small knife over in his hand, Dax jammed it into the ghost's neck. It slid through the skin like wet cement, the wound spurting black ink.

Aka Manto screamed loud enough to make Dax's bones shake. The creature retreated in a flurry, hurling back toward the toilet, where it compressed into the bowl with a violent hiss.

Shuddering out a breath, Dax wiped the knife clean on a paper towel, then shoved it in his pocket and leaned against the back of the door. He gave himself five seconds to stop shaking. Then he closed his guitar case and walked out of the bathroom, past the barista and the blushing woman and the hope that maybe, one day, he'd have that too, and into the cold night.

It was time to pay some old friends a visit.

OWEN

Owen balanced on a tree limb of metal piping and papier-mâché, green eye shadow glittering behind his thick framed glasses, faux fur vest clinging to his lean chest. He grinned cleverly down at Mike Tran—tonight's Lysander—as he chased a very annoyed Helena across the stage, before tossing a cocky grin to the fairy king in the tree beside him.

"Captain of our fairy band," he said loudly, with a hint of a British accent the Traverse student paper had reviewed as "believable and smoking hot" after opening night last weekend. "Helena is here at hand. And the youth mistook by me, pleading for a *lover's fee*." He leaned a little extra on the words this time, and Dante Salvaro—their lead Oberon—gave a breathy, not at all kingly, laugh.

Interesting, Owen thought, and tucked that information away for later.

The pipe digging into the arch of his feet, he leaned over a bushel of plastic leaves, careful to keep his right arm flexed to showcase the cut of his deltoid as he pointed down at Hermia. She sent him a raised brow and slid her shimmering gown a little lower down her pale shoulder.

He tucked *that* away for later, too.

"Shall we their fond pageant see?" he asked Oberon with a suggestive wink into the crowd, then sucked in a quick breath through his nose to nail the play's pinnacle quote.

"Lord, what . . ."

Movement under the glowing red exit sign caught his eye.

Annoyance rushed through him—the audience was supposed to

stay seated until the curtain—but there was something off about the way this boy stood. Even across the dark theater, Owen could see his arm extended before him. The point of his pale finger. The precarious way he balanced on his toes, as if he were standing on the same narrow platform Owen was.

This guy, bathed in red light, was mimicking him.

"Fools," muttered Dante. When Owen's gaze flicked his way, the feigned amusement had faded in Dante's now wide eyes. "Lord, what fools . . ."

Owen's throat grew thick, but he hid it with a wicked smirk. He turned back toward the audience, but that same asshole was there. Who was it? Shadows hid his face.

Owen's hand lowered slightly, just as the boy's did. He tilted his head, and the boy matched him. Unease speared through Owen's chest. It was as if he could anticipate what Owen would do next.

Pain shot up his leg as Dante stepped purposefully on his toes.

"Lord, what fools these fools be!" he cried. He was supposed to laugh heartily, but the line—the one he'd practiced a million times, that he'd auditioned for this lead role with—soured on his tongue.

"Lord, what fools these *mortals* be," he corrected quickly, at half the volume.

He smiled, but Puck was slipping off him like a shed skin. He tried to cling to it, but he couldn't. Stares from the crowd hit him sharp as knives without his shield. Humiliation flushed up his neck, under the thick stage makeup on his face.

He reached into the sewn pocket of his green tights, where he'd tucked his lucky stone. His fingers curled around the smooth, cold surface.

Oberon laughed boisterously to cover for the fuckup, but Owen couldn't find a single sound inside of him. He scanned the dark sea below the wooden stage, up the aisle, and there he was. Still mimicking Owen's every move.

Fury straightened Owen's back, and as the boy followed, his face was revealed in a wash of red light.

"Ian?"

But how—

Owen's foot slipped off the hollow tree limb. Releasing the lucky stone, he grabbed a hunk of plastic leaves to steady himself. With a loud rip, they tore free, exposing the white cast molding under the brown painted branch.

"What the hell?" Dante caught him under the arm, keeping him from toppling backward off the hidden pipe. Whispers rose in the crowd as an oblivious Lysander and Hermia darted around below their feet. Offstage, the student director was motioning for Owen to keep going, but he shook his head and swung down to the stage.

Behind him, the entire branch cracked, and Dante tumbled into a plastic bush.

Shouts and laughter erupted in the auditorium. Owen took a step downstage, past the now stunned Lysander and Hermia.

"What are you doing?" Mike whispered under his breath.

Owen's breath boomed in his ears. Ian was still standing under the red light. *Ian.* He was wearing a white button-down shirt. Nice pants. A tie. He was okay. More than okay. He looked good.

He'd always looked good.

"I . . ." Owen tried to swallow, but his mouth was suddenly dry. "I'll be right back."

"You'll *what*?" said Mike.

Owen jogged to the edge of the stage. The students in the crowd hollered louder. Another crash came from behind him as the tree branch hit the stage. He had the sudden urge to bow. People would love that. It would be all over social. But the thought slipped from his mind when Ian pushed through the door, out of the theater.

Owen leapt off the stage, bringing the crowd to their feet. He sprinted up the aisle toward the door. It banged against the stopper with a metallic clang as he shoved it open.

Breathing hard, he scanned the tiled foyer. No one. The posters advertising the play, an ACT prep course schedule, a hand-painted pep rally banner. But no one.

The door to outside was swinging on its hinges.

"Ian?" Owen raced toward it, his green fairy slippers silent against the floor, his heart in his throat. "Ian!"

As he broke outside into the misty spring night, a wave of dizziness made him stumble. Shaking it off, he searched the school parking lot.

In the back, where asphalt submitted to the woods, Owen saw him.

Owen ran, dodging around the parked cars. Ahead, Ian raced into the trees with a laugh. Owen choked on that laughter, on the joy in it, on the joy it echoed through his own chest. He remembered the sound of it, four years later. He would remember it fifty years later.

"Wait!" Owen called as he stepped off the asphalt onto a patch of grass. The bright circles from the parking lot lights didn't reach through the trees, but the moon was bright enough to guide his way.

The woods thickened, heavy pine boughs reaching across his path. He heard footsteps ahead and sprinted on, ignoring the rocks that dug into the flimsy soles of his slippers.

"There you are," he said when he spotted Ian ahead where the trees cleared. The moon gleamed off his dark hair in a silver halo. The play was real. The fairies had put a spell on him and sent him into the woods for this. For *him*.

Ian turned, his face so familiar Owen ached. This wasn't the boy he'd left behind four years ago. He'd aged. Of course he'd aged. It was only in Owen's nightmares that he'd been stuck thirteen. Ian was taller now, broader. He'd always been thin, but his cheeks had lost the childish roundness, and all the lines of his body were sharp and taut.

"It *is* you," he murmured with a dry swallow.

Ian nodded. His eyes weren't blue anymore, but silver clouds, a swirling storm. Was that strange? Owen couldn't tell. His head felt foggy. His ears were ringing.

"Come here," Ian said.

Owen jogged toward him, stopping at the edge of the clearing, ten feet away.

"How'd you . . . What are you doing here?" He could barely catch his breath to speak. How far had they run?

Ian smiled. Owen smiled back.

"I'm so glad you're here," Owen said.

Voices filtered through the trees. People laughing as they walked to their cars. What was so funny? A hard ball of ice formed in the pit of his stomach. His smile faltered. What was he doing outside? He couldn't even remember coming here.

His hand slid under his furry vest, into the pocket of his tights, gripping his lucky stone.

The temperature plummeted as Ian walked toward him. Snow fell—quiet, fat flakes that stuck to his hair and eyelashes. As he came closer, goose bumps rose on Owen's arms. His glasses fogged with the heat of his breath. In the back of his mind, a warning sounded. Questions speared through it—where have you been, and what happened—but they were too slippery to grasp.

Ian's hand rose. He brushed away the crinkle that had formed between Owen's brows with a gentle slide of his finger. His skin was like ice. The snow was falling heavier now, a glittering curtain of white around them.

"Are you cold?" Owen asked. Of course he was cold. It was freezing. Why was it freezing? It hadn't been earlier.

Owen's eyes caught on the scar on Ian's chin. He lifted his hand, tentatively pressing his finger to the pink loop. The small horseshoe that had once circled his fingertip now fit it perfectly. With another soft laugh, Ian turned, once, then twice. The snow followed his lead, spinning around them in a whirlwind.

"Wow," Owen said, his teeth beginning to chatter. "How'd you do that?"

Ian moved closer, his gray eyes dazzling. His marble skin inhumanly smooth. He placed his hand under Owen's collarbones, within the V cut of his vest. His palm was like ice, making Owen shiver. He wrapped his fingers around Ian's, trying to warm him up.

"I missed you," Ian whispered.

Owen's heart staggered.

Ian's hand slid higher, around the back of Owen's neck. "Did you miss me?"

"Yes," Owen admitted.

Owen gasped in surprise as Ian's lips pressed against his, cool and firm. His frozen fingers prickled along Owen's scalp. Ian sighed, making Owen's teeth ache from the puff of frigid air.

He wound his arms around Ian's waist, unable to feel his fingertips as they climbed the thin fabric that stretched over Ian's ribs.

Ian inhaled, and Owen choked. He couldn't catch his breath. Panic lit inside him, but Ian only kissed him harder. His fingers spread across Owen's jaws, pulling him closer, locking their mouths together as he sucked in another breath, this one deflating the air from Owen's lungs.

Anxiety shot down Owen's spine, tightening his stomach. The blood was pounding in his ears. Every cell was on fire now, icy flames licking his raw nerves.

"Wait," he tried to say, pushing back weakly.

Ian's kiss deepened.

Owen's feet went numb. His ankles and calves. His arms dropped to his sides—he lacked the strength to hold them up, but Ian was strong enough for both of them. He held Owen in place, breathing deeper, taking more, until Owen's thundering heart began to sputter and skip, and Ian pulled back to whisper in his ear, "Are you afraid?"

With his last bit of strength, Owen shoved away.

This wasn't Ian. It couldn't be. Ian would never hurt him. As Owen's head cleared, he watched the boy before him change. His pale skin turned sallow. His gray eyes widened. Owen scrambled back as the tie around Ian's neck grew unforgivably tight, cutting the skin around his swollen throat. Ian scraped at it with his fingers, ripping the collar of his shirt open in the process. Everywhere he touched, he bruised, fingerprints and lines of purple and brown on his dewy chest.

Owen gasped, his frigid lungs filling.

"Find me before dawn," the thing that looked like Ian groaned.

Then his skin, no longer able to hold the pressure within, burst, black rot spilling across the ground. Bone shards lodging into the trees and dirt. In the sludge left behind a scrap of skin remained. A pink horseshoe.

Owen screamed.

MADELINE

Madeline stared at the south entrance of Traverse High School, her heels bouncing against the floor of her Audi, her stomach in knots.

"It's fine," she told herself. "No one would still be here if anything bad happened."

The lot was full. People were flowing out of the theater. Groups of underclassmen were waiting on the curb for their parents to pick them up. Safety in numbers.

Her eyes darted from the glowing white sign over the theater for *A Midsummer's Night Dream* to the athletics wing on the west side of the school, where the sleek stone building that housed the pool waited in the dark.

Her throat went dry.

Forcing her eyes down, she checked her phone. Nothing from Emerson, who'd said they all needed to meet—*tonight*. With each minute that passed, Madeline believed more and more that she'd been pranked.

It made sense. Emerson had issues. Madeline wouldn't have put it past her to pay some kid to scare her at the pool, then call her in a panic, like *she'd* been the one in trouble. Emerson was probably laughing about it right now.

Unless whatever Madeline had seen at the pool had gone after her, too.

Madeline wrapped her arms tightly around her chest. She could still see the odd tilt of Ian's head. The way his hair clung to his face.

Finish the game.

A knock on the window. With a scream, she spun in her seat to find a stranger standing outside, peering at her with dark eyes.

A dingy leather jacket covered his red hoodie. Dark hair stuck out from under the hood, framing his angular face.

Impossible.

"Dax?"

He cocked a brow, and her heart gave a lurch. The same it had given when they were kids, but harder now, giving her the sudden sensation that she had missed a step on the way down the stairs.

The years condensed between them like a physical thing. She'd kept track of Emerson and Owen online, but Dax, like Ian, had disappeared. No social media. No mention of him in any high school sports or clubs or activities. She'd assumed that, like Emerson, he'd dropped out. The shock of his presence sent an echo of fear panging through her chest, and her legs flexed with the sudden urge to run, like she had the last time they'd been together.

He stepped back from the door, unfolding to his full height. She'd been taller than him when they were kids, but not now. Even before she stepped out of her car, she knew she'd have to look up at him. Instead of meeting his gaze, her eyes dropped to the strap that cut across his chest, attached to a large case on his back—a guitar? He'd never played an instrument before.

"You going to stay in there all night?" he called through the window.

She hesitated. Was he whistling? She thought she caught a verse from "Material Girl" as he ran a hand over the hood of her car.

With a frown, she tucked her phone into her coat pocket and opened the door into the cool spring night. Her eyes scanned the lot as she took a cautious step outside. A couple people were laughing near a pickup under the streetlight. A few more were coming out of the theater. No one looked particularly traumatized, but she kept the engine running just in case she needed a quick exit.

She looked up at Dax. He *was* taller, but that wasn't the only difference. His gaze was more serious, his jawbone sharp and flexed. She had a hard time reconciling him with the kid who never took anything seriously.

"What are you doing here?" she asked, hugging her chest.

He grinned. "Hi, Dax. How are you? Good to see you. It's been a while."

"Hi," she said.

He snorted. "Maddy."

"It's Madeline now."

His other brow lifted. She crossed her arms tighter.

"Wow."

Madeline turned sharply to find Emerson striding between the row of cars. She was wearing a threadbare sweater and loose gray pants cinched to her narrow waist by a belt. Her boots clomped over the asphalt, making Madeline aware of her own pristine sneakers, and how her leggings and Traverse swim team fleece clung to her body.

"Is this the part where we hug?" Emerson planted her hands on her hips, as if she dared anyone to try.

"You're late," Madeline told her, staring at Emerson's hair. Was she joining the army, or had she just gotten tired of dealing with it and hacked it all off?

"Not all of us have wheels, Butterfly." Emerson's tongue flicked across her lip ring as she narrowed her gaze on Dax. "What rock have you been hiding under?"

"A big one," Dax answered. "Nice look by the way. Very anti-establishment."

She ran a hand over her head. "Aww. Keep it up and you'll make me blush."

Madeline's brows drew together. She'd figured Emerson had called him. How else would he have known to meet them here?

Maybe he wasn't meeting them. Maybe he and Owen were still friends.

She frowned.

"So, to what do I owe the pleasure?" Dax asked. "Did I miss a birthday? Or are we all here for a little culture." He motioned to the *Midsummer's Night Dream* sign.

Emerson's hands fell to her sides. The sudden sag in her shoulders brought a pinch to the base of Madeline's throat.

"I saw him," Emerson said, paler than before.

Madeline went still.

"Who?" Dax asked.

"Ian," she murmured. Then she gave a strained laugh and slung a hand around the back of her neck. "Now that I say it out loud, it really does sound insane."

A chill crawled up Madeline's spine.

"It's not insane," she said. "I saw him, too. At the pool."

"Doing what?" Dax asked. "Going for a swim?"

She stared at the ground. "Maybe."

"So where's Mr. Popular?" Emerson asked. "You said he'd be here."

Dax, Madeline had written off, but Owen hadn't been hard to track down. He was a compulsive social poster, and his latest photo had been of him getting his makeup done for the show tonight, with the tag #Ifeelpretty.

Madeline's gaze turned to the school, her hands fisting in the sleeves of her fleece.

"He's in the play," she said. "He should be out soon."

"Why wait?" Emerson asked, waving a hand toward the theater. "Let's go find him, Butterfly."

"Don't call me that," Madeline said. Emerson didn't get to make cuts about swimming like she knew anything about it.

Madeline blew out a tense breath. Owen was a part of this, whether she wanted to admit it or not. He needed to be here.

She cut her engine, locked her doors, and, side by side, they walked toward the school. A strange sense of familiarity fell over her. When she looked down, she saw all three of their footsteps were in sync, and she deliberately took longer strides to offset their rhythm.

"Did he say anything?" Dax asked, pulling on the strap of his guitar. "Ian. When you saw him, did he tell you anything?"

Madeline could feel the quake inside her, starting at her organs and pressing out to her bones. The cool spring air was dewy on her face, too warm, but maybe it was just her blood pumping too fast. Her stare shot from streetlight to streetlight, from the shadow of someone's borrowed mom van to the woods that bordered the lot behind them.

"He said, *finish the game*." She blew out a thin breath. "I don't know. He was on the other side of the pool. It was hard to hear. I-I thought it was a prank at first, but he was there. Did you see something tonight?" she asked Dax.

"Yeah," he said. "But it wasn't Ian."

"I know," said Madeline. "It didn't look like him. But it was him. It just . . . it was." A wave of dizziness hit her. She didn't want to be here. It was one thing to hallucinate a friend on the anniversary of his presumed death. It was another if three of them had done it.

"What if we were wrong?" she whispered as their steps quickened. "What if he didn't . . . if he isn't . . ."

"Shut up," Emerson snapped. She looked behind her, but the people at the truck had piled inside, and the kids waiting for rides were too far away to hear.

"He's gone," Dax said, moving closer as they walked. "He never came out of that cave."

"But what if he did?" Madeline pressed. "What if he's out there?"

"What do you want us to do?" Emerson asked. "Go to the cops? 'Sorry, we weren't exactly honest four years ago. I know we said we went to the coffee shop, not the river, but now there's this dead guy trying to bite me through a mirror, and—'"

"Not the cops." Madeline's gut sank. They couldn't go to the police. *She* couldn't go to the police. For as long as she could remember, her mom had taught her to be cautious of how she was perceived by others. To go to the cops now and say she'd lied—about a missing white boy, no less—meant the kind of trouble she couldn't afford.

"Then what do you propose?" Dax's leather coat creaked softly as he pulled back his sweatshirt hood. There was an edge to him that put Madeline on edge, a tension in every sharp movement he made. It wasn't just that he was dressed for the cold, it was that she felt cold around him, not just chilled, but wary, as if his presence made all of this that much more serious.

"I say we find Owen, to start," said Emerson.

Madeline's pulse quickened as they neared the sidewalk surrounding Traverse High. The theater would be dark inside, like the pool.

"Look, it's after eleven," she said, falling behind the others. "The cast should be leaving anytime. Let's just wait out here for him."

"She's afraid someone will tell Mommy she was out with a couple high school dropouts," Emerson stage-whispered to Dax without looking back. "One of them a *musician.*"

"Who said I was a dropout?" Dax asked. "Just because I've missed a little school—"

"I'm serious," Madeline interrupted. She didn't have time for Dax's humor now. Emerson was right. Her mom had made it explicitly clear that Madeline wasn't permitted to speak to Emerson after she'd withdrawn from Traverse sophomore year. She'd never even uttered Dax's name, as if it would bring bad luck. Madeline didn't get the luxury of associating with whomever she wanted. She had to stay out of trouble and get a good education. She was Black, and even with a white parent, she had to be twice as good as everyone else to survive.

"I'm not going inside." She pulled her keys from the pocket of her fleece. Her fingers curled around the metal.

Dax whistled, as if impressed, and when he turned he gave her a small smile.

"What?" she asked.

"Nothing," he said, his gaze lowering over the brand-name leggings she definitely had not gotten on sale. "Just remembering when you had a backbone."

Emerson's sarcastic wince made Madeline's face hot.

A muscle ticked in Dax's throat, and Madeline had the sudden urge to shove him. In a rush, she remembered *all* the times she'd wanted to shove him. How he used to make up songs with her name in them just to annoy her, and beg her for the answers to homework when he knew full well Emerson had finished it first. All the times he'd teased her about that perfect wedding dress she'd put on her seventh-grade mood board, and that one Halloween he'd worn the same exact retro Pikachu costume and told everyone he'd gotten it first.

She was about to tell them both this had been a bad idea when a figure stumbled out of the woods on the far side of the parking lot and charged toward them.

She jerked back in surprise, lifting her keys like a weapon. Dax had one too—a knife he'd pulled from his pocket. Madeline's heart skipped. The boy running looked drunk, pitching sideways as he glanced back over his shoulder. As he drew closer, she recognized his dark hair, now dusted with what looked like snow, and his thick-rimmed glasses.

"Owen?" she called.

He reached Emerson first and grabbed her sweater with both hands. With wide, terrified eyes, he stared at them, frozen beads of sweat stuck to his jaw and forehead. He gasped for breath; under the streetlight his lips looked faintly blue. Even the fur on his strange costume vest was prickly with shards of ice.

His voice broke over a single word.

"Run."

EMERSON

Emerson pressed hard on the gas, barely slowing for a stop sign as she sped out of Traverse's parking lot, down the narrow roads. Madeline's Audi was more sensitive than her dad's old Honda, and when she jerked around a corner, Dax braced against the passenger window.

"Take it easy!" Madeline ordered from the back seat.

"You want to drive?" Emerson shot back. If she recalled, Madeline's hands had been shaking too much to stick the key in the ignition. If Emerson hadn't stepped in, they'd still be huddled around her car in the parking lot.

"Where are you going?" Dax asked between his teeth.

"I don't know!"

She caught a glimpse of Owen in the back seat through the rearview mirror, leaning over his knees, gripping the sides of his head. Beside him, Madeline was huddled against the car door.

"It looked just like him," Owen was muttering. "Exactly like him."

"Ian, right?" Emerson switched lanes with a squeal of tires, barreling through a stop sign onto the curving road that led up the hill to the conservatory.

"How did you know that?" Owen asked.

"You're not the only one seeing ghosts tonight," Dax told him. Lights from the road slashed over his face, making his grim expression more severe.

"Yūrei," Owen whispered.

"What the hell does that mean?" Emerson asked as the backlit glass of the conservatory's greenhouse whipped by. From the higher ground, she could see the woods where Owen had seen Ian snaking between the houses in her rearview mirror and the tops of the city high-rises before her. She lived in the shadows of those buildings. Could she make it? Would they be safe there?

"Yūrei. Dead people who come back to the living world," Owen said. "Apparitions. They usually have a message, or unfinished business, or they can't let go. He's back because it's our fault—"

"He told you that?" Madeline interrupted.

"No," Owen said. "But he didn't have to. He was upset. You could tell."

"How?" Dax asked. "What did he do?"

"I don't remember all of it." Owen shifted, making Emerson think this might not be completely true. "He asked if I was afraid. He wanted to punish me." In the mirror, Emerson watched him absently run the back of his hand over his mouth.

"They feed on fear," Dax said. "It makes them feel alive. The more they take, the stronger they become."

"They?" Emerson asked. "There's more than just one?" She glanced over at him again, thinking of Owen's blue lips. His wide, panicked eyes. She cranked the heat up.

"Oh, wow." Dax leaned forward. "Are we actually going to have a conversation about this? You sure you don't want to pretend nothing's wrong for another four years?"

"What's wrong?" she asked. "What are you talking about?"

Dax fell back in his seat. "And we're back to denial."

"I'm not denying anything!" she shouted, cutting off a blue car to merge onto Columbia Parkway. To their left, the Ohio River gleamed in the moonlight.

"You've seen something like this before?" Madeline asked him.

"Okay," Dax said. "The innocent act is cute, but . . ." He was quiet a moment, the whirring of the tires overtaking the conversation. "Wait. Is this the first time you've seen one of them?"

"How many ghosts are there?" Emerson demanded.

Lines tightened around Dax's mouth, bringing a cold chill to her gut.

"Yōkai," Owen muttered. "They come if you're bad—if you steal or talk back to your elders or blow off studying for a test. They eat shitty attitudes for breakfast, that's what my mom always used to tell us. *Be good. Don't feed the yōkai.*"

"Ghosts are . . . dead people," Emerson said, when no one else seemed able to state the obvious. "They can't touch you. They just float around and . . . I can't believe I'm having this conversation." She gave a breathy laugh. "Ghosts, yūrei, yōkai . . . they *aren't real*. They're the coping devices of people who are grieving or can't explain strange phenomena. What we saw tonight . . . it can't be a ghost. It can't be *Ian*."

When she swallowed, her throat felt like it was filled with sawdust.

"Then how do you explain all of us seeing him?" Madeline asked.

She couldn't. But there was an explanation for everything. That was the law of the universe. Dead was dead, alive was alive, and there was nothing in between.

"When I saw him at the pool, he said we had to finish the game," Madeline said.

"You really saw him too?" Owen asked.

Madeline nodded. "He said something about dawn."

"Find me before dawn," Owen said with a scowl.

Emerson remembered the smudges on her mirror she'd wiped clean. She'd thought she was seeing things. Now she wasn't so sure.

"What if he was talking about the cards?" Madeline asked. "The ones we found in the cave. What if that's the game?" She gripped the back of the driver's seat, making Emerson lean toward the steering wheel, away from her.

"What if you're all high on something I clearly missed out on?" Emerson asked, but she could see the playing cards in her mind. Old pieces of thick paper, worn at the edges, painted with Japanese characters. Owen, who'd been taught some kanji by his mom, had been able to piece together their meanings.

"The cards." Dax scratched a hand down his jaw. "Karuta."

"Karuta's just an old matching game," Owen said, his cheeks turning pink. The way he said the word was different than how he used to. The *t* was softer, matching how Dax said it. "We didn't even play it right."

"How are you supposed to play it?" Madeline asked.

"I don't know," Owen said, raking a hand through his hair. "Half of a quote or a riddle is given, and you have to find the other half on another card. But we didn't have the cards with the riddles, so we just acted out the answers because we were bored and stupid, and that's what bored, stupid kids do."

He was right, at least about that. They'd made up a game to pass the time. Madeline and Dax were looking for answers where there were none.

"So we have to finish playing a made-up version of Karuta by dawn and then the ghost of Ian will leave us alone?" Emerson gripped the wheel harder. "Do you realize how ridiculous that sounds?"

The tires whirred against the road in answer.

"It is ridiculous," Owen said. "But what if it's true? What if he's stuck somewhere and it's our fault?"

"We didn't do anything wrong!" Emerson argued.

"We lied," Madeline said.

The cold in Emerson's gut was spreading through her chest.

"If it's true, we owe it to him to make it right," Dax said.

"We don't owe him anything," Emerson said, biting hard on her lip, feeling the metal ring press back against her teeth. "He's dead. He's gone. That's it."

Sickness churned in Emerson's stomach at the thought of him being out there all this time, in some form, waiting for them to come back.

"We have to do it," Madeline said, her voice hollow. "We have to play the game again."

"And what?" Emerson replied, but her voice was weaker now. "We're going to find a clue on a card that will miraculously bring Ian back from ghost land?"

"I don't know, maybe!" Madeline said.

"Shit," Owen said. "This is a bad idea. I haven't been back there since . . ."

He didn't finish, but Emerson knew. Since the day they let Ian die.

The car slowed as her foot eased off the gas pedal. She couldn't believe she was considering this. She'd sworn to herself never to go back to that place. Never to speak about what had happened.

Never to talk to these three people again.

Madeline's hand came over the seat and gripped her shoulder.

"If it was you, wouldn't you want us to go back?"

Yes.

Madeline was right. If—and it was a very small *if*—Ian was trying to send them a message, if there was a chance they could help him in this life or some other, they had to.

He'd been there for her when she'd needed him. When Mark DeWine had said she was flat as a dollar bill, Ian had responded that Mark's IQ matched his shoe size. When her dad had lost his job and had to go on unemployment, Ian had promised her it would pass. And on the sixth-grade overnight trip, when Maddy had gotten the flu and gone home and Emerson had no one, Ian had snuck into the girls' bunks and played Go Fish with her until she'd fallen asleep.

She swung across two lanes of empty traffic and took the first road toward the river.

⸺◆⸺

The walking paths at Smale Riverfront Park closed at dusk, so Emerson parked on the curb behind the baseball stadium to avoid any attention from a patrolling police car. In silence they left the car, thin spindles of wary anticipation connecting them in a delicate net. The hazy glow from downtown stretched soft shadows over the gravel path along the river. Dax led, Owen and Madeline just behind him. Maybe they were right about the yōkai, maybe not. Either way, she was proceeding with caution.

As she walked, the dark took shape around them, bending the light that sifted through the trees, turning the thin branches to fingers that curled around her ankles as she walked. Her breath was hot against her lips, and she hugged her arms against her body, fighting the cold.

"My parents are going to kill me," Madeline muttered, tugging on the bottom of her fleece quarter-zip.

Emerson felt a pinch in her stomach, remembering her own parents' fight over her GED. They were always arguing about her now.

"It's just one night," she said.

"You don't understand." Maddy tucked her braids behind her ears. "I don't do this."

Emerson snorted. "Which part? Midnight ghost hunting, or wearing those white shoes after Labor Day?"

Madeline shook her head. "When did you become such a jerk?"

"About the time you became a pretentious shit heel, *Madeline*." Emerson grinned. "Don't worry, there's a first time for everything."

"It's not the first time," Madeline said quietly, glancing down the path Emerson hadn't been on in four years.

They needed to change the subject.

"Dax seems fairly unsurprised by the whole ghost angle," Emerson whispered, watching Dax stride through the dark without hesitation, while Owen, holding the flashlight, picked his way through the brush two steps behind. "It's weird, isn't it? That he's been gone all these years, then this happens?"

Madeline's brows pulled together. "What are you saying?"

"I don't know." She couldn't name it, but there was something off about his arrival.

But it wasn't just Dax. It was Madeline, too. Madeline, who lived in her three-story historic home wrapped in her designer clothes. Who was a swimming champion, and top of her class, and never looked back after what had happened with Ian. And Owen, in his ridiculous fur vest and green tights, walking around after dark like a grounded Peter Pan.

She hated these people.

"There it is," Owen said, carving a path through the rocks that dropped to the river's bank. Dax followed him toward the black gap in the gray stones.

Emerson felt a tug in her stomach. It was as if the cave had a current, dragging her closer against her will. She'd felt it every time she thought of this place. It was there in her nightmares, when she heard Ian calling for help from inside the tunnel.

It wanted them to come back.

She followed Dax and Owen, hearing Madeline on her heels.

"I say we pull straws. Smallest one goes in," Owen said. He'd pulled something out of his pocket and was gripping it in his fist. When he caught her looking, he put it away.

"We all go in," Dax said.

"I didn't bring the right shoes," Owen argued, looking down at his green felt slippers.

Emerson grinned. "Want to borrow mine?"

"Just a quick look," Madeline said. "If we can't find the cards, we go."

They all muttered their agreement.

Emerson stopped outside the cave's entrance—a mouth, ringed by jagged stone teeth and flossed by strands of limp ivy. Owen shined the light from his phone into the black gaping hole, but the dark seemed to swallow the glow. Dax crouched, absently rubbing the heel of his hand over his chest.

A knot of nostalgia rose in Emerson's throat. The last time they'd been here together, they'd looked at this tunnel and seen an adventure. They'd trusted one another because they couldn't imagine not.

It was too quiet now. No crickets, or night birds calling. Emerson could hear her own heart pounding over the gentle rush of the river behind them.

"I've dreamed about this place," Owen said, his voice thin.

"Me, too." Dax glanced at him. Looked away with a frown.

Emerson took a step closer, even as a cold sweat broke out on her brow. She didn't want to go inside, but the call was getting stronger. She felt as if the world had tipped, and she was sliding forward, into the cavernous mouth.

Madeline's hand closed around her wrist. "Wait." Her eyes were bright with worry.

But Dax was already climbing inside.

Owen followed.

"Let's go," Emerson said, pulling Madeline after her.

Emerson and Owen used her phone light to guide their path. As they crossed under the entrance, the cave creaked, reminding Emerson of old mine shafts and sending shivers across the back of her neck. Madeline gripped her arm.

Emerson shook her off.

The air grew cool and thick, bringing a bitter, metallic taste to the back of her jaw. Moisture dripped down the ragged walls, filling shallow pools at their feet.

Dax kicked a bottle and they all jumped. Braced for something to climb from the shadows and attack.

Nothing came.

"Don't fuck around," Emerson snapped at him.

"Or what?" Dax asked.

She shook her head, wishing she had her flamethrower.

Owen pointed them around the bend, to the right.

"Hello?" he called, his voice low. "Anyone there?"

Nothing.

"Look for the cards," Owen said, but he didn't sound certain. How could they still be here after four years? The water and bugs must have turned them to compost by now.

They searched the ground but found only broken glass and trash. Doubt circled Emerson's chest. Madeline had been grasping at answers, and they'd all been eager to find an explanation for what had happened.

But now that she was here, she couldn't leave.

Something bumped her ankle as she walked, but when she looked down, she saw only gray gravel.

Another step, and she felt it again. Dark soil covered the toe of her boot. She tried to lift her leg, to shake it off, but the ground held solid, as if she'd stepped in wet cement.

"What the hell?"

Her other foot began to sink into the soft ground.

"Emerson?" Madeline stepped back quickly, jerking on Emerson's arm, but then gave a shriek as her own foot plunged down to the ankle.

"Maddy!" Dax grabbed her arm but couldn't pull her free.

Emerson gasped as the ground bubbled, then hissed, then swallowed her up to the knees.

"Help!" She reached for Owen's outstretched hand, but it slipped through her fingers. Her heart galloped; panic narrowed her vision. She reached down, dropping her phone, digging at the ground to free her legs.

She threw herself backward as a flame shot out of the ground at her feet. It broke through a crack in the floor, like a gas leak, and glowed green.

The Choke.

"What's happening?" Madeline shouted.

"Hold on!" Dax yelled at her.

"Owen!" Emerson reached for him again as the ground turned to quicksand, compressing around her thighs. It climbed up her hips, sliding into her shoes, beneath the cuffs of her pants, and up her sleeves. Faster, she went under. Her arms were trapped underground. Her head tilted back, her mouth open to gasp for breath. The green flames spread, circling around them, stretching to the cave's ceiling. Tiny granules of sand sifted through her hair and into her ears. The urge to fight, to survive, overwhelmed her, and she bucked and thrashed, her muscles searing.

"Help!" she cried, but the word was cut off as she gagged on cold, damp earth.

MADELINE

Cold wormed through Madeline's veins. It traced out to the tips of her fingers, filled her chest.

"Maddy."

She heard her name, but it was drowned out by the crackling of flames. The imprint of green fire remained behind her eyelids, brilliant and deadly.

"Madeline, wake up!"

As steadily as it had come, the cold fire loosened its hold, drawing back like blood into a syringe. Her eyelids fluttered open. With a pop her ears cleared, and she could hear the clatter of tree branches and the rush of nearby water.

She gasped, frigid air scraping her throat. Her teeth began to chatter.

A filthy Emerson leaned over her. Mud covered her clothes and streaked her face. Madeline looked down at her own fleece and leggings. She wasn't any better off.

Dax crouched beside them, shaking clumps of earth out of his dark hair. "Everyone all right?"

"What the hell happened?" Owen's voice came from behind Emerson, and when Madeline tilted her head she found him cleaning his glasses on his muddy vest. After a moment he gave up and put them on anyway.

"I don't know." Her head was throbbing. She pressed her fingers to her skull. Bits of leaves had collected in her box braids. The last thing she remembered was standing in that tunnel, the dirt churning beneath her feet, a strange green fire slithering through the cracks in the ground. Now a blanket of fog surrounded them, lit by the fragile glow of a sickle moon.

"We must have fallen through a sinkhole," Emerson said.

"And ended up in the woods?" Madeline asked, picking a small stick from her hair.

"We were gassed," Owen said. "Did you see that green fire? It must have been some kind of toxin."

"Oh my god, we've been abducted. I've been drugged." Madeline pushed to her knees, searching frantically for their captors.

"That's your go-to?" Dax said. "Drugs and kidnapping?"

"You've got a better idea?"

"Calm down," Emerson said, the fog behind her shifting like a living thing.

Madeline's heart beat faster. She reached into her pockets, but they were empty. "Who has a phone? My dad . . . he'll come pick me up."

"Where are you going to tell him we are?" Emerson said. "This isn't the park."

Madeline searched for landmarks. A sign, a path, *anything* even remotely familiar. But she didn't know this place.

"I left mine backstage before the show." Owen scowled.

"I must have dropped mine," said Emerson.

"I don't have one."

Owen stared at Dax. "Who doesn't have a phone?"

Dax shrugged.

Madeline forced herself to breathe.

Ian pressed through her thoughts, dripping and pale blue from the reflection of the pool. She turned to Owen. "Is this part of the game?"

A muscle ticked in his throat. "How am I supposed to know?"

"Ian didn't say anything to you about the woods, or . . . or the sinkhole, or fire?"

"He didn't exactly hand me a rulebook."

"Well what *did* he say?"

"Didn't you see him too? What did he tell you?"

"Quiet!" Emerson snapped.

Silence settled between them. Madeline held her breath.

"What is it—" Dax was cut off by a rumbling growl. At first

it was barely audible, but it grew until Madeline's bones began to vibrate like the hard hit of a bass. She spun, trying to locate the source, but it seemed to come from all around them.

"We need to move," Dax said.

Owen was already nodding. "Yeah, no shit."

They pushed through the fog, racing over dead branches and crackling pine needles. Madeline's breath puffed in front of her face. The mist obscured their path, making it hard to see more than two steps ahead. Behind them, she could hear a rustling in the brush. Tears stung her eyes. She didn't dare look back.

"Over here!" Emerson called.

Madeline tripped over a rock. A branch scraped her hands as she fell forward, but she hardly felt it. Dax grabbed her arm, roughly hoisting her up. They raced after Owen, toward Emerson's voice.

"There!" Dax pointed ahead.

Emerson's shadow came into view, bracketed between two cedar trees in the soupy mist. Behind her stood a small cabin. Madeline took it in in pieces—the gaping hole punched in the roof, the sliding front door. A light came from inside, flickering in the ragged patches of panel between the intersecting beams of wood.

Her steps slowed.

"What is this place?" she whispered. The shack was all wrong. It didn't belong in these woods, in this *time*. Small, but too solitary to be a utility shed, with no driveway or path out.

"Those are shōji sliders," Owen said. "Is this some kind of Japanese historical reenactment? A festival or something?"

"No idea," Dax said. "Why don't we stay out here and talk about it?"

Another howl ripped through the night. Without waiting for the rest of them, Owen charged up to the cabin. The tattered sliding door vibrated beneath his fist as he knocked on the wood frame.

"Hello?" he called.

Soon Madeline was knocking beside him. "Is anyone there?"

"Wait," Emerson said. "That Ian thing that attacked Owen . . . What if there's one inside?"

"You want to stay out here, be my guest," Dax told her.

Before he could shove the door open, it slid slowly to the side, and an old Japanese woman appeared in the threshold, her silhouette outlined by flickering candlelight.

"Hello, Madeline."

With a quick intake of breath, Madeline jerked back into Emerson. There was something strange about the woman's speech—something Madeline couldn't quite pin.

"How do you know my name?" she asked.

"Do not be frightened," the woman said. "Come in. Come in. I have been waiting a long time for you." Wrinkles curled around her mouth, her eyes, her sagging cheeks and neck. Her black kimono was like the mofuku Owen's mom had let Madeline borrow for a report in seventh grade, a robe of mourning fastened around the waist by a simple black obi, that she'd made certain to learn the purpose and history of to avoid cultural appropriation. The old woman had a kind look about her, but that made Madeline even more wary. Why was she here in the woods by herself? She had to be ninety years old. For all they knew, she could have been responsible for their abduction—maybe the others weren't convinced they'd been drugged, but Madeline wasn't ruling it out.

Madeline's gaze shot behind the woman, taking in the single room—splintering plank walls, a rolled mat in the corner, some shelves with threadbare blankets, and a low table. There were no outlets or electronics. No light switches. No windows, even.

"How am I understanding you?" Emerson asked the woman, her brows scrunched.

"All who play will know our words," she answered cryptically.

Madeline rocked back on her heels, realizing that the strangeness of the woman's voice wasn't because of her tone or the cadence of her words. It was because she was speaking a different language entirely.

And somehow Madeline understood it.

"Come in, and I will explain. I have been waiting a long time for you," their host said with a gummy smile. "For Madeline. Owen. Emerson." She looked over to Dax, and the lines around her eyes tightened. "Dax."

"Is this a prank?" Owen asked. "Who put you up to this?"

When she reached up, her pale hand marked with olive age spots, Owen flinched, but she only patted his cheek.

"No pranks," she said, then she turned and went back inside.

Madeline looked to the others. "I'm not going in that house."

"She's old," Emerson said quietly, glancing over her shoulder. "She can't hurt us."

"I wouldn't count on that," Dax said. He flicked open the blade of a small knife in his hand, a habit that apparently hadn't died in the four years he'd been MIA. Madeline scoffed. As if a two-inch blade could possibly protect them.

"I don't think she's dangerous," Owen said. "I mean, I don't think she's a yōkai."

"And you believe this because of your vast experience and research?" Dax asked.

Owen glared at him through his grimy lenses. "My mom used to say you could tell when a yōkai was near because it would get cold. Her hand wasn't cold." He touched his cheek absently.

"It's freezing out here," Madeline said, hugging her arms to her sides. "How would you even be able to tell?"

A howl cut through the night, raising the hair on her arms.

"Taking my chances with the old lady," Owen said, then rushed inside, Emerson behind him. Dax waited for Madeline to go ahead of him, and when she didn't, he gave her a strange look before stepping over the threshold.

Not willing to stay outside alone, she hurried after them, sliding the squeaking door shut behind her.

"Now," the old woman said, clasping her hands. "Isn't that nice?"

"Who are you?" Dax asked, the pocketknife now hidden in his fist.

"I am Shinigami," she said.

Madeline wasn't sure if that was her first name or her last, but the way she said it—like she assumed they'd been looking for her— spread unease through Madeline's chest. There was something wrong with this woman, with all of it. Her odd house. Her calm smile. Their mutual comprehension despite their different languages and the way she'd known their names.

Madeline hugged her arms around her chest.

"Nice to meet you," said Owen, almost as a question. "Can you tell us where we are? We seem to have gotten a little turned around." He glanced at her black kimono, a frown pulling at his lips.

"You are in Meido," she said.

"Is that a place?" Emerson asked.

She looked up at them, her smile broadening. "It is the game."

Madeline inhaled sharply, Ian's words buckling her knees. *You have to finish the game.*

"You mean the card game?" she asked. "The one in the cave?"

"Hai." Shinigami motioned to the low, dusty table topped with a candle. Wax rings spread out from its nubby wick nearly to the edge of the wood, as if it had been burning for days. How long had Shinigami been waiting here?

"I'm sorry, I'm a little confused," Madeline said. "What do those cards have to do with where we are?"

Realizing that the old woman didn't intend to answer until they sat, Madeline kneeled on one of the tatami mats around the table. Owen and Emerson followed, the dry weave crinkling beneath their weight. Dax stayed standing near the door, flicking the knife open and closed in his hand.

"All those who start the game must finish it," said Shinigami, clearly pleased with their choice. Slowly, she shuffled to the shelves at the back of the room, where she retrieved a flat, black teapot and five chipped ceramic cups, which she set around the table. "They are tethered to Meido until they complete their tasks."

"What tasks?" Dax asked. "And what do you mean, *all*? Everyone who plays the cards?"

"Is she talking about Ian?" Owen asked. He turned to Shinigami. "Do you know our friend Ian Spencer?"

Shinigami hushed him with a hum. She knelt carefully on one of the mats, wincing as her knees touched the floor.

"Hey," Emerson said as Shinigami began pouring yellow tea

from the pot. "Lady. We're not here for teatime. We're looking for our friend. If he's in your creepy forest, we need to know."

"He is here."

Madeline winced.

"Where?" Owen demanded. "Is he okay? Is he hurt?"

"He is running out of time."

"What does that mean?" Owen pressed.

"Dawn," Madeline murmured.

Shinigami looked to her and gave a slow nod.

"What happens at dawn?" Emerson asked. "What do you mean he's running out of time?"

Shinigami wafted a hand over the first cup as if it might be hot, but unless the old kettle was self-heating, Madeline wasn't sure how that would be possible—there wasn't a heat source apart from the candle that she could see. She glanced to Dax, fearful that they'd be asked to drink something offered by a stranger in the woods, but Dax did not return her gaze. He was still watching the steam from the first cup, which had now risen over the table in a thick white plume.

"Everyone sees that, right?" said Owen.

Madeline scrambled back in fear, but Emerson grabbed her sleeve.

"Wait," she hissed.

With a wave of Shinigami's hand, the steam gathered into the shape of an animal, a pitiful creature that stood on matchstick legs with a concave chest and a rounded spine, and had two skinny horns that twisted skyward. It wore wide pants and a billowing top, but its face was too broad, inhuman, even in the steam.

"That's a neat trick," Dax said quietly.

"What is that?" Madeline managed. It certainly wasn't Ian.

"Sit. Please," said Shinigami.

Slowly, tentatively, Madeline returned to the mat, Dax lowering beside her.

"Once there was a demon—an oni—who fell in love with an empress," said Shinigami. She moved her hands over the second cup, circling them to draw more steam from the yellow tea. As it rose, it took the shape of a woman. She lifted her arms, the long sleeves of her kimono swirling around her, dancing like her long hair and her clever smile. Madeline found her own lips curving in response, the steam woman pulling at some invisible string inside her chest.

"Empress Izanami was a good and fair leader, but she did not return the oni's love."

With the third cup, Shinigami sent a cloud around the monster and his queen, stripping away Izanami's smile and pushing the demon down until it stood on its hands and feet like a wolf, and its clothes faded away.

"For seven years, he offered his heart. He swore his allegiance to her," she said, a twist of her wrist making the oni bow low, his chest and head pressed to the ground at her feet. "And for seven years she shunned him."

Madeline swallowed in awe as the empress figure turned her back.

"Why is she telling us this?" Owen asked.

"Shut up," Emerson said. "Maybe it has something to do with the game."

Shinigami fanned the fourth cup and a gray mist rose, spearing through the chest of the demon with an awful, silent prong. The creature seemed to swell in all directions, wiry hairs poking from its back, sharp teeth protruding from its mouth. Its eyes deepened, empty wells in the gray mist.

"Izanami's dismissal made the creature mad."

Dax flicked his knife open and closed with a click.

"And so he pursued her one last time." Shinigami leaned over the low table, blowing on the last cup. From it came a faraway scream, a sound that grabbed Madeline's spine and brought a cringe to her lips.

Before them, the empress shattered, each section of her form sharp as glass before dissipating into the air alongside the boy.

Madeline caught her breath, sweat on her brow, as the room fell silent. She looked to Emerson, whose cheeks had flared pink in surprise.

"From her body, he took seven pieces," Shinigami continued, the glow of the candlelight making her face look wide and disfigured as she drew away from it. "One for each of the seven years she shunned him. Stained by kegare—the pollution of her blood and death—they turned to stone. He hid them throughout Meido, spreading darkness and disease wherever he went."

Madeline felt a strained laugh building in her throat. She was losing her mind. That was the only explanation for any of this.

"Fun story," said Dax. "What does it have to do with Ian?"

Shinigami met his gaze, her eyes too dark, the pupils too large. "Complete the game. Retrieve the seven stones and return them to the empress. Only then can you find what you seek."

"Ian," Madeline breathed.

Shinigami nodded. "If you cannot reach him by dawn, he will belong to the game, forever tainted by kegare. Forever unclean."

Madeline couldn't make sense of Shinigami's words. Ian was dead. She'd learned to live with it—not just his absence, but the lie they'd told the day he disappeared.

If he was here, that changed everything.

If he was here, that meant they really had left him in the dark.

Guilt rolled through her, slick and bitter on the back of her tongue. Yes, they'd run, and they'd told their parents and the police they had been at the coffee shop, just like they'd promised to be, but they were kids. They'd been terrified. What happened wasn't their fault.

"How do we find the stones?" Owen asked.

Madeline's gaze shot toward him. "You're not serious. There could be more yōkai out there!" She stumbled over the word, the *o* coming out shorter than when Owen said it, but she was too scared to be embarrassed.

"Many more yōkai. Cursed by the oni's violence."

"See?" said Madeline. "There you go."

"It doesn't matter what's out there," Owen said, his face paling. "Ian's in trouble."

"He's right," said Emerson. "We finish this by morning, we find him, we go home. It's a classic quest design."

"This isn't a stupid video game!"

"Are you sure?" Dax asked. "Look around. This isn't normal.

We've been dragged into something, and I, for one, would like to get out of it."

Madeline balked. She looked from Dax to Emerson to Owen, then stared at the floor, unable to believe that not a single one of them could see how insane this was.

"So that's it? This is happening?" She hugged her knees against her chest.

"You have something better to do?" Dax asked her.

With an eerie grin, Shinigami stood and moved to the back of the room, where a reed basket sat. She lifted the lid, pulling out a stack of old paper.

Not just any paper, Madeline realized. Thick cards, yellowed with age and worn at the edges.

Her stomach bottomed out.

She remembered it all vividly then. The pitch in Ian's voice when he'd told them it would be like Karuta, the matching game. How she'd guessed with the others what Owen and Ian were acting out. How the walls had boomed like a heartbeat.

Beside her, Owen sputtered.

"These are yours?" Madeline whispered, looking up to Shinigami. If they were, then she was to blame for them starting this game in the first place. For Ian's disappearance. For them being here now.

All of it went back to these stupid cards.

Shinigami made a tutting noise, her black eyes moving from Madeline to Dax. "They belong to the one who begins the game."

Madeline's hands clenched, nails biting into her palms. A temper she hadn't felt in a long time flared up her neck, clenching her jaw. This wasn't a game—it was their lives. It was *Ian's* life.

"Playing was Ian's idea," Owen said, his voice dropping. "He found them that day. These aren't his."

"They are yours now," Shinigami said. Carefully she set them in a pile on the table. The kanji on the first was faded but readable, the black slashes of ink like the cuts of a knife.

"To complete the game, you must complete seven challenges," Shinigami said. "Tests of loyalty. Fear. Cowardice. Lies. Wounded hearts." Owen choked as she flipped the first card over and the thick paper clicked against the table. "Honor. And finally, bravery. Upon completion of each challenge, you will be given one of the seven stones, and the next challenge will begin. But be wary; if you attempt to fool the game, you will be punished. Meido does not suffer cheaters."

"Wait," Madeline said. "Punished how?"

Shinigami smiled.

"Punished how?" Madeline repeated, louder now. "And what happens if we don't finish these challenges? How do we get out of here?"

"All those who start the game must finish it," Shinigami said. "If you do not, you will never wash yourself clean of the pollutants of Meido."

Madeline huffed a breath, but the air felt thinner than before.

"Hold on," Owen said, springing to his feet. "No one said anything about staying here forever."

"Take it easy," Dax told him. "There's got to be a catch."

"The catch is we're screwed," Owen snapped at him. "She's saying we can't leave!"

"We've got another problem." Emerson scrambled backward as the black of Shinigami's robe spread down her wrists and up her neck. The darkness rolled over her face like a wave, until the whites of her eyes were all that could be seen. "Shinigami? Hey! Can you hear me?"

"What's happening?" Madeline's pulse hammered in her ears. She backed toward the door, but the walls had gone dark too. It was as if the entire shack were being swallowed by shadows.

"The cards!" Emerson shouted. "Grab them!"

Madeline, closest to the table, gathered the cards into a messy pile. The hard papers snapped against one another as she gathered them in her damp hands. As soon as she picked them up, the table faded and disappeared.

"Dax?" she cried, feeling him bump against her arm. "What is this?"

"How should I know?"

The darkness pressed out around them, thinning to a gray mist. As it cleared, Madeline could make out the black sky overhead. They were back in the woods, soil and dead leaves beneath their feet, naked trees wagging their spindly silver branches at them in the breeze.

The shack, and Shinigami, were gone.

"Where is she?" Madeline gripped the cards in her shaking hands. "What was that?"

"That was making an exit," Owen said with a short burst of laughter. "She just smoke bombed us like a magician."

"She wasn't a show," Dax said. "That was real."

"Everything's a show," Owen told him. "All the world's a stage, my friend. Sometimes it's an old lady tossing out monologues and cloud puppets in the woods, sometimes it's a jackass in a leather jacket pretending he isn't scared shitless like the rest of us."

Dax grinned. "Anything else?"

Owen picked a leaf off his vest. "Oh, I'm just warming up."

"Shut up," Emerson told them, glaring at the clearing where the shack had been moments before as she rubbed her hands together. "She's an NPC."

"A what?" asked Madeline.

"Non-player character. They're placed in games with limited roles, with the purpose of explaining the game to the player." She clapped her hands. "It makes perfect sense. She appears out of nowhere, like a guide. Then she disappears when she's no longer necessary."

"So she isn't real?" asked Dax.

Emerson nodded. "She's a function of the game—Meido. That's why we understood what she was saying. That's how she can just poof into thin air. If what she was saying is true about this place, then she's a part of it."

"This isn't a game!" Madeline shouted. "We need to get out of here. We'll backtrack, and then maybe we can find our way to the cave."

"We can't leave without Ian," Dax said, his gaze cool.

"Don't do that," she said, marching toward him. "It's not like I don't want to find him. But even you have to admit that we're a little out of our league here."

"Guys?" Owen said.

"Who are you?" Dax leaned closer, invading her personal space. "The Maddy I knew wouldn't have thought twice about going after a friend who needed her."

"Yeah, well, I grew up," she said between her teeth. "And maybe you should, too."

"Oh, get over yourselves," Emerson groaned. "I'm not spending the rest of the night listening to you two fight."

"Guys!" Owen grabbed Madeline's sleeve, his green eyeshadow dull in the low light. "Listen!"

Madeline braced, hugging the cards against her chest. She waited for the howl they'd heard earlier, but it never came. There was only the clattering of branches in the breeze above.

Then a heavy *whoosh*, swirling the fog around their legs.

Madeline's mouth went dry. "What was that?" she whispered.

Through the dark came the smacking of jaws, and the horrible squish and tear of meat. Somewhere close an animal—large, by the sound of it—was devouring something.

Owen stumbled backward, falling into Madeline's side. She gripped his arm and held her breath.

Footsteps approached, crackling over the ground. Madeline spun just in time to see a white man dart through the trees toward them. He was wearing tattered clothes, and his feet were muddy and bare. In his hand was a long spear.

She dove to the side as the rest of her friends scattered, but the man barely glanced at them as he whipped by. Her last glimpse of him was of his back, and the tattered corner of paper tucked into his frayed rope belt.

"Hey!" Emerson called, but he didn't stop. "He's got a card!"

"You think he's playing, too?" Owen asked.

"I'm about to find out," she said, then raced after him. Dax followed, and after a brief hesitation, Owen did too.

"Wait!" Madeline called, shoving the cards into the front of her zip-up. She sprinted after them, hurdling over a fallen branch. Terror chased her, making her heart pump too fast. Was the man running from the animal they'd heard? Or hunting it? She glanced over her shoulder, but whatever they'd heard had returned to the darkness above.

The woods opened ahead, the thick gray trunks drawing back to reveal a clearing as big as the park near Emerson's house, lined with silvery hedges reflected by the moon. A cold, wispy fog filled it, raising goose bumps on her arms. Making her shiver.

"What are they doing?" Owen asked, his breath coming out in a puff of steam.

Madeline followed his gaze to the center of the clearing, where long shadows stretched into human shapes. She recognized the man they'd seen amongst them, the spear braced in both his hands as he stepped tentatively over the ground. A woman beside him in scarcely more than her underwear pointed overhead into the mist. There had to be a dozen others, all with their faces upturned, all waiting. Their silence made Madeline hold her breath, made her flinch at the crackling sound under her shoes as she shifted her weight. What were these people looking at? What did they see that she could not?

Another *whoosh* came from above, followed by wings and a snap of teeth.

Then the woman was plucked from the ground and, with a stunted scream, she disappeared into the fog.

Madeline toppled backward in surprise, tripping over something behind her heels. With a grunt, she fell on her hip, cold pressing through the thin fabric of her leggings.

"What was that?" Emerson said. "Did anyone see it?"

"Holy shit." Owen raked his hands through his hair. "Holy *shit*."

Madeline's gaze dropped from the sky, latching onto what looked like a bruised patch of skin in the dirt beside her right foot. As the wind scattered the leaves, its length was revealed—an arm, bent at its knobby elbow, and severed at the shoulder in a knot of white bone and sinew. In its still-gripped fist was a rusty knife.

She screamed.

Before she could finish the breath, Dax was there, pressing his cold hand to her mouth. The rough scars on his palm smashed her lips against her chattering teeth. He shook his head quickly, as if to tell her, *Don't make a sound.*

Tears streamed from her eyes. She scraped at his hand with her fingers. This was wrong. She needed to go home, to her room, to her pool and her schedule and her rules. She couldn't do this.

He leaned in, pressing his forehead to hers.

"Tell yourself it isn't real," he whispered. "Tell yourself it's a dream. Just keep it together."

She met his gaze, steadied by the stillness in his eyes.

When she nodded, he slowly pulled back his hand.

"How do we get out?" Owen asked, his whisper strained. "How did we get *in*?"

Madeline's eyes shot toward the exit. It wasn't a trick of the light, or a curtain of fog. The brush had closed behind them, brambles and vines weaving together to sew their exit shut. The silver shoots climbed skyward, disappearing into the dark sky above.

"We're trapped." A buzz rose in her ears. The man with the spear crouched across the arena, mist moving around his ankles like waves in a pond. His slow turn revealed the card on his back. Around him, the others readied their weapons—spears and knives, rocks and makeshift pitchforks made of branches. Mud was smeared across their faces and skin as camouflage. They looked like they were preparing for battle.

"He's playing now," she whispered, the realization sinking like a stone in her gut. "They're all playing. What if this is it? What if this is the first challenge?"

"Loyalty," Emerson said.

A scream came from the center of the ring, followed by another loud *whoosh.* Madeline jumped toward Owen, and they pressed against each other, shoulder to shoulder. Emerson dropped, snatching the knife out of the severed arm's grip. She braced it before her.

Quickly, Madeline removed the cards from her shirt. She showed them to Owen. "Are there directions . . . or clues . . . *something*?"

"There isn't a card for loyalty," he said, flipping through them.

"Shinigami said loyalty was first," Emerson said.

"Are you sure?" Madeline asked.

Owen held up a card. "Fear is first. Unless they're out of order."

Madeline grabbed the cards. "There're only six! Did you drop one?"

"Me? No! You were carrying them!" Owen said.

"Why don't we figure this out later?" Dax said as the fog began to ripple like waves in a lake.

"They're coming," called the man with the spear, his voice low and bitter.

"What?" Emerson asked. "What are they?"

"Tengu."

"What's that mean?" Madeline asked, stuffing the cards back into her fleece.

"Tengu are monsters." Owen paled. "Flying monsters."

"Excellent." Dax knelt, picking up a rock from the ground. Owen moved closer to his side.

"We have to fight," Emerson said, lifting the rusty knife.

Panic gripped Madeline's spine. "I'm not fighting anything! I—"

A cry split the night, loud enough to make Madeline clap her hands against her ears. The fog split, ripped in half by a thunderous punch of wind. It tossed them apart, flinging Madeline to the edge of the clearing. She hit the brush barrier hard, a thorn the size of her thumb stabbing into her shoulder, pinning her in place. Pain seized her lungs, but she swallowed her cry. Through the fog came a massive black creature—a bird, as big as a full-grown man. Its beak was hooked and gleaming, its eyes like tar pits. Leathery, bat-like wings spread wide as it swooped toward them.

"Move!" Dax shouted.

She twisted, pain shooting across her back as she slid her shoulder free. The sticky silver leaves clung to her shirt. Branches tangled in her braids. The more she struggled, the more stuck her left arm became.

"Help!" she cried. Behind her, she could hear the screech of more birds. Feel the bitter wind from their flapping wings. She didn't know how many there were. She could only hear the screams of those they attacked.

Emerson appeared by her side, bits of leaves stuck in her sweater, a weeping cut on her chin. She pulled on Madeline's wrist, trying to tear her shirt free. Pain sang down her arm and prickled across her scalp.

"Hold still," Emerson muttered, her breath a puff of steam in the cold. She lifted the knife and sawed through the sleeve around Madeline's elbow.

Madeline fell forward to her knees, her shirtsleeve left in the brush behind her, as a bird dove toward them.

With a roar, the man with the spear charged into its path, a patch of bare skin on his side catching the moonlight as he braced the weapon against the ground. The tengu twisted to the side, and with its pointed talons speared the man through the chest, fixing him to a patch of gravel.

Madeline covered her mouth as his blood spattered across the dry leaves before her. He writhed, the Karuta card protruding from the edge of his fist, as the animal opened its beak to feast. She couldn't look. Curling into a ball, she hid her face as the man's screams suddenly went silent.

"It's not real," she told herself. "It's a dream. It isn't real."

The bird was gone when she peered out from under her arm. It must have taken the man with the spear, because all that remained was a wash of red and his broken weapon.

"Emerson?" she called quietly. Had the bird taken her, too? Madeline's vision dimmed at the thought.

"Please," moaned a woman. "Please help."

Madeline looked up. The woman was high up in the brush, dangling sideways, as if she'd been flung that way and stuck. Her skirt was pulled up around her thighs, revealing a thorn that had punctured straight through her calf and another through her thigh. Three more points emerged from her chest.

Madeline gave a strangled sob. Her breaths came faster as the sharp scent of blood rose in the air.

"Just a dream," she said.

She forced herself to stand on shaking legs. She needed to get out of here before the tengu caught her. If the entrance was gone, she'd have to climb.

Reaching for a vine, she pulled on it to test her weight. When it held, she found a foothold, avoiding the metallic thorns and sticky leaves. She fought the urge to gag—the brush had a rotten stench, like raw chicken left out too long.

A high cry had her head jerking back toward the center of the arena, to a felled log two people were hiding beneath. One of the birds had landed on top, its broad, inky back hunched as it scratched and pecked at the rotting wood. Madeline's stomach twisted as she caught sight of Emerson's boots tucking under the log, and Owen's arm sticking out the other side.

"Just a test," she said, her voice shaking. "Not real."

When she turned back to the brush, she came face-to-face with a man hanging upside down. His jaw was decaying, graying skin turning to paper over his cheeks. He had no eyes, just empty sockets, and his wrists and hands were slender knives of bone.

Releasing her hold, she fell backward onto the ground, staring up at him in horror as a hot breath puffed from her lips. She didn't know how she'd missed him when she'd started climbing. The silver glare of the brush wasn't bright enough to hide his short auburn hair or his white button-down shirt fluttering in the breeze. It was as if he'd grown out of the brush itself.

"Help me," he moaned. Bile rose in her throat. As the fog cleared, her gaze followed the hedge wall, and she shuddered as she found one body after another in the gleaming thorns. They begged for help in strange accents, in languages she didn't know, but understood.

How were they alive? How could they possibly still be breathing?

"I'm sorry," she whispered, pedaling backward. "I'm sorry. I can't."

A bird squawked behind her, and when she spun, she saw the creature perched on the log over Emerson and Owen, snapping its giant beak. A rock came careening through the air, puncturing its outstretched wing. The monster tilted back its head and, with an angry scream, hurled itself toward Dax.

Her heart stalled as he leapt to the side and rolled across the ground. It followed, stomping at him with its onyx talons.

"Dax!" Madeline screamed.

As the creature's head swung down, Dax punched a fist up, a flash of silver catching Madeline's attention. With the small blade of his knife he stabbed the creature in the eye, and it stumbled backward, wings flapping.

"Come a little closer, honey."

Madeline spun to find a woman in the brush behind her, her clothes torn, great hunks of flesh revealed, some picked down to the bone. Silver spiked thorns, tacky with old blood, stuck through her chest and thighs, pinning her in place.

"A little closer, that's it." With her free hand, the woman motioned her over. "I know the way out."

Madeline knew she shouldn't believe her, but desperation made her weak. She inched nearer, wariness tightening the muscles between her shoulders.

"I should have kept him safe," the woman said, one eye rolling back in her skull. "It was my fault. My fault. My fault."

Madeline fought the urge to run. Something was wrong with this woman. She looked half dead. Maybe she was a living yōkai, like Shinigami had mentioned. If so, Madeline didn't want to know.

"Where's the way out?" Madeline asked. "Please."

"Closer," she groaned.

Madeline glanced back to see Emerson snatching the broken, bloody spear off the ground. *I'm sorry,* she thought. She wasn't like her. She couldn't do this.

"One more step," the woman prompted gently.

Madeline stepped closer, tears hot on her face.

Like lightning, the woman grabbed the collar of her fleece, knotting her fist in the fabric. Madeline choked, off-balance, as it tightened around her throat. She scratched at the woman's hands, crumbling away her skin like dried clay.

The woman ripped down the zipper of her fleece, her cold fingers skittering over Madeline's chest as she grabbed one of the cards and raised it to her mouth.

"Help!" Madeline cried. "Someone help!"

She twisted, just in time to see Emerson toss the spear to Dax, who jammed it into the tengu's chest. The bird gave a wild scream.

"My fault," the woman said, her gaze latching on Dax over Madeline's shoulder. "My fault, my fault, my fault."

"Please," Madeline said, but she'd stopped struggling. She swayed, the fight gone out of her.

She was going to die here. They would all die here.

As she heard the tengu Dax stabbed fall dead to the ground behind her, the woman, still eyeing Dax, shoved the card she'd taken into her own mouth. It tore in her jaws with an awful crunching sound. Her hot breath burned Madeline's eyes.

The woman grabbed one of Madeline's hands and moved it to her mouth as if to eat her too. A new terror rolled through Madeline, potent and heavy.

Then the woman opened her mouth and, with an awful crackling, her teeth began to fall out. A molar dropped into Madeline's palm, small but weighty.

The card was gone.

Madeline finally jerked free of the woman's grip, and as she watched, the brush began to move before her, growing and twisting apart, swallowing the woman and other nearby bodies within its braided tendrils.

An opening appeared, and beyond it, Madeline could see the dark woods through a thin veil of jade flames.

"Dax!" she shouted. "Emerson! Owen!"

Without waiting, she charged through the exit. Cold fire licked her skin as she leapt out of the arena, the tooth still nestled firmly in her closed fist.

EMERSON

Emerson sprinted after Madeline, her breath coming in staggered bursts. They skidded to a stop at the edge of a cliff, kicking small rocks and debris over the side as they scrambled back. Emerson's feet tangled in the gnarled roots that curled over the drop-off like claws. She chanced a dizzying glance down, finding a shale wall that stretched down toward a silver river, maybe five stories below, then spun back, peering into the gloom.

The tengu hadn't followed them.

"We're out," she said, a pulse-pounding victory exploding in her chest. "You guys, we're out!" She rose quickly to take a head count of the others. Madeline stared into the woods behind them, one shaking fist gripped against her chest. To her side, Owen hunched over his knees. Dax leaned against a tree, breathing hard.

"We passed the test?" Owen looked back, but the gate that had appeared in the bushes was gone. His hands patted his head, the ridiculous furry vest over his chest and stomach, finally landing on the crotch of his ripped tights. He sighed in relief. Then he whooped, his breath visible in a steamy huff, and raised both middle fingers at the dark sky. "Suck it, Meido! We did it!"

"Technically Dax did it," Emerson said. "You hid under a log, and I sawed Madeline out of a bush."

Dax snorted as Madeline's hand shot up to her shorn sleeve. She rubbed at her forearm, scratching away the splatters of mud that had dried on her skin.

Emerson should have held on to that weapon. It might have come in handy.

"He wouldn't have done anything if I hadn't provided a distraction," Owen argued.

"You're a regular hero," Dax told him.

"Did you hear that, Emerson?" Owen cupped one hand to his ear, his green eyeshadow gleaming. "Dax, say it again."

"Shinigami said we'd get a stone if we finished it, right?" Madeline interrupted. "Well, look."

She unfurled her fist in a narrow beam of moonlight, revealing a small, white rock nestled against her palm. As Emerson stepped closer, its shape became clear.

"Is that a tooth?" she asked.

Madeline nodded.

Dax leaned closer. "Where did you get it?"

"You don't want to know," Madeline said with a visible shudder. "But someone took one of the cards and gave me this, and then the door opened in the brush."

"You traded one of our cards for someone's molar?" Owen asked, scratching his head. "How exactly did that conversation go?"

"I didn't really have a choice," Madeline said, looking away as Emerson met her gaze. "She took it when Dax killed that bird."

Emerson grabbed it between her thumb and forefinger, examining it for clues. There was no minute writing on it. No directions for what to do next. She offered it back, but Madeline shook her head, looking more than happy to give it up. With a sigh, Emerson tucked it into her hip pocket.

"So this is a new level?" Owen looked up. "Please tell me there are no more tengu."

"In a game, each level usually has a new encounter," Emerson told him.

"Because I'm sure this ancient death trap works exactly like your video games," Madeline grumbled, slapping the dust off her fleece and leggings.

"You have any better ideas?" Emerson asked. "Please, by all means, let's hear them."

Madeline glared at her.

"If it *is* following a gaming pattern"—Emerson sent her a pointed look—"then each encounter will get harder."

Owen's shoulders slumped. "Of course it will."

"So where is it?" Dax asked, his leather coat creaking as he turned in a slow circle. "Where's the next nightmare?"

Emerson pulled gently on her lip ring, frowning. The arena had been close when Shinigami's house had disappeared. If she had to guess, their next challenge would be, too. She looked around for a sign of where to go, but didn't know exactly what she was searching for. A path? A road sign? A map would have been nice.

As she turned downriver, a chill crawled up the back of her neck. She squinted into the dark of the woods, bracing for some danger, but none came. Still, there was something unsettling about this way. A strange intuition that this was right, even while it grated her senses.

Gamer's luck.

"Let's head downriver," she said, stepping over a knotted root. The bare trunks on either side seemed to lean into her chosen path, making her suck in her belly and try to make herself smaller.

"Hold on," said Madeline, gently prodding the bloody wound on her shoulder with two fingers. She'd been stabbed clean through by one of those thorns. The fact that she wasn't doubled over either meant she was tougher than she looked—which Emerson was not about to point out—or riding too high on adrenaline to feel it. "No one named you team captain. Maybe we should take a vote."

Emerson stopped, sending her a cold smile. "You're right. All in favor of following the girl who just got stuck in a bush, say aye."

Owen scratched the back of his neck. Dax gave Emerson a narrowed stare.

Madeline's jaw flexed. "Why do you have to take it there? Not everything has to be a fight."

"All in favor of finishing this so we can find Ian and go home, come with me."

Emerson didn't wait. She turned and headed into the woods, her sweater, still damp from sweat, chafing her skin. They didn't want to follow, that was fine. Good luck to them. It wouldn't be the first time she'd taken the road less travelled.

When she heard the crunch of their footsteps behind her, her shoulders relaxed.

She kept her eyes roaming, searching for some sign of their next challenge, but it was hard to get her bearings. Everything was different here. The dark was thick. The heavy air breathed cold over her skin. They followed the edge of the cliff and below them, the river twisted like a silver serpent, reeking of mildew. Even the current didn't sound right—more a groan than a babble.

Shinigami had said the oni's wrath had made this place unclean. She could feel it now. Like a cold, slick oil on her exposed skin.

Where was the next challenge? The clock was ticking. It had been almost midnight when they'd gone into that cave. How much time had passed since then? An hour? More? Wariness churned in her stomach. Shinigami's house and the tengu arena had both appeared and then disappeared as if they had never been there at all. How could you beat a game when the playing board was constantly changing?

A quiet hum reached her ears. A song she recognized—*I . . . I will survive. Just as long as I know how to love, I know I'll stay alive.* She peered through the gloom to find Dax's hulking shadow.

"Nice job back there," she said, shivering as she recalled the giant creature landing on the log she'd dived under. "I'll have to remember the old pocketknife-to-the-eye maneuver. Might come in handy."

He was quiet a moment. "What happened to you?"

"What do you mean?"

"You and Maddy. I never thought you two would be on the opposite side of anything."

"*Madeline,*" Emerson said, as snobby as possible. "Why don't you ask her?"

"Because I'm asking you."

Emerson jammed her hands into her pockets as they walked.

"I don't know. After that day at the cave, things changed. You went who-knows-where. Owen hooked up with the drama nerds. Madeline's mom took her to swim team tryouts, and she made a whole bunch of fancy new friends."

Friends who were singular in every way. Swimmer. Female.

Straight. The kind who fit into boxes that romantic, but not physical, introverts could not.

"I wasn't who-knows-where."

"Wow," said Emerson. "So vague and mysterious. The vibe really goes with that jacket."

He glanced down at his worn leather coat. "What's wrong with my jacket?"

"What's wrong with my answer?"

He sighed. "I was locked up. A psychiatric hospital."

Her eyebrows shot up. "Seriously?"

"Turns out not everyone sees the ghosts that are trying to kill us." A twig snapped beneath his step, and she flinched. "My mom sent me to a facility in New York to get some clarity."

She blew out a stiff breath. "Lucky you."

Dax's mom wasn't big on parenting. When they were kids, he'd never had a curfew, or a lunch to bring to school. Emerson hadn't pushed him to talk about where his dad was, or why his mom never came to meet the teacher nights, but she noticed, just like she noticed how he always wore the same baggy jeans and Green Day shirt, and that when he'd finally gotten new clothes, they looked a lot like Ian's old ones.

"It wasn't so bad," he said. "We had waffles on the weekends. And I learned to play guitar."

She remembered the case he'd been carrying when they'd met outside the theater where they'd found Owen. He must have left it somewhere.

"How long has this ghost thing been going on for you?" she asked, staring into the gloom to her right. It could have gone on for miles, or stopped just beyond the nearest trees. In the dark it was impossible to tell.

Still, she couldn't shake the feeling that somewhere in the shadows, something was watching them.

Dax cleared his throat. "It started right after Ian disappeared. I lit the apartment on fire trying to get away from one."

"Oh," she said. "I see now why therapy was on the table."

He snorted.

"How did you even survive this long?" Without Dax in that arena, she wasn't sure she'd still be here. She couldn't imagine facing all those monsters alone.

"Good luck, I guess."

"I guess," she said, but it didn't sit right. A game of this magnitude only worked if the rules were consistent, and yet they'd been broken before the real playing had even begun. They all should have entered on even footing, but Dax had been fighting yōkai for four years. Maybe he'd somehow selected the hard mode, or never stopped playing when they had.

Maybe Dax wasn't telling her the whole story.

She gave him a sidelong glance. A beam of white moonlight cut through the branches, lighting a patch of ground an eerie, bruised hue. His face was streaked with dirt and purple blood—the tengu's, most likely—making him come off even more severe. He definitely had experience fighting monsters, and she was sorry about that. But she wasn't sure if that meant she could trust him. Even though he had killed that bird, they weren't friends. They were teammates, at best.

"And you?" he asked. The branches thatched together above them, black, spindly fingers blotting out the moon. It was hard to see the ground before her, to see her feet at all as they tromped over the dirt and fallen leaves. Worry quickened her stride. Had she been wrong to choose this direction? If she'd made a mistake, Madeline would never let it go.

Emerson lifted her chin. "I dropped out of school and became a menace to society."

"Why?"

"Why'd I become a menace, or why'd I drop out?"

"Drop out."

She shot him a glare. "I don't know. Wasn't for me."

"Yes it was."

"Oh, is that right? Well, I could have really used your guidance sophomore year, asshole."

"Maybe you should have picked up the phone then."

"Like you would have answered."

"I would have. For you." He glanced over his shoulder. "For any of you."

She missed a step, then quickly caught up. Was he being serious? Dax was never serious. The old Dax hadn't been, anyway.

"The phone works both ways," she finally said. "Why didn't you call me?"

"I did."

"No you didn't."

"We going to fight about it?"

She groaned. "I'm kind of busy now, between the giant monster birds and the corpse bushes."

He chuckled, his voice low and disembodied in the dark. "Well, pencil me in sometime in the future then."

She shot him a glare, but as they walked on, something shifted inside her, loosening her tongue. "Things were different after Ian. School just . . . it didn't matter. It wasn't important. Not like they were teaching anything useful anyway. My history teacher freshman year didn't even know about the Tulsa Massacre. The curriculum is so whitewashed." She was still disgusted.

From behind her came a scoff. She spun to find Madeline shaking her head. How long had she been listening? From the way she was avoiding looking at Dax, Emerson guessed she'd heard a lot.

"Is there a problem, Butterfly?"

"Not at all," said Madeline. "I hope you got a trophy for being such a great ally."

A heat spread in Emerson's chest. She looked to Owen, but his gaze was fixed on the ground.

"What's that supposed to mean?" she asked.

"It means your whitewashed curriculum answer is a little convenient. All curriculum is whitewashed, because it was created by a culture steeped in white supremacy."

"But I—"

"You dropped out to make a stand, which is a privilege—"

"A privilege?" she sputtered.

"That's right. A privilege. One not everyone can afford without becoming part of the narrative that they were never going to make it anyway."

The heat in Emerson's chest was searing now, spreading up her throat. She'd always supported Madeline, and Owen, and everyone who'd been affected by this messed-up, hateful system. She'd marched for their rights in Washington Park.

At least, she had before she'd left school.

"I'm the one picking fights, huh?" she muttered.

This was bullshit. She knew how Madeline had struggled growing up—that she always had to be perfect. One step out of line, and her mom was all over her. At first, Emerson had assumed that was just how her family was, but as they'd gotten older she'd realized it was more than that. She couldn't play by the same rules. She couldn't even wear the same sweatpants and crumpled shirt to school that Emerson did without getting a note sent home. Emerson had been there through all of it—not as some kind of white savior, but as her friend.

But now she was an outsider in Madeline's life. Ignorant and privileged.

She felt sick.

"What's that?" Dax pointed ahead.

Her heart leapt as the trees cleared before them. In the distance, she made out a bridge spearing through the fog, a dull red arch stretching high over the treacherous cliffs it connected. She picked up her pace to an awkward, stumbling jog as the dark woods thinned. Soon, she could make out an entry gate at the bridge's base—two simple wooden pillars in the ground, connected across the top by a beam that flared at the edges.

Determination lifted her chin.

"Come on," she said, pushing on. Behind her, she could hear Madeline and Owen hurrying to catch up.

As they left the shelter of the trees, the moon revealed itself, a fingernail of white in an empty, black sky. It provided more light now that they were in the open, but night still muted the colors, graying the scattered branches, the rocks, and the dead, patchy moss beneath their feet. It was as though the whole place were decomposing.

They were exposed out here, open to attack. On the bridge, they'd be even more visible.

"Look," Madeline said, her voice pitching. "Is that . . ." She pointed to the right pillar of the gate, a dusky red beam decayed by time and weather. Sharp splinters stuck out at all angles. It looked as if bugs had feasted on the right side, whittling down a spot near the top.

Just below it, carved into the wood, were two letters.

I.S.

Emerson's heart tripped.

"Ian Spencer," Dax whispered as Madeline's hand dropped to her side.

"He's here," Owen said.

"Let's not get ahead of ourselves," Emerson said, though she couldn't stop the hope from blossoming in her chest. Ian had been gone for four years. The searches had been called off. The police had told everyone the chances he was alive were slim to none.

But what if they'd been wrong? What if they could really bring him back?

She hadn't truly believed it might be possible until this moment, and it frightened her just as much as the tengu. What if they'd come all this way just to find out they were too late?

"Maybe he was trying to complete the challenges," Madeline said quickly. "Do it all on his own. Maybe this is a bread crumb he left behind for us to follow!"

"Didn't the bread crumbs get eaten by birds?" Dax asked.

"Please don't talk about birds." Owen winced.

"The marks are old." Emerson reached up, her finger pressing into the cuts in the wood. "They could have been made years ago. 'Ignatius Sociopath' could have carved them into this arch for all we know."

"It's a torii," Owen corrected, clearing his throat. "Not an arch. It marks a sacred space. My grandparents used to have one outside their shrine."

"Sacred space," Dax said with a scowl. "Does that translate into dangerous space?"

"We're about to find out," Emerson muttered, glancing again at the letters *IS*. Time seemed to quicken as she stared at them, the seconds ticking by in her brain. "We have to try it, at least. If we don't complete the other six tasks and get the stones before dawn, we're stuck here, remember?"

She stepped onto the first plank.

When it held steady, she grasped the arm rails and tilted her weight forward. Madeline watched her, balancing on the balls of her feet, hands fisted at her sides.

Two more steps, and Emerson was standing on a rickety plank over thin air. She held her breath as she went a few more without a problem.

"It's all right!" she called.

The bridge creaked as the others began to follow.

Step by step, she made her way up the incline. Her hands gripped the railing like a kid riding the wall at an ice-skating rink. Beneath her feet, the planks revealed a slice of river five stories below, brown and frothy as it whipped through the ravine.

She winced.

"Don't look down," Madeline said, just behind her.

She forced her eyes forward. "Thanks for the tip."

They reached the place where the bridge disappeared into the clouds, the cotton wisps close enough to touch. The thick, gray air swirled and parted around her fingertips as she reached up.

Wonder blossomed in her chest. Owen was right; it did feel sacred.

"Where exactly did Shinigami say Meido was?" Dax shouted over the far-below roar of the river. He must have been last in line judging by the volume of his voice, but she didn't dare glance back.

"She didn't," Madeline said.

"Well it's not Cincy," Owen said. "I'm not sure Meido is even on Earth."

Emerson considered the strange things they'd seen—Shinigami, the yōkai, the sacred arch, the tengu that swooped down from the sky. The game had to be Japanese in origin—Owen recognized parts of it, even if they weren't in a form he had ever seen. It was as if they'd fallen into another world where mythology was reality.

Except spirits, demons, and monsters *were* real to a lot of people in her world. It wasn't a matter of believing. Of faith. Her Western cultural lens was trying to filter things into categories—real and imaginary, alive and dead—when in reality, they just *were*. This world, and everything in it, existed, just as she existed.

"It's another dimension," said Emerson.

"A what?" Dax asked.

"A different dimension!" she called back. She took another step, carefully shifting her hand higher on the railing. "An alternate reality. A glimpse behind the veil. Scientists say it's possible that there are replicate universes are out there. Maybe this is some kind of pocket reality. Somewhere that's been here the whole time, and we just haven't seen it."

She thought of how the quicksand had pulled them under, and how she'd woken in the woods, a shimmer of green flames around them. Shinigami hadn't said how they'd come, only that they had to finish the game to leave.

"If it's the Japanese pocket, how'd I get here? I'm not Japanese," Dax yelled. "Unless my mom meant 'your father is Asian' when she said 'your father is Satan' all those years ago."

"Ian wasn't . . . *isn't* . . . Japanese either," said Madeline.

Emerson started to point out that their races didn't matter, but shut her mouth before the words came out. The last thing she wanted was Madeline pointing out how woke she was again.

"Well this isn't *my* fault," Owen said, his voice pitching as the bridge creaked beneath him. "I didn't sign us up for Japanese Monster Camp."

"I don't think this game cares about who we are personally," said Emerson carefully. "Shinigami never said anything about only Japanese people being admitted here. Clearly we're all welcome to play."

"An equal opportunity nightmare," Dax mused. "That's nice."

"For all we know, our world is the pocket world," Emerson said. "And this game is where it all started."

"Our world is the knockoff?" Owen said. "No way."

"Why not?" Emerson said, the mist thick and white around them, dewing droplets of water on her skin. "I mean, whole civilizations have been erased by genocide and colonization. Some Christian conqueror could have killed the storytellers or destroyed records of the real origin of our world, just to hide the fact that the universe as we know it is . . . is . . ."

"Just a storage unit for players in this master game."

Emerson glanced back to Madeline, framed in clouds, her braids whipping wildly in the breeze, and remembered, just for a second, what it was like to be her friend. The certainty that came with it. The knowledge that they could face whatever challenge arose together.

"History's made by those who tell the stories, right?" Madeline asked quietly.

Emerson nodded, and the heat in her chest finally cooled.

"I don't buy it," Dax said. "There are billions of stories that could have come from pocket worlds. Why'd we end up here, and not, I don't know, Valhalla? Or Atlantis? The chances of us finding our way into this place, together, should be virtually impossible."

"Agreed," said Owen.

"So how do you explain it then?" Emerson asked.

Owen hesitated. "It's a game, isn't it? This could be a large-scale escape room."

Emerson barked a laugh. "It's impossible that pocket worlds exist, but you think there's an escape room big enough for all *this*?"

"I'm still working out the details!" Owen threw back.

"Quiet!"

She froze at Dax's command, gripping the railings with both hands. They were nearly at the top of the bridge, the mist below them now like a false floor.

"Look." Dax's voice had gone rough with warning, and though

she braced for tengu, none came. There was only the open sky and the moon, moving over a faraway wisp of clouds.

She blinked. That wasn't right. The moon should have gone *behind* the clouds, not the other way around. But before she could make sense of it, the moon began to shift across the horizon, the silver sickle lurching sideways across the horizon.

"What's happening?" Owen whispered.

"It's not a moon," she realized, tracing the top of it with her eyes. Making out a head, and wide shoulders. A slow, swinging arm. "It's an eye."

The mostly closed eye of an enormous monster lumbering slowly across the skyline.

What would happen if it opened that eye? If it looked at them?

Just as her mind wrapped around it, a low howl cut through the clouds, and set her heart pounding to a new frantic rhythm. She recognized it immediately—they'd heard that sound before in the woods outside Shinigami's. It was closer now, more urgent.

Owen looked back over his shoulder. "What was that?"

Emerson looked back, but they were too high up to see where the bridge met the ground. She remembered the feeling she'd had earlier that they were being watched. Whatever was making that howl could have followed them, and they wouldn't have known.

Beneath her feet, the bridge began to shake.

"Go," Dax said. "Get off the bridge!"

The board below him gave a loud crack, and Dax threw himself forward just as it broke and dropped through the air. Emerson stared into the gaping hole where it had been, eyes wide. The river below thrashed, hungry.

"Emerson!" Madeline pushed her forward, throwing off Emerson's balance as another board ripped loose of its mooring before them.

"Jump!" Madeline shouted, and Emerson did, landing bent over the railing with a terrifying view of the water beneath. The bridge was quaking now, the boards rippling like piano keys. The wood crackled like kindling, snapping and whining. Splinters shot through the air as more boards dropped away to the river below.

They were going to fall.

"Dax!" Owen shouted.

Emerson looked back in horror to find Dax stretched across a gap, his chest and hips suspended over thin air, his white-knuckled grip wrapped around the base of the railing. Owen was crawling toward him. He grabbed Dax's wrist, then planted his feet against a shaking board to haul him across the gap.

"We can't stop," Madeline shouted, pulling at her arm as she slipped by. "We have to go!"

But Dax had killed that tengu. They'd only made it to this level because of him. They needed him.

She dropped to her knees, reaching for Owen's shoulder. Hooking her arm around his, she pulled with all her might, every muscle straining over the quaking boards. Sweat stung her eyes.

She didn't see the crack in the board below Owen until it was too late.

With a snap, it gave way, and when Dax and Owen fell, she was dragged into the sky after them.

———

The air slapped her face, whipped her clothes. She gasped for breath—short, desperate sips that didn't fill her lungs. She was in a free fall, spinning, flipping, arms pedaling wildly.

She hit the water hard on her side. Pain slashed down her leg, up her ribs, jarring her spine. Her head whipped to the side, and for a moment everything went hazy.

Brown water. White sky. She tasted blood in her mouth.

Something slimy was sliding up her pant leg.

She cried out as its circled her ankle. Bubbles erupted from her mouth. Panic beat a rhythm between her temples. With another bubbly cry, she tried to kick it away, but it dragged her down. Her arms extended, trying to slow her descent, but it didn't help. Deeper into the river she went, her sweater rising over her face, her boots weighing her down.

Her lungs burned.

She couldn't breathe.

A cold, slick sensation climbed up her opposite pant leg. It tightened like a noose around her calf, and then pulled hard, speeding her descent.

The rope's coil tightened, cutting off the circulation in her foot. Another wrapped around her left wrist. She blinked through the brown water, seeing a black snake spiraling up her arm.

Not a snake. An eel.

Panicked, she smacked the creature aside, but it attached to her leg, sinking white teeth through the fabric of her pants with a sharp sting. She was still going down. The river was bottomless; her head was pounding from the pressure. Renewed desperation streaked through her as the eels took shape before her, a swirl of black into a torso, legs, arms, a head with long black strands of hair.

A girl made of eels.

She wrapped her arms around Emerson's chest, pressing her face to her neck. A row of eel teeth flashed as she opened her wide mouth and bit into Emerson's shoulder. Blood stained the water, drawing a dozen more eels from all directions. So many that the water churned above them.

A splash came from her side, and when she twisted, a shadow was streaming toward her. She tried to struggle away, but it was coming too quickly. Like a battering ram, it burst through the eels, tearing them apart. Emerson made out dark, braided hair, and a fleece with a golden logo.

Maddy.

Arms streamlined before her, Madeline cut down through the water, legs kicking hard. The eels encircled them, a hundred wriggling snakes. She peeled away one on Emerson's leg, then another at her waist. When two more were gone, Emerson could shimmy free, and with the last of her air searing her lungs, she kicked up hard out of the black tornado.

She broke the surface with a gasp, air scraping her throat. A white shoreline came into view, and she could see Owen dragging himself onto it. Driven by instinct, she swam toward him, dragging herself out of the water with a sob as soon as her feet touched solid ground.

"Help!" Madeline called.

Emerson turned, and her knees weakened.

Madeline was dragging Dax to shore. He was limp, his head hanging back. His jacket was gone, and his clothing was soaked. Owen grabbed his other arm to help heave him onto the sand, and when they set him down, a pointed black tail swiped across his bottom lip.

Every swear word Emerson had ever heard crossed her mind as she opened Dax's jaw, reached into his mouth, and before thinking too hard, pulled two feet of slithering black eel free of his throat.

With a jerk, Dax gagged and spit up a lungful of water.

"Dax?" Madeline's hands ghosted over his chest and arms, as if ready to grab another eel off of him at any moment.

He coughed and gasped.

"You're alive," Owen said. He pulled off his now crooked designer frames, sticking his finger through a missing lens. "Oh man, my glasses are broken."

"Seriously?" Madeline asked, exasperated.

"I can't see without them!"

Emerson's fingers dug into the cold, grainy beach. She was still breathing hard. "Do you have the cards?"

Madeline reached into her shirt, pulling out the heavy pieces. Beads of water clung to the paper, but did not seem to have soaked through the coarse surface.

"Are they all there?" Emerson asked as Madeline thumbed through them. "Did we get another stone?"

"I didn't get one," said Madeline.

"Me either," said Owen.

"I ate an eel," said Dax.

Owen snorted, then laughed. Madeline buried her face in her hands and began to giggle. Emerson joined them, and even Dax was chuckling—a rasping, coughing sound that stripped away the image of his still body in her mind.

Their laughter faded into shivers and coughs.

She sagged. Was that not the challenge? Or had they somehow failed? The bridge remained upriver, though she failed to see any broken planks. It was almost as if the structure had put itself back together. The waves down below had smoothed now, the eels quiet beneath. She shuddered to think what might have happened to her if Madeline hadn't been there.

Emerson glanced over at her, now blue-lipped and shivering on the riverbank. Why had she done that? The girl was scared of her own shadow. If she'd thought Emerson hadn't seen her trying to climb over the wall in the arena to escape the tengu, she was wrong.

Madeline looked up, and Emerson followed her gaze toward the trees that climbed the craggy cliff behind them, rubbing her arms. The cold air cut through her sopping clothes.

"If that wasn't the challenge, what is?" Her breath fogged in front of her mouth.

"I don't know," Owen said. "But if we don't warm up, we're going to catch hypothermia."

"Don't be dramatic," she said, but he was right.

With his back against a gray boulder on the bank, Owen sat on a hunk of driftwood and pulled off his tattered felt slippers. He pulled off his green costume leggings, baring his lean legs. His soaked fur vest came off next, revealing a fit, V-shaped chest.

"Who wants to snuggle?" he asked, turning a lens-less wink toward Emerson. "What? We have to share body heat."

"You make me the little spoon, I cut your balls off," Emerson said, quickly stripping down to her cotton boy-short underwear and black cami. The frigid air raked over her stomach and chest, but it was still somehow less cold without her sweater on. Before she set her pants on a nearby rock, she checked the pocket to make sure the tooth was still there. With a sigh of relief, she tucked it into the bra of her camisole.

Then she sat next to Owen, his goose-bumped leg and arm pressed against hers.

Worrying her bottom lip between her teeth, Madeline frowned at Dax, who with a resigned sigh began hacking at a branch with his pocketknife to make curled wood shavings for a fire.

"Let's go, Butterfly," Emerson told her.

Madeline didn't object to the name as she toed off her boots.

Her soggy fleece dripped as she wiggled out of it, setting the wet cards on the ground. Turning away, she peeled her leggings down her blotchy thighs. Her shoulder, punctured from the thorn wall in the arena, had stopped bleeding, but had stained the back of her pink bra copper. Even though she lived half her life in a paper-thin swimsuit, she didn't act like she was used to people staring at her. One arm crossed over her stomach, the other over her chest, like she was self-conscious.

In a flash, she was pressed tightly to Emerson's side.

"So if the bridge and the river eels weren't part of the next challenge," Owen said, "what's next?" He had one arm around Emerson, the other fisted against his thigh. Most of his eyeshadow had washed away in the river, but a small glimmer of green lined the creases of his lids.

Emerson leaned forward, reluctant and stiff. She laid out the cards, side by side.

"What do we have?" she asked Owen.

"Wounded hearts," Owen read. "Bravery. Cowardice. Lies. And honor."

"They're out of order," Dax said, his throat still rough from the eel. He rubbed two sticks together over his small pile of bark and moss. "Bravery was last."

"I think honor was last," said Madeline, giving a small frown.

Emerson rearranged the cards. "We never got one for loyalty—we figured that out before the tengu encounter. And fear is gone now, right?" She looked to Owen, who nodded. "Which means next should be cowardice." She tapped the card with the matching kanji.

"Are you sure?" Madeline asked.

She nodded. "LFCLHHB. Live Fast, Cry Loud, Heal Hate, Breathe."

"Did you see that on a bumper sticker?" said Owen.

"It's a mnemonic device," Madeline said, squeezing the water from her hair. "You use it for memorizing lists. Live Fast—that's loyalty and fear. Cry Loud is cowardice and lies."

"Heal Hate is wounded *hearts*, honor, and Breathe for bravery," Emerson finished. "So we got our first stone—the tooth—in exchange for the fear card. Maybe we lost the loyalty card when Shinigami's house disappeared."

"What does that mean?" Owen asked. "Can we not finish?"

"There's got to be some way to get it back," Emerson said. "I just need to figure out the sequence."

She'd played some version of an RPG all her life. When she'd been a child, she'd made up quests from books and comics she'd read. Then there was old-school D&D and strategy board games she'd played with her dad, and finally video games, like *Assassin 0*.

They almost all followed a pattern, and learning it was essential to beating the game.

"Dax killed the bird, then we got the tooth, and the door opened to the next level," Emerson said. "Solve the card, get the stone, level up."

"Finish all seven challenges by dawn," Madeline said, then shivered. "Is that when the giant opens his eye?"

"Let's hope it gets a full eight hours and isn't a light sleeper," she said, lowering her voice just in case it was. "What else do we know?"

"Don't cheat or the game will punish you," Dax said.

"I still don't get that," Owen said. "What's this place going to do that's worse than what it's already doing?"

"Well muscle up, Buttercup," she told him. "Dax beat the fear challenge by overcoming his fear and killing that bird. If the next level follows suit, we'll have to be brave to beat the cowardice challenge."

She tucked her chin closer to her chest. The shared body heat seared warmth back into her fingers and toes. It made her aware of the rough hair of Owen's thigh beside hers. The hard muscle of Madeline's arm.

"How many people do you think have played?" Madeline asked.

Emerson thought of the people they'd seen fighting the tengu. There could have been dozens in the mist, hundreds stuck in the thorned walls of the arena. She rolled her shoulders, cringing at the strain of knotted muscles.

"The guy with the spear looked like he had a plan, like this wasn't his first time," Madeline said.

Emerson nodded. All the fighters had old, worn clothing, and when they'd looked to the skies, they'd known what was coming.

"The woman who took the card," Madeline said quietly. "She kept saying, 'My fault.' Over and over. What do you think that means?"

"Probably that it was her fault," Dax said.

"What was?" Madeline asked.

"The birds. The thorns. The weather. Take your pick." His voice had thinned. He snapped a twig.

Madeline's jaw twitched. "Why do you always have to do that?"

"Do what?"

"Act like you're above it all." She gestured sharply toward the sky, making him snort. "Like you're not as scared as the rest of us."

"Of course he's scared," Emerson said. "He'd be stupid not to be."

"Then he should stop making the rest of us feel like idiots," Madeline snapped at her.

"He's not making me feel like an idiot," she replied. "And Owen's too self-absorbed to care about anyone's opinion but his own."

"She's not wrong," said Owen.

Madeline glared at Emerson. She smiled.

"So it's just me," Madeline said. "Why?"

Dax scowled, and Madeline's chin lifted. Emerson cocked a brow as Dax slung a hand around the back of his neck.

"You make me nervous," he said quietly.

"Sure I do," she snapped.

"I don't think that was sarcasm," Owen said under his breath.

Maddy huffed, but when she looked to Dax for confirmation, he had turned away.

"Anyway," said Emerson, past ready for a change of topic.

"There was this lady in the facility in New York," Dax said after a moment, then hesitated, his shoulders bunching as he worked on the fire.

Emerson could feel his anxiety.

"Perhaps you recall from eavesdropping in the woods, but Dax got thrown into a mental health hospital because no one believed he saw ghosts," Emerson said. "Everybody over it? Great."

She looked from Owen, quickly nodding, to Madeline, whose brows pinched but whose mouth remained shut.

Dax cleared his throat. "She used to say the same thing—'It's my fault.' Something happened with her kid—an accident, I think. She couldn't get over it. The repetition was a side effect of the meds."

"So those people in the arena were drugged?" Madeline asked.

"What is it with you and people getting drugged?" Dax asked, but his tone was softer than before. "I just meant that maybe she got stuck and couldn't move on."

"That guy with the spear was a player," Emerson said, her stomach sinking. "We saw his card. And he knew what to expect."

"He can't pass the challenge," Madeline said.

Emerson shrugged. "In a video game, if you fail the level, you usually have a chance to do it again."

"Lovely," Owen said. "That's what Shinigami meant by getting stuck here. An endless cycle of dress rehearsals. Hell week forever."

The thought sent a violent shiver through Emerson. She couldn't imagine spending every hour of every day facing the tengu.

A small tendril of gray smoke twisted into the air from Dax's hands.

With a hoot, Owen left Emerson's side to gather kindling. Dax kept the fire small, a reminder that they weren't alone in these woods. He propped their clothes on rocks and branches beside it to dry them, then peeled off his sweatshirt with a pained wince from the cold. His shirt beneath was black and threadbare, with the words GREEN DAY and an electric guitar across the front.

"Seriously?" Emerson laughed. "How does that shirt still fit you?"

Dax looked down. "It stretches." He seemed to debate taking it off, then in a rush shrugged out of it, stripped down to his boxers. After tucking the knife into his waistband, he sat on the other side of Madeline, an arm's length away.

"So now we're all modest?" Emerson asked, annoyed. She reached over Madeline to drag Dax closer. When he moved, the back of Madeline's shoulder aligned with his chest, and her legs overlapped his thigh.

Madeline cleared her throat.

Dax stared straight ahead.

You make me nervous.

It was like they were back in middle school, Dax pretending he wasn't staring at her in pre-algebra, Maddy writing his name in loopy script in her notebook.

"You know, there are other ways to increase body heat," Owen offered.

"Gross," said Emerson.

"Doesn't have to be me," Owen said. "You could pair off with Madeline, and I could . . ." He looked over their heads to Dax, who rolled his eyes. "Enjoy some alone time."

"Seriously, what is wrong with you?" said Madeline.

"It's just a suggestion," Owen said. "You can tell me when you've lost three toes to frostbite that it wasn't a good idea."

"I would give three toes right now for you to shut up," said Emerson, shifting in her seat. She became overly aware of Madeline's pink cheeks, and Dax's rigid posture. How easy it was for Owen to talk about sex, like it meant nothing.

Why did everything have to devolve to that? Why couldn't people just like each other, love each other even, without that part of it?

Because that's not how people were made. She was the one who'd been built without that need—a piece she'd thought would come as she'd gotten older, or when she met the right person, or when she watched the steamy scenes in movies. But it hadn't come. And seeing Dax and Madeline spark together reminded her how different she was.

It was fine. She liked being who she was. But occasionally it would have been nice to know what all the fuss was about.

"I'd give three toes for a fat-free vanilla latte from The Bean," said Madeline.

Emerson could feel her gaze on the side of her face, and felt like her thoughts had been acted out behind a thin sheet of glass.

"Forget the latte, I'd give three toes for a burger," Owen said. "And Wi-Fi."

"Status update," Emerson said, with a sudden burst of chattering teeth. *"Hell's colder than I thought, but at least the company's shit."*

Owen laughed.

"I haven't had a burger since freshman year," Madeline said. When Owen gasped, she added, "It's not exactly approved by my nutritionist."

"What is?" Dax asked.

"Lean proteins, some grains, and vegetables, mostly."

Owen looked offended. "No doughnuts?"

She shivered. "Doughnuts don't maximize your physical effectiveness."

Owen's spine straightened. His arms bent at rigid angles. "Must maximize effectiveness," he said in a robot voice. "Insert vegetables. Shit excellence. Beep. Bop. Beep."

Dax laughed.

When Emerson joined him, Madeline groaned. "I hate all of you."

Their laughter faded, but Emerson felt the wake of it, warming her from the inside out. It made her squirm. She remembered that kind of comfort too well. It was all-encompassing, and safe, and when it was ripped away, it hurt like hell.

"We should keep moving," she said, pushing up. They didn't know when the giant would open its eye, but she could feel dawn chasing them.

"But Dax just got the fire going," Owen whined.

"You want to stay here forever, be my guest." She started to round the fire to reach for her pants and sweater, but caught movement on the far bank of the river out of the corner of her eye.

She froze.

"What is it?" Dax was beside her in an instant.

"Nothing," she said, scanning the shoreline for any sign of life. An animal. A person. She squinted, stepping closer to the water, but there was nothing except the dark, creepy woods, and the sharp cliff stretching up behind it.

A creak came from behind them, then a deep voice, quaking in excitement.

"Look what has washed up on my shore!"

Emerson spun to find a man on the opposite side of the fire, leaning heavily on a cane. He was as old as Shinigami, and no taller than Dax's shoulder, with a slender build and a peppered topknot. His wide pants and tunic were a patchwork quilt of shiny leather, which rustled as he stepped closer to their drying clothes.

Instantly, Emerson became aware of how exposed she was—apart from her underwear and camisole, she was naked, every freckle, dimple, and swell of her skin on display. A flush crept up her chest, needling against the cold. Beside her, Madeline tried to cover herself, leaning behind Owen when he stood.

The man's words reached Emerson a moment later, and she glanced past Dax, now crossing his arms over his chest beside her, to the red arch connecting the shale cliffs upriver.

"We had a small problem crossing the bridge," she said, carefully moving in front of the cards, which were still splayed across the ground. The man seemed pleasantly surprised to see them, but unconcerned by their state of undress or that they'd clearly taken an unplanned swim.

He chuckled. "Ahh, yes. My bridge will not suffer the weight of strangers."

Dread lodged in Emerson's throat. Still, there could be a reason for his visit. He could be a guide like Shinigami. He might have information about the game or their part in it.

"Does that mean we failed our second challenge?" she asked.

"Crossing is a challenge, one you certainly failed." He gave a wide smile. "But worry not. There is no harm done. Not too many bumps or bruises from the fall, I hope. You have a nice flush to your cheeks." He tilted his head to examine Emerson's legs, and she snapped her fingers and pointed back to her face.

"Eyes up, old man."

Madeline stood, still hiding her chest and underwear behind her arms.

"Our clothes," she hissed at Emerson. "Get our stuff!"

"He said it was *a* challenge, not *the* challenge," Dax said quietly to Emerson. "If it was, we'd have to redo the bridge, right?"

"Like the guy with the tengu." Emerson nodded.

Dax was right. They wouldn't be here if they'd failed. They were still moving forward, which meant their next challenge could start at any time.

She looked at the old man, wondering if it had already begun.

Owen crossed in front of them to reach for his pants, but before he got there, their visitor bent and gathered their clothing into his arms.

"Oh, such rags!" he said, curling his nose in disgust.

"That costume was hand sewn, thank you very much," Owen told him.

The man threw the pile of clothing into the fire. Though they were wet, they went up like dead leaves, sparking in a thrust of orange flames.

Emerson jerked back. Madeline gaped.

"Whoa!" Owen said. "I've got four more shows! Not cool."

"Not cool," the old man agreed, patting his chest. "Keneō," he pronounced slowly, as if that was what Owen had meant to say before. "Come. I have what you seek."

A dark curiosity drew Emerson's shoulder blades together, but before she could ask any more, Keneō had turned and was walking into the woods.

"He's leading us to the next challenge. That's got to be what he means." She checked that their first prize was still in her cami and stepped forward to follow.

"What about our clothes?" Madeline asked, scrambling to pick up the cards.

"My mom gave me that shirt," Dax grunted.

"I'm not fighting a monster naked," Owen said.

Emerson wasn't thrilled about the idea either, but they didn't have much of a choice. Their clothing was gone, and the strange man who claimed to have what they needed was quickly disappearing into the trees.

"Eyes open," she said. "And whatever happens, be brave."

They picked through the woods barefoot, following Keneō over the fallen leaves and white, chunky sand. The uneven ground bruised and poked at Emerson's soles, but she kept a watchful eye as they cut through a break in the cliff. The shale walls squeezed in on either side, the eye-lit sky above framed like a bolt of lightning. Cobwebs tickled her bare shoulders. Just as claustrophobia was mounting between her temples, the cliffs parted again. A new section of the woods appeared, filled with fat, gray trees, their spindly limbs twisting in all directions. Strips of thick, leathery fabric hung in the branches, swaying gently in the breeze between old oil lanterns encased in glass.

The light spread across the ground and through the trees, twinkling and soft, and yet filling Emerson with an opposite pressure—where before she hadn't had enough space, now she had too much. As she walked, she kept her hands loose and ready at her sides. She braced for something sinister to be hiding behind the heavy curtains. Another one of those mutilated people like in the brush, or something worse.

Owen moved closer behind her.

The path opened to reveal a small, round clearing edged by trees. They grew so densely that only slivers of the woods could be seen between them. More lights glowed from boxy lamps hanging from the branches. Tables made of knotted roots were covered with more stacks of the fabric from the trees. It looked like her mom's sewing table at home—half-finished projects piled up and hanging over the backs of chairs.

"You must be hungry," Keneō said.

At the mention, an ache panged through Emerson's hollow stomach. Her throat burned with thirst. They hadn't had anything to drink or eat since yesterday, but she hadn't been truly hungry until now. Whether that was because of his suggestion or the consistent run of adrenaline, she didn't know.

She turned to Dax, who slowly flicked the blade of his knife open in his hand. Madeline was behind him, hugging the cards against her chest, while Owen spun in a slow circle to take in their surroundings.

Keneō led them to a table set with dusty dishes. Beside each of them were a set of long lacquered chopsticks and a folded napkin made of thick, beige cloth.

"Sit, sit." He motioned to four straight-backed chairs. Emerson didn't want to do what he asked, but Keneō waited patiently, blinking like an owl. "There is no need to be afraid. You are safe here. These old trees are stronger than any engimono." He patted a nearby trunk fondly.

Slowly, Emerson perched on the edge of a chair. After a moment the others reluctantly followed.

"Ah, good." With a smile, Keneō turned toward another table piled with more dishes.

"What's an engimono?" asked Madeline under her breath, the cards now on her lap. When Emerson glanced down she saw the kanji for "cowardice" on top and lifted her chin.

"It's a good luck charm. I think." Owen scratched a hand through his hair. "My mom used to tell a story about how a girl had one that kept her safe from yōkai. She lost it in a lake, and . . ." He drew a line across his throat with his finger.

"So it's protection," Emerson said.

"We could use some of that," Dax added.

"I'm not a hundred percent," said Owen, flustered. "Maybe it was bad luck and that's why she drowned."

"Maybe we'll pass on it, then," said Dax.

Emerson's gaze fell to a nearby table. There were sewing materials—needles and bobbins of thread. Maybe this was a shop, or a tavern, and Keneō was meant to give them clothes and protection for their journey.

"After you have some food in your bellies, I will measure you for the finest clothes in all Meido," said Keneō.

He returned to the table carrying a huge knife with a wooden handle, the fat sickle blade the length of his forearm.

Emerson jumped in her seat. The rough wood of the chair chafed the backs of her bare thighs. Her eyes remained on the blade as Keneō tapped it against his plate twice.

The trees behind the table moved.

At first, Emerson thought it was a trick of the light. She blinked, but the gnarled trunks twisted aside, creating an opening into a small room behind them. When a man stepped through, Madeline shrieked.

The new arrival was wearing loose pants like Keneō, but his chest was bare and mutilated. The skin had been flayed away, revealing red blood and white tissue, bones sticking out of the muscle and fat. His face was normal on one side, a scruffy beard lining his square jaw, but the flesh on the other side had been carved away, leaving his yellow teeth and eyeball protruding grotesquely.

Bile climbed up Emerson's throat, burning away any hunger and thirst.

"What the hell?" Owen jerked, tipping over his chair with a loud clatter. Dax knocked into a swinging lamp from above as he jolted up. Their sudden movements didn't seem to bother Keneō or their new visitor in the slightest.

The man who'd been summoned stepped obediently to Keneō's side, and Emerson watched as their elderly host lifted his knife. For a moment, she thought Keneō would turn on them, but he tugged the side of the man's pants down his hip and sawed away a chunk of meat, which he slapped on a dusty plate on the table.

Beside her, Madeline turned and retched.

The man stared ahead blankly. Blood soaked his pants below the new wound, dripping down the rough seam to the hem, then to the ground below.

"Eat!" said Keneō, passing the plate. "There is much to go around."

"No," said Dax, and when the man turned his knife toward him, Dax added, "Thanks."

Emerson's mouth was dry. She couldn't speak. The man hadn't even flinched in pain when he'd been cut. His eyes were empty and dark, as if he were in a trance.

Cowardice. The word banged around her mind. This was it. This had to be the challenge. She had to be brave, but a thin tendril of horror was sliding down her spine. She thought of the players who'd fought the tengu. Was this man the result of a failed level? Had his cowardice been the reason he was now getting his ass shaved off for dinner?

She straightened her back, working hard to swallow.

"Don't be afraid," she muttered to the others. "Thank you," she told Keneō, trying to keep her voice steady. "But we're not hungry."

Keneō frowned. "Not hungry?" He didn't seem to understand.

"I'm not eating that," Owen said. "I'll lose the challenge. I don't care."

The thought that they'd have to choke down human flesh sent another wave of nausea through Emerson.

"We need to get out of here," Dax said, a steadying hand on Madeline's arm. She'd grabbed one of the napkins on the table to wipe her mouth but looked as though she was about to be sick again.

"There is no leaving," Keneō told them, his words closing their entrance through the trees behind them with a creaking braid of branches. "You crossed into my woods. You belong to me."

"I don't think so," Dax said, raising his knife in his fist. Keneō glanced to his own larger blade and grinned.

Emerson stood slowly, grabbing Madeline's arm to hoist her upright. The cards on her lap drifted to the white gravel beneath their feet—all but the cowardice card, now fisted against her stomach. She pressed the napkin to her mouth as she gagged again.

"We didn't know," Owen said. "We're sorry. Sumimasen. We'll leave right away."

Emerson lowered slowly to retrieve the other cards. But as she reached to gather them, she realized that the white gravel wasn't gravel at all, but pristine white fragments of bone, and withdrew her hand.

A sea of fingers, and pieces of spine, and fragmented skulls.

Madeline seemed to realize the same thing, and dropped her napkin she held to her lips at once. It spread across the ground at Emerson's feet, a square tapestry of moles and freckles and a raised pink scar.

Skin.

"What do you want?" Emerson asked. Maybe if they gave the man something, he would exchange their card for the next stone without a fight.

Keneō motioned to the trees around him, to the fabric, waving in the breeze. "You have such beautiful skin. It will look lovely on my trees."

Emerson's gaze fell to Keneō's hand, now smoothing his tunic over his chest. She could see now that it wasn't leather at all—it was dotted with tiny brown freckles that seemed to pebble under his touch like goose bumps.

Emerson's knees threatened to buckle.

Don't be a coward.

"I like my skin where it is, thanks," she said, again feeling that slickness inside her. Was it kegare that had made Keneō this way? A pollutant that had infected his mind?

Keneō looked disappointed. "Then who will volunteer? You?" His head snapped toward Owen, who stumbled backward. "You?" He looked to Madeline, whose eyes were glassy with tears.

"You skipping me?" Dax asked, stepping in front of her. "You're going to give me a complex, Keneō."

"So many scars," Keneō said with a frown, motioning to Dax's hands. Dax glanced down at his palms, which were a pale braid of knots. He'd gotten too close to a fire when he was little, he'd told them once. Emerson had forgotten they were there.

Tension thinned the air as Keneō waddled toward her. She longed for her clothes, anything to hide her body from his hungry gaze.

"Such delicate feet," he whispered. "The calf skin pulls off easily when detached from the ankle. Up it rolls, straight to the base of the hip."

"Stop it," Emerson said shakily.

"The back gets a little sticky," he said. "So much muscle. But those arms . . ." He blew out a quaking breath, spittle gathering on his chin. "Oh, how tender they will be."

"Leave her alone," Dax warned him.

Ignoring him, Keneō leaned around Dax toward Madeline. "Now this is a different taste. So much strength. Such little fat for flavoring. But the skin will stretch nicely, I think. A fine kimono you will be, my dear."

She tilted forward unsteadily, a greenish tint to her cheeks. A sob raked through her.

"Madeline," Emerson warned. She wanted to tell her not to be afraid—they needed to be strong now, but she could feel the panic rising in her blood.

"No? Then maybe the boy." Keneō turned toward Owen. "His hair will make such a lovely collar. I'll keep him nicely preserved until I find a use for the rest."

Owen was breathing hard. "Stay away from me."

"Well it must be one of you," Keneō said. "One, or all."

A line of sweat dripped down Emerson's temple. The challenge was cowardice, so they had to fight, but would they get the stone if he took one of them? Her gaze shot to the maimed creature, and she imagined one of them taking his place. Shinigami had not said that they would all finish together, only that they all needed to play.

She shook her head, sweat stinging her eyes. There had to be another way.

"Time is running short," Keneō said. "Is there no volunteer?"

"Doesn't look like it," Dax muttered.

Keneō laughed, then stomped one foot against the ground. In response, the bones beneath their feet trembled.

Owen shouted something to Emerson, but she couldn't hear it over the blood rushing through her ears. The bones began to roll into piles, toppling up over one another as if gravity had been reversed. They covered her bare toes, scraping the skin over the tops of her feet as she shuffled backward.

In an instant she was locked in place.

Behind her, Owen had grabbed a tree, and was trying to pull himself out. Dax was jabbing his knife at a skeletal hand gripping his ankle.

Madeline was frozen.

At first Emerson thought Keneō had done something to her

to make her so still, but as she watched, Madeline's shoulders bounced with quick breaths, and her lips trembled. Fear rolled off of her in waves, crackling in the air between them.

Keneō slowly ambled toward her, his cane in one hand, the knife in the other.

"Stop." Emerson struggled to free her feet. "Madeline!"

When he reached Madeline, he lifted the gleaming blade and ran the side of it slowly up the arm she held tucked against her chest. The card in her fist shook as she squeezed it.

"Hold her," Keneō said.

The man Keneō had been feasting on limped toward them, one lidless eye glaring blankly at Madeline, one muscle-torn leg dragging behind him. Fresh blood from his flank dripped onto the white ground, smearing a crimson path in his wake.

"Madeline!" Emerson shouted. She threw her weight forward, stretching out her hand. She skimmed Madeline's fingers, and with another strained reach, grabbed her wrist.

Madeline turned to face her, and their gazes locked.

Emerson remembered the twisting current of the river. The eels, wrapping around her ankles. The way Madeline had been brave when Emerson had been terrified.

Her heart thundered in her chest.

"It's not real," Madeline whispered, the words hollow. "It's only a dream."

Her fear broke something loose in Emerson. A hot flash of steam, bursting through her blood. A red curtain around her vision.

Releasing Madeline's hand, she reached for the nearest chair and hurled it into the bleeding man. Without enough muscle to stay upright, he toppled over, his backside making an awful sound as he hit the ground.

She turned to Keneō, her teeth bared.

"You want some skin? Fine. You can have all of us, you sick fuck. You have no idea what we've been through. None of us are cowards."

As the words left Emerson's lips, a ringing filled her ears. Fog floated into her mind, softening the sharpness of her breath, sand-ing away the edges of her thoughts. She was suddenly sleepy, her eyelids drooping closed. Her muscles grew heavy, her fingers clumsy and thick.

When she blinked, she saw men in uniform standing over her chair in her shotgun kitchen at home. Her mother sat next to her, arm over her shoulders. Her father was sitting across the table, his head in his hands.

"Where were you after school?" the policeman asked.

"At the coffee shop," she answered, just like she'd rehearsed. "Studying, with my friends."

"She already told you that," her mom said.

"And afterward, where did everyone go?"

"Home," she told him. "We all went home."

She was in trouble. She needed to call Maddy. Something was wrong—they all needed to meet.

"Ian didn't make it home, Emmy," her dad said, lifting his heavy gray gaze to hers.

The room around him grew fuzzy, and then his face fell out of focus. She looked to her mom, but she was already gone. The policemen faded, blending in with the cabinets behind her.

Ian didn't make it home.

The words sifted out of her mind, like sand through her fingers.

She opened her eyes, feeling lighter. Like she'd just taken off a heavy backpack and could finally stretch. She shook her head to clear it, rocking back on her heels.

The smell of blood jolted her back.

"Shut the fuck up, Emerson!" Owen was shouting. "What's wrong with you? I'm not giving some serial killer my skin so he can make a new suit!"

Emerson looked to Maddy, and reached again for her hand. No longer frozen in place, Maddy threw herself forward, one foot breaking free to step out of its prison. She gasped, glancing down at the card in her fist, now black and crumbling.

Keneō's laughter cut short as the draping skin in the trees at the edge of his house began to billow, the ends dragging across the ground. From the bottom, the skin twisted and creaked, braiding into a thick arch. A green light streamed through, the crackle of flames rising over the grumble of bones.

Keneō bared his yellow teeth. *"No."*

"That's it!" Maddy cried. "That's the exit!"

With one last heave, Emerson pulled Maddy free. Maddy opened her hand, and where the card had once been was now a white stone ball, marked in the center by a black circle.

An eye.

"Stop!" howled Keneō.

"Hurry!" Emerson told Maddy, snatching the cards off the bony ground. Owen had kicked free from the bones and was racing through the gap.

"Dax!" The ground beneath Emerson's feet slid like a moving rug as she bounded toward him. Kicking aside the jaws closed around his forearm, she helped him up, and they ran.

As they passed through the gate, the skin groaned. As it stretched, goose bumps prickled the fine hair that covered it. Emerson bumped against the side, feeling its clammy grip rub against her shoulder before she leapt through the fire.

Then Keneō's cries were silenced, and the skin gate was gone.

OWEN

Owen squinted through the remaining lens of his designer glasses at a mossy boulder, resting where the curtains of flayed skin had just closed. Ashes, tinged bright green, floated in the air, the last remaining signs of the cold fire they'd sprinted through. A harsh shudder worked from his heels to the roots of his hair. He checked his arms, his legs, his neck and face. Apart from a large bruise on his hip where he'd fallen on the lucky rock he'd tucked into the waistband of his boxer briefs, he was in one piece. His skin was still his.

With one hand, he covered the missing lens. The forest had changed, or maybe they'd come to a different place in it. The old, gnarled trees around Keneō's home were gone, replaced by saplings, some of them no taller than his chest. Those that reached higher were thin and fragile, limbs barely able to hold the gray budding leaves and blossoms at their tips. The air here smelled cleaner, not so rotten.

The sudden shift in landscape caught him off guard, and he dug his bare toes into the soft, warm soil, ready to run. The woods were clearer now than they had been on the previous challenge. The night sky, not so dark. He checked the giant's eye, finding it wider than before—a curved white slash on the horizon. Panic trickled through him as the scar on Ian's chin came to mind, and he rubbed absently at the tightness that formed in his chest.

"We did it!" Emerson shrieked, pumping one fist in the air. "Look! Maddy's got the second stone!"

Madeline gave Emerson a strange look, then opened her fist to reveal what looked suspiciously like an eyeball.

"Well done, *Maddy*," Owen said, narrowing his gaze on Emerson's glowing smile. He hadn't seen her this happy once since they'd reconnected, and it felt as out of place as he did in this game.

"Don't call me that," Madeline said, her pink lacy bra now scuffed and dirty. "Anyway, Emerson's the one who did it."

"You can have all of us, you sick fuck." Dax sneered, lifting his fists like he was ready to box. His mouth turned up in a grin. "That was brutal."

Emerson bowed dramatically, fanning the leftover cards behind her.

"Are you concussed?" Owen asked her. "You're giddier than I was during my audition for *ELF The Musical*."

"I don't think so." She frowned. "My name is Emerson Olive Bell. I'm seventeen years old. We're in Meido. Meido backwards is O-D-I-E-M. The date is May fifth—at least it was when we came here. But it seems like it's after midnight, so now it's probably the sixth."

"She's fine," Madeline said, but the look she gave Owen said she agreed their companion was a little too punchy.

"Two down, five to go," Dax said.

"We'd better hurry," Owen said, pointing to the sky. "Time's ticking."

Dax looked to the giant's eye and scowled. "That's not good."

"It changes with each challenge," Madeline said.

"An eye can only open so far," Dax said. "Ian said until dawn. That must be when the moon's full."

"Or it becomes a sun," said Emerson.

Owen's fingers tapped against his bare thighs. A phase of the moon for each challenge. A steadily opening eye, counting down to their fate. The clock was going too fast.

Emerson reached into her cleavage to take out the tooth Madeline had gotten in the arena. She set it beside the eyeball in Madeline's hand—two smooth, gleaming pieces that were dirty in their own way. *Unclean*—as Shinigami had said. Tainted by the pollution of death and blood. Owen didn't want to touch them. For all he knew, that's why Keneō was the way he was.

"The stones are body parts." He cringed, tearing his gaze away from the eye and crossing his arms over his bare chest. "Cute."

"Shinigami did say the oni chopped the empress up," Dax reminded him. "Now we have a little memento of the act."

"That makes me feel so much better," Owen said.

Emerson scooped up the pieces and tucked them into her bra top. Then she fanned out the remaining cards like a hand of poker.

"Cowardice, check. Next up in our Live Fast, Cry Loud, Heal Hate and Breathe lineup is . . ." She pointed to Owen.

"Get lost?" He turned a slow circle, sick of his missing lens, but saw no discernable path.

She groaned playfully. "Lies. Don't worry. You'll get it." She patted him on the shoulder.

"What got into her?" he muttered to Dax.

"She beat the last challenge," Dax told him. "She's happy. So what? She earned it."

Owen scoffed. Happy wasn't part of the equation, not here, and not after what she'd done.

"She lost her temper and almost got us murdered," Owen said. All he'd wanted was to get away from Keneō, to get out of that room with the half-eaten man and the skeleton garden, but Emerson was only thinking about herself.

"At least she wasn't a coward," Dax said, picking a white bud off the end of a branch.

Owen's chin pulled inward. "What's that supposed to mean?"

Dax shrugged.

"For your information, I've performed in front of hundreds of people. I learned to *dance* to get a lead in *West Side Story*. You think that doesn't take guts, you're wrong." \

"Being brave is more than just acting like it," Dax said.

The fight deflated inside him. He wanted to tell Dax there were other ways to be brave than just using your muscles. That he wasn't the sniveling little mouse he used to be. But looking at Emerson, now examining the cards for clues, and Dax, scanning the woods for danger, and even Madeline with her ripped shoulders and six-pack, he felt decidedly less.

A high-pitched giggle came from the woods to his left. His eyes met Dax's, dark with warning.

"Is that . . ." Owen started.

"It sounds like a kid," Emerson said.

Another laugh joined the first, this one lower.

"Kids," Madeline corrected, then shivered.

"Great." Owen smiled tightly.

"Don't worry," Dax told him, grabbing a stick off the ground to use as a weapon. "They can't be any worse than the murderous cannibal and the flesh-eating birds."

"I'm fine," Owen muttered, but his heart was racing.

He picked up a stick like Dax had, only his was bigger. Dax quirked a brow at him.

"What?" Owen said, gripping the end like a bat. It was flimsy, and arched under its own weight. Not the old, crunching branches they'd stomped through before, but green wood.

"Shh." Emerson held a finger to her lips. "Someone's coming."

They closed ranks, standing back-to-back.

A screech of delight and then a wild flutter of laughter came from Owen's left, raising the hair on the back of his neck.

"Owen! Dax!" shouted a girl's voice. "Come out, come out, wherever you are!"

A cold punch of fear rocked Owen back on his heels. "You all heard that, right?"

"Look over there, Maddy!" shouted a girl.

"I think . . ." Emerson said, her voice thin. "I know that voice." With a glance to the others, she stepped out of their circle.

"Wait!" Madeline grabbed her hand. Emerson looked down at where they connected, and smiled.

"It's all right," she said. "I think we're supposed to follow them."

"Should we also eat the candy from the guy in the unmarked van?" Madeline asked, exasperated, but she let Emerson drag her forward.

Owen and Dax followed, soon catching movement between the trees. The shadow of a boy, lit from behind by a yellow beam of light, jumped out from behind a short maple tree and ran away with a happy shriek. They hurried after him, the branch swinging in Owen's hands. Ahead, one bouncing light joined another, too direct to be from any lantern.

"Those are flashlights," he said, his heart quickening. He hadn't seen anything even remotely modern in Meido. "Maybe they're players!"

Emerson stopped, and Owen braced for a fight. But instead of a monster, he found four children zipping through the woods, dodging one another in a game of tag.

"No way," Dax said. "That . . ."

He didn't have to finish. Owen's eyes had landed on the girl with two high buns in her hair. She was curtain-rod thin, with narrow hips and jeans that dragged on the ground at her heels. Shiny red stripes covered her rumpled shirt.

"Oh," Madeline breathed.

The girl noticed them, and broke away from the group. As she came closer, Owen could see the gleam from her braces, and felt as if the wind had just been knocked out of him.

"Hi," the child said bravely. "I'm Maddy."

She couldn't have been more than ten.

Madeline could only nod. A white girl wearing a purple backpack raced after Maddy, her strawberry blonde hair in a ponytail. Beside Madeline, Emerson touched her own shaved head and stared.

"This is Emerson," said Maddy. "And that's Owen."

Owen lifted his chin to find his younger self striding stiffly toward them. He wore the same frown Owen did now, a look that said he didn't trust the stranger before him. His hair was neatly trimmed, his shirt tucked in. He was wearing the tie Owen remembered getting for Christmas when he was ten or eleven. Blue, with tiny peaches on the front, for the story "Momotaro the Peach Boy" his mom always used to tell.

"Are you playing hide and seek?" Emerson asked the girls.

"Onigokko!" the younger Owen said, the mention of an oni making the older Owen's jaw clench.

His three companions looked at him to translate. He took a step back. Normally, he liked being the one who knew things. But here, he wished he didn't have to. They were counting on him too much to get it right. Just because this game was Japanese, and he was Japanese, didn't mean he knew everything. He was only half Japanese anyway. It wasn't like he was some kind of cultural expert.

"It's tag," he said, steeling the worry in his voice. "The oni is it."

"Is the oni here?" Madeline asked, her gaze darting from kid to kid.

Maddy gave her a look that suggested she was dense.

"You want to play?" Little Dax rushed toward them, pulling up his jeans, which were too big. He was wearing his old retro Green Day shirt, only it was baggy now. "You play, you're the oni."

"How is this possible?" Dax asked, examining his younger self. "He looks just like me."

"Amazing," Emerson said, circling the smaller Emerson, who gave Little Maddy a strange look. "It's like the game accessed our memories and created our younger selves."

"What is she talking about?" Little Maddy whispered to the smaller Emerson.

"No clue," said Little Emerson.

Owen scratched his head. This was weird, but it beat the other stuff they'd seen. "Are we supposed to play with them?"

"The challenge is lies," Emerson said quietly back. "So we have to tell the truth."

Before her, the younger Emerson tightened the straps of her backpack.

"In that case," Owen said, glaring again at the boy before him, "how did you all let me walk around like this? I look like I'm in *Book of Mormon*. Unironically." The last time he'd worn a tie not for a part it was loosely knotted, and balanced out with a half-tucked-in shirt and bed-head hair.

"You look better than you do now," Dax said, motioning to his underwear.

Owen shot him a look. "All I'm missing is a sign that says, 'Please take my lunch money and shove me in a locker.'" He stepped forward as his younger self frowned. "Hey, kid. Want some advice? Lose the tie, and stop letting Mom buy your glasses from Dr. Lens. There's a way better assortment online."

"Like yours?" the younger Owen asked, pointing the beam of his flashlight directly in Owen's face.

Owen squinted at him. Was he being a smart-ass? That wasn't like the younger him. It took another beat to realize he was serious.

"You want to trade?" Owen asked.

His younger self grinned. "Sure!"

They traded glasses. The prescription wasn't exactly right, but his eyes hadn't gotten too much worse since he was a kid, and though the wire frames were snug and painfully out of style, it was way better than walking around with a missing lens. At least no one had a phone anymore to take a photo for blackmail.

When he turned, Dax was smiling at him.

"What?"

"I was just wondering," the older Dax said, suddenly serious. "How do you get giardia?"

"From contaminated water," he said, his stomach knotting as he thought of the river and the gulps he'd inhaled when they'd fallen off the bridge.

"What kind of animals carry leprosy?" Little Emerson asked.

"Armadillos."

"Was it wrong of me to lick the handrail on the bus yesterday?" Madeline asked him, tapping her chin as if confused.

The worries rising in Owen were squashed by a wave of irritation. His smile flattened as he glared at them.

"I can't believe I'm taking shit from Boots McGamer, a girl who won't eat cheeseburgers, and the guy who's worn the same shirt since the fifth grade."

"Boots McGamer!" Both Emersons cheered.

"Don't be shy. I think you're cute." Dax wrapped an arm around Owen's shoulder and ruffled his hair.

Owen flipped him off, which made the younger Dax cover his mouth and howl. A pair of glasses didn't change who Owen was now. Still, he couldn't hide the flush when it rose up his chest. He was sick of being practically naked. Maybe he should have taken the kid's pants and shirt, too.

"Okay, okay," Emerson told the younger version of herself. "You don't have any stones for us, do you?" When Madeline balked, she added, "We have to be honest, right?"

"What kind of stones?"

They all turned to find a lanky boy striding across the grass toward them. He was taller than the rest of the kids, though the same age, and swiped his hair out of his eyes with a careless shove.

At the sight of him, the air punched from Owen's lungs.

"Who . . ." Emerson trailed off.

"Ian," Owen whispered. Emerson's head whipped toward him, her brows furrowed, but Owen couldn't deal with whatever suspicions or game logic she might try to throw at him. There was only room in his brain for shock.

"Ian?" Emerson asked, as if she didn't recognize him.

Owen would have recognized him anywhere. At any age. In any world.

Ian smiled, a dimple digging into his right cheek. He looked so real. So *alive*. It was like he'd been plucked straight out of Owen's head, every detail perfect, from the holes in the knees of his jeans, to the T-shirt that hung off his bony shoulders, to the horseshoe scar on his chin, pinker than it had been when he died.

He'd seen that scar a thousand times since Ian had disappeared. In a curved shadow or a hammock. The U in the *Midsummer* poster at school had been an almost perfect match. Owen shivered at the memory of how it had topped the pile of remains when the ghostly Ian had blown up outside the play. It was a shape that haunted him, and now that it was real, he could barely breathe.

"Well? What kind of stones?" Ian looked to Owen, but any possible response disintegrated in Owen's mind.

He was *here.*

"We can take him home," he murmured. Then, mouth dry, he turned to the older Dax. "We found him. We can take him home."

"Easy," Dax warned. "That's as much Ian as those kids are us."

He was right. This wasn't real. It was a trick. A *challenge.* Owen's temples were pounding. A dozen memories of Ian at just this age flashed through his mind. Fragments, unimportant moments. The tilt of his lips. An eyelash on his cheek. As quickly as they came, they fled, and soon shame was breathing down Owen's neck. The longer he stared, the hotter it got, until he had to turn away.

"I don't know," he told Ian, forcing a careless shrug. "We're trying to find stones that look like body parts, maybe."

The younger Dax began to giggle.

"Not those body parts," Owen told him, though he wasn't exactly sure that was true.

"I might know where to find some of those," Ian said, flipping his flashlight from hand to hand.

Owen's brows lifted.

"But first, let's play a game."

Owen's breath staggered again. How many times had he heard Ian say those words? He was always the one picking what they'd play next.

It's a challenge, he told himself. This wasn't the real Ian. This Ian was a kid.

"Do we have to?" Madeline asked with a tight smile.

"*You* don't like games?" Maddy asked her, hands on her hips. The younger Emerson tugged on the straps of her backpack and laughed.

"Why do I feel like I'm being judged right now?" Madeline muttered.

"Truth or dare," Ian told them.

The younger crew sat in a half circle at their feet. They tilted their mismatched flashlights together in a cone shape, like a campfire. It was enough to cast an eerie glow over their faces, but the way they smiled and leaned in punched Owen in the gut.

They looked right together. At home with one another. It had been a long time since Owen had felt that ease with anyone, even the theater crew at Traverse. He couldn't remember the last time he'd played a game where he might look stupid, unless that stupidity would get him a laugh.

He cleared his throat. "So who's getting this thing started?"
Ian grinned.

That grin felt like a knife to the heart.

"Truth or dare?" Ian asked him.

"What kind of dares are we talking about?" Owen asked, then
sent a pointed look at Ian when he laughed. "You want me to streak
or hold my breath, sure, okay. But if these dares involve cannibal-
ism, it's a hard pass."

Ian laughed. "Easy stuff. Don't worry so much."

"Sure," Owen said, taking a seat between Madeline and Dax.
"Fine. Let's go with truth just in case."

"True or false—are you actually allergic to that antiseptic spray
they use in the skates at the roller dome?"

All eyes turned his direction. Emerson hiccupped a laugh.

In an instant, he was back on the bench under the neon lights,
watching his friends weave across the glossy floor. He looked across
at his younger self, watching the way his ears turned pink. Feeling
the blush creep up his own neck.

"Lots of people are allergic—" he started.

"Don't lie," Madeline whispered.

"People stick their sweaty, nasty feet over and over into those
skates and what does the rink do? Spritz a little vinegar in, as if that
even gets deep enough inside to do anything. It's so disgusting."

"So?" Ian asked.

Owen groaned. "False. You're right, you got me. I'm not allergic. I'm hygienic."

Across the ring, the younger Dax gave Maddy a high five, as
if they'd just won some unspoken bet. Owen glanced to the older
Dax, pulling his knees closer to his body.

Being brave is more than just acting like it.

Dick.

"Your turn!" Ian said.

Pressure mounted between his temples. Could he ask about the
stones yet, or was that off-limits until they finished this game? Ian's
question had been relatively benign—maybe he should stick to that
route for now.

"Truth or dare?" he asked Little Emerson, who'd moved her backpack into her lap and was hugging it fondly.

"Truth," she said.

"What's in the bag?"

"A human head."

Owen jolted to his feet. Dax shoved backward with a spray of dust.

The younger Emerson laughed so hard she fell into Maddy's shoulder. "I'm kidding! I took some pond water samples to look at under my microscope later."

She unzipped the bag, revealing a small plastic box filled with glass slides.

Owen slowly sat again.

"Can I have that bag?" Emerson asked. When her younger self nodded, Emerson took the backpack and tucked the tooth and eyeball into the front pouch, then put all the cards except for lies inside. "Thanks, little me."

"You're welcome, big me."

They gave each other a fist bump.

"Truth or dare?" Little Emerson asked Dax.

"Say dare," said Little Dax. "Come on, say dare!"

"Fine. Dare," Dax said, making his younger self pump the air with his fist.

Little Emerson bit her lip, trying not to giggle. "Yell, 'I have a crush on Maddy,' as loud as you can."

Older Dax sputtered. Across the circle, his younger self fell backward laughing and hiding his face, shaking his legs in the air. Little Owen and Ian were cracking up, while Maddy tackled Little Emerson in a fit of laughter.

Madeline glanced to the older Dax, trying not to smile.

"Wow, I. . . ." He looked slightly mortified. "I mean, just for a little while when we were kids. It was nothing."

"That's nice, but you didn't say truth, you said *dare*," cried Little Emerson. "So suck it up, you big weenie!"

Dax snorted. "Fine." He laughed a little. Was he seriously embarrassed?

So much for *a little while when we were kids*.

"Being brave is more than just acting like it," Owen reminded him.

Dax shot him a grimace, then stood. Circling his hands around his mouth, he sucked in a deep breath, and then, as loudly as he could, shouted, "I have a crush on Maddy!"

He sat quickly, the kids laughing hard across the flashlight fire. Beside him, Emerson was chuckling, and Madeline grinned.

"Impressive range," Emerson told him.

"Yeah, yeah," Dax said. "My turn. Truth or dare?" he asked his younger self.

"Dare!"

"I dare you to tell me what the deal is with this empress."

Little Dax looked disappointed. He'd probably wanted to do a handstand or burp the alphabet or something. "What do you mean?"

"Is she for real? Is this whole place really cursed because of her?"

"Of course she's for real," said the younger Dax. "This is her empire."

"I thought Meido was a game," said Emerson.

"Her empire *is* the game," said Little Dax. "When she died, it changed. It doesn't like being this way. It wants to go back to the way things were."

Owen's brows drew together. "The game doesn't like being this way?"

Little Dax nodded. "Can't you feel it? It's tired. It wants the empress back."

"So the game is . . . alive," Dax clarified.

"It's like a kid. Constantly growing up. Learning new things. Well, maybe not like you. But the rest of us," said Little Owen with a grin.

"Nice," said Dax flatly, shooting Owen a hard look, as if the jab had been his fault.

"It becomes something different every time it's played," said Little Emerson.

Her meaning slipped through Owen's grasp. How were they

supposed to beat a game that was constantly changing? That didn't like being the way it was? This place was worse than him picking outfits before homecoming.

"If it's changing, how are we supposed to solve these challenges?" Madeline asked.

"Enough questions!" Little Dax said. "It's not your turn, it's mine." He looked to Emerson. "Truth or dare. Say dare."

"Nice try," she said. "Truth."

Little Dax sighed, then narrowed his eyes. "Why'd you shave your head?"

Emerson's hand lifted to her buzzed hair.

"To piss off my mom," said Emerson. "I am a total teenage cliché."

Little Emerson crinkled her nose. "I thought we were better than that."

"You and me both, kid," Emerson told her. She looked to Little Owen. "Truth or dare?"

"Definitely truth," he said, and Owen couldn't help feeling a little disappointed, even though he'd taken the safe path as well.

"Where's the empress?"

A hush fell over them. Little Owen hugged his knees against his chest, squinting at Owen through his missing lens. "Yomi no kuni."

"Where is that?" Emerson asked.

"You'll find it when you're ready," Ian said.

"The game is alive, we'll find it when we're ready," Owen said, frustration sharpening his tone. "You guys are tossing out a lot of riddles."

"That's part of the fun," said Ian, leaning closer to the upturned lights. He tapped Owen's younger self's thigh.

"Truth or dare?" he asked Madeline.

"Let me guess, truth," said Little Maddy with a roll of her eyes.

Madeline balked. "Dare." She crossed her arms over her chest, making the kids all "Ooh" at her excitedly. When Owen glanced over, Dax was smiling.

"Make her kiss someone!" said Little Dax.

"Yeah," said Little Owen. "Kiss . . . um . . . Emerson!"

Madeline's arms dropped. She looked to Emerson, who'd stiffened beside her.

"I choose truth instead."

"Come on," said Maddy. "Don't be like that."

"I'm not being like anything," said Madeline. "I meant truth."

"But you chose *dare*," said Ian. "Are you not going to do it?"

Madeline rolled her shoulders.

"Wow," said Owen, wondering if she objected to him as well. "Didn't peg you as a homophobe."

Madeline shot him a scathing gaze. "I don't care that she's a girl. She doesn't like being touched like that, you idiot."

Emerson stared at the ground in front of her bare feet, as if it were the most interesting thing in the world.

"Really?" Owen asked. He never knew. He wondered if she was aromantic or ace, or bi like him, or panromantic. A strange sense of affection rose in him for her. Suddenly her badass, you-can't-hurt-me attitude made a lot more sense, and he wished he could have been the one to stand between her and whoever had forced her to turn so harsh.

"It's fine," she said, a flush rising up her neck. "It's just a game, right?"

She smiled, in a way that hurt to look at. He'd smiled like that once too, before he realized he didn't have to.

But her smile changed as he watched. Lines tightened around her eyes, then her mouth. Her full cheeks began to droop, and her eyebrows, light brown just moments before, lightened and thinned.

He blinked, anxiety running down his spine. He rubbed his eyes under his younger self's glasses, but she was still different. *Older.*

"Owen?" she said, her shoulders heaving with quick breaths. He followed her gaze to his hair, and when he pulled on the ends to see for himself, he could see that the tips were gray.

"What the hell?" he asked.

"What's going on?" Madeline pushed to her feet, the roots of her wavy hair grown out to a steely gray, as the ground around them trembled. When Owen peered into the dark, he could see that the young trees were growing—their trunks were fattening, their branches stretching longer.

It was as if the entire forest was aging, and them along with it.

"Stop this," he said, looking to the kids. "Whatever you're doing, stop!"

"She broke the rules," said Ian.

"I didn't know we'd all jump a few birthdays if I said no to a dare!" Madeline argued.

"You're a team," said Ian. "Win together, lose together. Anyway, you didn't break the rules." He looked to Emerson. "She did."

Emerson gaped. "What did I do?"

"You said it's fine," Owen realized, panic racing through him. "But it isn't fine."

Emerson paled. "I wasn't intentionally being deceitful," she argued. "*That's* lying."

"So not lying," said Ian, holding out one hand, then the other. "But not telling the truth either."

Emerson's cheeks flared red.

"Why do you care if she was being vague?" Owen asked. "Madeline was supposed to be doing a dare anyway."

"That doesn't mean people can go around being dishonest," Ian told him with a shrug. "You said you wanted to play."

Owen's hands itched, and when he scratched them he found wrinkles lining the backs and hair on his knuckles.

Was this permanent? He looked to the kids, but they seemed unaffected. He felt sick. Out of control of his own body. The sudden urge to shower—wash his hands at least—overwhelmed him. As if he could clean the old away.

"How do we get the next stone?" Emerson asked as the trees grew quiet.

"It isn't your turn," said Ian. "Madeline lost, so it goes to Maddy."

Madeline knelt slowly beside Owen, sweat glimmering on her temples.

"Truth or dare?" Maddy asked Madeline.

"Why am I up again?" she muttered, desperation pinching her voice. "Truth."

"Have you ever stolen anything?"

"Of course not."

"False!" Maddy cackled. "You stole fifty bucks from Mom to plant a money tree, remember?"

Madeline's mouth rounded with panic. "Wait. That was . . . I was six. Maybe seven! That doesn't count! It wasn't a lie, I just forgot."

The trees began to creak and groan again. Roots stretched under Owen's knees, cracking the ground and toppling the flashlights. Leaves fell and regrew. Owen pushed off from the dirt, but his arms were tired and his back couldn't pull straight. What was happening to him?

"Owen?" Dax stepped closer, taking Owen's arm before he lost his balance. His hair had fallen over his eyes, keeping the shadows over his face. Still, he didn't seem to be aging as fast as the rest of them.

"It's not happening to you," he said to Dax. "Why isn't it happening to you?"

"I don't know!"

"Good luck, I guess," said Ian.

"Stop," Emerson moaned, doubling over her stomach. Her skin was sagging on her sides and back. Her thighs were wasting away. She twisted in pain.

"Knock it off," he told the kids, who were sitting and watching as if nothing extraordinary were happening. "This challenge is about lying, right? We aren't lying. Madeline couldn't remember. That's different!"

The woods went quiet again. Owen's bones ached in the wake of the last seconds. As he caught his breath, he shook out of Dax's hold.

"Why are you doing this?" Dax asked, horror in his eyes as he stared at the changed Madeline before him.

"This is a game!" his younger self said. "A game within a game!"

"How long do we play?" Owen asked, fear nestling in his gut. "When does this end?"

"When someone wins," Ian said. "Don't you want to win?"

"Who *are* you?" Emerson asked incredulously.

Owen forced himself to breathe. If winning meant completing the challenge, they had to win. They needed the lies card to turn to get out of this level.

"My turn again," Maddy sang, and Madeline closed her eyes, her gnarled hands covering her face. "Owen, truth or dare?"

"I can't," Owen said, his knees and hips weak.

"Are you forfeiting?" Ian asked, and at his words, the forest around them seemed to shudder, as if waiting for his permission to grow.

"No," Emerson moaned. She reached for Owen's hand, skin over bones, and squeezed lightly.

"No," he said, pinching his eyes closed. "Truth."

"What's your biggest fear?" Maddy asked, wiggling her eyebrows at him.

"I . . ."

His pulse was pounding weakly, too slow.

"Well?" Ian asked.

Owen looked up, meeting his youthful blue eyes, feeling time stretch between them.

How many times had he imagined Ian sitting beside him at lunch, or lying across the floor of his bedroom on his stomach like he used to do? Sometimes pretending he was alive was the only way Owen could get through the day.

Ian's blue eyes filled with pity, but Owen didn't want his pity. He was the one who'd left Ian. He was the one who'd lied about where they'd been that day, and who'd kept lying, even when Ian's mom had come to their house, crying, *begging* for information. Saying she'd retraced her son's steps from The Bean over and over, trying to figure out what had happened, when all the while Owen had done to Ian what he'd been most afraid of all his life.

"Being alone," he said quietly.

"I don't mind being alone," said Little Emerson. "I thought you were going to say snakes or something."

"Not being alone." Owen scowled, staring at his wrinkled feet. "Being left alone."

"Abandoned," said Ian.

Owen glared at the ground.

"When have *you* ever been abandoned?" Dax asked in a way that managed to be both condescending and incredibly fragile.

"Your dad," said Madeline, the muscles of her broad shoulders now thinned.

This was stupid. Why were they talking about his dad? It wasn't therapy. It wasn't Dig Into Owen's Past Time. He wanted to agree with her and move on, but something told him the kids would know if he was lying, and they'd be hit with another consequence.

"He was sick," Owen said. "There was a problem with his thyroid."

"I'm sorry," said Emerson.

He forced a shoulder up, feeling a twinge in his neck. "It's not a big deal. I was four. I barely remember him."

"What do you remember?" Ian asked.

Owen closed his eyes, seeing flashes of a white room with a bed with bars. Hearing the beep of the robot beside his bed, and the lightning-bolt line that counted the beats of his heart.

"Washing my hands," he said, looking down at his lined palms. "We had to wash our hands all the time. We wore masks sometimes. We couldn't chance bringing in germs."

He frowned. He hadn't thought of that in years. Pressing his palms together, he had the sudden urge to wash them again, scrub until they were red and raw.

"Well you aren't alone anymore," Madeline said, one hand on her rounded back. "You're one of the most popular people at school."

It should have made him feel better, but it didn't. He didn't know why. He had lots of friends. People knew him when he walked down the hall. That's what being onstage did—it made it impossible for people to forget about you.

"Did I pass?" he asked, his voice scratchy and unfamiliar.

Ian smiled. "Your turn."

Owen looked to his younger self. "The loyalty card. Where is it?"

"You already solved it," Little Owen said. "Don't you remember?"

Owen's brows furrowed.

"What is he talking about?" Madeline asked.

"I don't know," he said.

"It disappeared when you solved the first challenge," Younger Dax told him. "In the cave, don't you remember?"

He didn't understand, even as memories spilled into the front of his mind. Quaking walls. The ceiling, caving in over Ian. He'd been too terrified to move.

Ian's gaze held Owen, piercing blue, dislodging the careful walls he'd built around that day. He tried to look away. Tried to fight the sudden flood of sensation, but it was too late.

With a gasp, he was swallowed by the past.

4 YEARS AGO

"This," said Ian, "is the creepiest place I've ever seen."

He crouched in front of the cave entrance, blue eyes round with awe. Cold air funneled out, needling through his eighth-grade cross-country T-shirt and the holes in the knees of his worn jeans. Behind him, Owen pushed up his wire glasses on his nose. The end of a T. rex tie, his mother's latest addition to his collection, brushed against the back of his hand, sending goose bumps up his arm.

"You sure it's safe?" Owen asked.

"I'm sure it's not." Maddy grinned, her teeth sparkling with braces she'd gotten red and blue bands on for eighth-grade pictures last week.

Dax raked back his shaggy, dark hair. "Ten bucks there's a dead body inside." He'd found the cave last week while Owen was studying and hadn't stopped talking about it since.

"You don't have ten bucks," Maddy told him.

"Do too."

"Do not."

Owen ignored them. The scent of damp earth and river water beckoned him closer to the threshold, toward the thick darkness of the cave's throat.

Ian knelt to reach for a rock, then tossed it into the black.

A clatter. An echo off the low ceiling. Then a groan, as if the cave itself had sighed.

"There must be another entrance to allow the ventilation." Emerson, cheeks pink with excitement, pulled a flashlight out of her back pocket, shining it into the gloom. "This probably connects to one of the old railcar tunnels."

"There's no subway here," Owen said, still well behind the others.

"It was never finished," she replied. "We literally just learned about this in history two days ago. The project lost funding in 1928."

"When all the workers mysteriously dropped dead," Dax added in a low, spooky voice.

"That's not funny." Owen looked at Emerson. "He's not serious, right?"

"Is he ever?" Giving Dax a playful shove, Ian crept deeper into the tunnel. "Come on, Foxtail Five," he called. Dax was the only one who didn't live on Foxtail Avenue, but he was at Ian's enough that it counted.

Tentatively, Owen followed. The gravel was rough beneath his sneakers, the ceiling low enough that he had to hunch to move forward. Graffiti covered the walls, thin and patchy, too old to make out. Again came the sigh, like an old man taking his dying breath. It raised the hair on his arms and dampened his palms, but he didn't back up. If Ian and Dax could do it, so could he.

Maddy, still grinning, hurried to catch up. She pulled a screwdriver from her belt beneath her tank top and braced it before her like a sword. He moved closer to her side, just in case.

At the end of the main stretch, the path made a hard right. The air was colder that way, and a steady *drip-drip-drip* echoed off the walls. As they crept around the corner, the entrance disappeared behind them. The beam of Emerson's flashlight cast an eerie yellow glow over the craggy walls. The ceiling lifted so they no longer had to hunch, and the path widened, allowing them to walk side by side.

"This is great, right?" Ian whispered as Owen came next to him.

"It's great." Owen's voice cracked, sending a surge of heat into his cheeks. "Especially if you want to be murdered by drug runners or bitten by rats."

"I've always wanted to be bitten by rats," Ian mused, bumping Owen's shoulder.

"They carry hantavirus, you know. And leptospirosis."

"You don't say."

"And plague. As in, the bubonic plague that wiped out Europe in the Middle Ages? Yeah, it's still a thing."

Ian smiled. "Poor rats."

The tunnel groaned.

Owen grabbed Ian's hand. It was warmer than his, and a little bigger. Their fingers threaded together, squeezing tightly, and Owen's throat felt thick when he tried to swallow.

Ian looked down, then pulled away.

"Sorry," he said, with a shy smile.

"It's okay." Warmth built in Owen's chest.

Ian hesitated, and Owen thought he might reach for his hand again, but he didn't.

"How'd you find this place again, Dax?" Maddy asked.

"I passed it walking home," he told her. "You can't see it from the path; you have to be down by the river." He'd taken out his pocketknife. It had been a present from Ian, back when they'd all met in the fifth grade.

Owen didn't know why it bothered him that Dax took it *everywhere*, but it did.

"If my parents knew I was messing around at the river, their heads would explode," Maddy said, miming the action with full sound effects.

"My mom doesn't care too much," he answered, picking at a loose thread on the retro Green Day shirt he always wore.

"Obviously," said Emerson. "You spent the night at Ian's every day last week. You don't even have a curfew."

Dax glanced to Ian, then looked away. "She's a pretty cool mom, I guess."

That was the most Dax ever said about her—that she was a dental hygienist or something, and that she was nice—but Owen had never met her. He couldn't imagine not having his mom around, asking him how his day was, making him breakfast before school. Dax never complained about it, but Owen knew there was a reason he stayed over at Ian's so much.

"It was hard enough getting my parents to agree to The Bean," Maddy said.

That was the alibi of the day—that they were all studying for a history test together at The Bean, a coffee shop near where they lived. It was close enough to school that Maddy's mom and dad let her walk there—as long as they stayed together—and the baristas were always so busy with the afternoon crowd that they never noticed if five kids had left through the back exit.

Dax didn't answer.

"Dax?" Maddy turned. Dax had been right beside them a moment ago, but now there was only a dark void. "Where is he?"

The beam of Emerson's flashlight bounced off the walls. The water drip was suddenly muffled by another voice from deep in the tunnel's throat—a whisper, seeming to come from all around them.

"Help me."

"What was that?" Owen's voice cracked again. "What's going on?"

"Just an echo," Emerson said, the beam of her flashlight shaking. They waited, holding their breath.

"Please."

Chills crawled over Owen's skin.

"Okay, ha ha." Maddy stepped closer to Emerson. "Dax, this isn't funny."

Drip, drip, drip.

"Guys, I don't think he's here," Ian said.

"I knew this was a bad idea," Owen muttered. "I told you guys when Dax brought it up. But did you listen to me? No. *You're paranoid, Owen. You're a hypochondriac, Owen.*"

"Calm down," Maddy told him, switching the screwdriver to her other hand so she could wipe her sweaty palm on her pant leg.

"Dax!" Emerson shouted.

The air grew colder. A clatter deep in the tunnel's core had them all whipping toward the tunnel's depths.

"I'm so . . . thirsty . . ."

Maddy screamed, the screwdriver falling to the ground. Her legs kicked out as she was grabbed from behind.

"Maddy!" Emerson lunged forward, grabbing one of her ankles just as Dax's laughter howled through the cave.

Owen picked up the light Emerson had dropped, shining it on Dax, who had his arms crossed over his narrow waist, cracking up like a maniac.

"You pothole!" Maddy kicked him in the shin, which only made him laugh harder.

"Hilarious," snapped Owen. "You're lucky Maddy didn't stab you in the liver."

"You're lucky *I* don't stab you in the liver," Emerson growled, snatching the flashlight from Owen. She linked arms with Maddy and marched ahead.

"Should've . . . seen your . . . faces . . ." Dax gasped, wiping away his tears. "Like you'd seen a ghost."

Before he could take another breath, Ian tackled him and they were wrestling across the ground. Owen jumped out of the way as Ian grabbed the ticklish spot above Dax's knee, squeezing until he kicked free with another howl of laughter.

"Okay, he gets it," Owen said, wishing he'd gone ahead with the girls.

Ian stopped suddenly and pushed Dax aside. "What's that?"

Owen leaned closer as Ian tugged on the corner of thick paper sticking out of the ground. When he pulled it free, Owen saw it was a card the length of his palm, rectangular and dense. As Emerson turned back with the flashlight, he could make out marks on it—graceful, weathered slashes of ink forming a single symbol on the sturdy surface. His gaze followed the curving lines to where they intersected with straight strokes, some thin, some heavy, each one deliberately drawn.

Recognition scored though him, making his heart beat faster.

"That's kanji," he said.

"Whoa." Maddy knelt beside them.

When Dax's brows rose, Ian added, "Japanese writing. Owen's mom taught him to read it." Owen instantly recalled the first time Ian had been to his house and had seen the small pieces of paper bearing the symbols for toilet and bed and everything else his mom had taped up on the walls. She'd basically refused to speak anything else to him until the age of seven, when she'd married Jim, and having someone outside the family see it had been mortifying.

"What's it say?" Dax asked.

Owen's forehead scrunched up. "There are thousands of characters. I don't know all of them."

"Do you know *any* of them?" Dax asked. Then added, "What?" when Ian gave him a sharp look.

"Those are the characters for honor," Owen said, pointing to what looked a little like a kite over a box, and a temple beside it. "And that one is hero . . . no, brave? Bravery."

"Let me see." Maddy elbowed closer.

"There's more," Dax said, dropping to the ground. He dusted aside the dirt to reveal two others.

"It's a game," Ian decided, looking to Owen. "Like the one we played at your house after your grandma's visit!"

"Karuta?" Owen asked. Ian was right, they looked like Karuta cards, but the kanji was different—not painted with images like in his grandmother's deck, but characters that took up the entire face.

"Look for the rest of them." Ian gathered the cards in his hands.

"Here's one!" Emerson said.

"I've got one too!" said Maddy.

"How do you play?" Dax asked.

Ian looked to Owen.

"It's a matching game," Owen said. "I mean, that's what Obāchan said."

"Obāchan," Dax sang.

"It means 'grandma,'" Ian told him with a shove. "She brought a bunch of old stuff from Japan when she came to visit. She was going to donate the set because half the cards were missing, but Owen and I said we'd take it. Since we didn't have the matches, we just acted out the cards."

Owen's cheeks darkened. He didn't know why he was embarrassed. They'd had a great time that night.

"Ooh, give me bravery!" Dax said.

"Give him bottom-feeder," Emerson said.

"Um . . ." said Owen. "There's not exactly a card for that."

"Give them all to Owen," Ian said. "We'll act them out and you guys guess what the card says!"

"In front of everyone?" Owen withered.

Ian leaned closer. "I'll be with you the whole time."

Owen's pulse skipped. "Sure. Okay."

The cards, though scraped rough at the edges, were still sturdy, and clacked against one another as Ian collected them. He made a pile that he set in front of Owen, who silently read the first card, then whispered to Ian, "I think it says, 'wounded heart.'"

Ian grinned. "Prepare the patient!" He whispered to Owen, "Lie down."

"On the ground?" Owen cringed.

"You can't talk!" Emerson pointed out.

"Who says?" Ian answered.

She rolled her eyes as Owen carefully lay down on the gravel. Ian knelt over him.

"Scalpel!" he called, holding out his hand for an invisible assistant to hand him the necessary tool. Owen snorted.

"Surgery!" Maddy called, and when Ian circled his hands encouragingly, she rattled on. "Broken bones! Lung transplant! Appendectomy!"

"Saw!" called Ian, then took his imaginary saw and began cutting into Owen's chest. Owen rolled his eyes, then gave a tiny jerk.

"Yes!" Ian whispered to him. "Keep going!"

Owen twitched and shook.

"Frankenstein!" called Dax.

"Frankenstein's monster!" shouted Emerson.

"That's what I said," Dax told her.

"It absolutely is *not*."

"We're losing him!" Ian cried. "Paddles!" He rubbed his hands together, then called "Clear!" and pretended to shock Owen's chest.

Owen flopped around but didn't rouse. "It's not working. I'm going to have to give him CPR."

"You can't give him CPR," Emerson snapped. "Isn't he under anesthesia?"

Ian touched Owen's warm cheeks, leaning closer. Without thinking, Owen reached up and touched his finger to the scar on Ian's chin—one he'd gotten when he crashed his bike over a speed bump in Washington Park a few years ago. The skin was smoother there, and for a moment, there was only Ian's scar and Owen's throbbing heart.

"That's not how you do CPR," Maddy said.

It wasn't until Owen saw Ian's eyes grow wide that he realized the pounding in his veins wasn't just his pulse. The sound came from all around them, from the walls of the cave itself. The vibrations grew faster, heavier, a thunderous boom making the gravel churn and dust rain down from the ceiling.

"What's going on?" Maddy cried, launching to her feet. "Is it an earthquake?"

"I don't think so," said Emerson. Her flashlight flickered, as if the battery might be dying. She slapped it against her leg, sending flashes across the wall like lightning.

"Dax?" Owen glanced up to find Dax covering his ears, his back rounded in pain. Maddy jumped beside him, lifting her screwdriver toward the dark recess of the cave.

Ian pulled Owen up, still gripping the cards in his hands, and breathing fast, his shoulders rising and falling in quick succession.

"Is it a cave-in?" Owen asked.

The walls shook harder. Small rocks and pieces of root fell onto their heads.

"We need to get out of here," Ian said. "Go! *Go.*"

But just as he took a step, a loud crack came from above. Owen looked up to see a chunk of earth break loose directly above him.

"Move!" Ian shouted.

Owen dodged out of the way just in time for a boulder to miss his head. It struck the ground in front of him and he twisted, tumbling face-first onto the cave's floor. Pebbles pelted his back. A landslide of dirt from the wall covered his right leg up to the hip. He tried to shake it free, but couldn't.

He was trapped.

"Owen!" Ian dove to the ground beside him, grabbing his hand. He tried to pull Owen free, but the earth was too heavy. Another groan came from the ceiling above them.

"Run," Owen said weakly. And then louder, "You have to go!"

"I'm not leaving you!" Ian shouted. His attention shifted to the ground by Owen's shoulder. With wide eyes, he reached to snatch something up, then he yanked back on Owen's wrist hard enough to crack it. Owen's body strained under the pressure. His shoulder felt like it would tear free.

Then his toes could move again. His right knee had just enough room to bend. One hand gripped Ian's, the other clawed at the ground. He shouted with the effort to get free.

The dirt loosened. He lurched forward just as Ian fell backward. They landed beside each other in the dust and rock. When Owen looked up, their gazes met, and held.

"Ian?" Owen's voice shook.

"Did you see that?" he asked, his fist wrapped around whatever he'd picked up off the ground.

"Are you all right?" Maddy reached them, grabbing Ian by the arm to help him up. Emerson and Dax followed.

"What's that?" Emerson said. "Something touched my foot!"

Owen felt it too, inching over the toe of his left shoe. He looked down, but couldn't see anything in the dark. Dax's cold wrist brushed against his arm. Maddy's sharp elbow pressed into his back. Their quick breaths filled his ears.

Then the ground trembled, and he sank to the ankles. He yelped in surprise.

"We have to get out of here!" Emerson cried.

Ian reached down to drag Owen out of the mud, a hard stone pressed between their palms. When he drew back, Owen gripped it, the cold rock like metal in his fist.

"Go!" Ian ordered, pushing Owen ahead. "Run!"

He ran.

Owen remembered it all now. How Ian had pulled him free. How tightly his hands had wrapped around Owen's. He could still feel the hot puff of Ian's breath against his neck when they'd fallen. He hadn't realized he was still holding the stone until he'd gotten home and pulled it from the imprint on his aching palm.

It might not always have been the twisted copper rock he'd carried in his pocket. It could have been one of the cards that they'd dropped after playing that stupid game.

Loyalty.

Ian won the loyalty challenge.

He pulled the stone from his waistband, his throat suddenly too dry to swallow.

"Is that one of the prizes?" Emerson snatched it from him with a dry, cracked hand, holding it up to the beam of the flashlight. "It kind of does look like a heart. Half of one, maybe."

"Why didn't you tell us?" Dax asked.

"I didn't know."

"How could you not know?" Madeline pressed, her thin frame warped by time she hadn't lived.

Resentment lodged in Owen's chest. "It was a long time ago, okay? Ian gave it to me."

"We're looking for stones and one Ian gave to you the day he disappeared didn't raise any red flags?" Madeline asked.

"I didn't think about it like that!"

"Well you held on to it all this time, so you must have known it was important," Dax told him.

"I kept it because . . . I just did, okay?"

"Where's the other half?" Madeline asked. "Did you break it? Did you *lose* it?"

"Some things just come in halves," Little Owen said. "Like half gallons of milk. And half a dozen eggs. And, I don't know, some of us."

"What does that mean?" asked Madeline.

"We're half Japanese," explained Little Owen. "And Dax is half something. You're half Black."

"She's Black and biracial," said Little Emerson. "She's not half of anything. You don't mix flour and sugar and get half cookies. You get cookies."

The older Emerson winced. "Maybe let her speak for herself," she said quietly.

The older Madeline turned to her with a half smile that might have been exasperation or might have been affection. Maybe it was both.

"Actually, you get flour-sugar," Ian said, making Little Emerson roll her eyes. "You'd have to add eggs and some other stuff to make them cookies. Chocolate chips."

"Baking powder," added Little Owen.

"Well this is all I have," older Owen said harshly.

Madeline shook her head. "We have a whole tooth and a whole eye. Why just half a heart? It doesn't make sense."

"It doesn't have to," Owen argued back. "Just because you want it to look a certain way—*be* a certain way—doesn't mean it will. Not everything comes in a neat package."

He was breathing hard now. Her words were needling him, plucking at insecurities he'd dealt with all his life. Why didn't he speak more Japanese if he *was* Japanese? Why, when he tried out for different parts, was it *interesting* to give the role to a boy like him? He was simply too Asian to be white, and too white to be Japanese. Madeline may have been able to combine both sides of herself, but he was always lacking.

And now they were counting on him to guide them through this place like he was sure about what it all meant, but he wasn't. He'd never felt more unsure of anything in his life.

"Remember that at dawn," Ian said.

"What?" Owen said. "What does that mean?"

Ian shook his head. "Take a dare, and I'll tell you!"

Owen spread his weak arms wide. "I can barely walk!"

The younger Dax jutted his chin forward, strutting around like a chicken. "Bok bok bok!"

"Do it," Emerson said.

Owen shook his head. "Dare." He could still kiss someone if it came to that.

"Stay behind," Ian said, then smiled. It wasn't the kind smile Owen remembered. It was the cutting grin of the Ian Owen had seen in the woods, just before he'd tried to kill him.

At once, the air was sucked from Owen's lungs.

"What?" Dax asked.

"Stay behind, the way you left me behind," Ian said, still looking at Owen.

"I . . ." Owen shook his head. "You want me to stay here? On this level?"

"What does this have to do with lying?" asked Madeline. "How is this part of the challenge?"

Ian stood slowly. "Do you forfeit?"

The trees, now so tall they disappeared into the dark sky, began to heave with anticipation. This had to be a test. He just had to say no—to be brave, like Emerson had. To tell Ian the truth. He could do that. He did it every time he stepped onstage. He pretended he was someone else, until he *was* someone else. Until Owen was gone, buried so deeply he never felt the sting.

Being brave is more than just acting like it.

Dax didn't understand. Acting wasn't just pretending—it was surviving. It was filling all the parts of him that weren't good enough or brave enough or just *enough* with someone else. He grabbed the lies card off the ground and lifted his chin. He was Puck in *A Midsummer Night's Dream*. He was Tony from *West Side Story*, and both twins in *The Shining*, and the funniest goddamn Buddy the elf Traverse High had ever seen.

He sucked in a breath. "I'm not staying here. I'm finishing this and going home."

Ian's grin widened. "That's too bad!" He giggled, but the sound was sharp as knives.

"Wait!" Dax said, but it was too late. Owen swallowed a gasp as his hands curled around the lies card, arthritic jolts of white-hot pain shooting up to his shoulders. His knees buckled and he fell forward, ankles crackling.

When he looked up, Emerson's hair had gone completely white. She aged before Owen's eyes. Fifty. Sixty. Seventy.

"No," Owen said, stumbling toward her.

Madeline was curled over her knees, her eyes turning cloudy. "I can barely see," she whispered.

"Stop this!" Owen groaned.

"Owen!" Dax grabbed his shoulder.

He turned to Dax, still teenaged and untouched by the mysterious aging affecting the rest of them, but before resentment could fully form in him, a curtain of darkness covered the moon, bathing the woods beyond their flashlight fire in inky shadows. Owen looked up, a chill crawling over his loose skin.

"It's coming," Ian said.

Emerson blinked at the sky. "What's coming?" Her voice crackled with age.

A howl cut through the woods, high and pained. It dragged out for too long, ending in a gravelly groan that raked over Owen's raw nerves.

"The oni," said Maddy, grabbing a rock off the ground. The fallen leaves began to stir, dancing on the breeze at their feet.

"That horned thing we saw in the steam at Shinigami's? The demon that cut up the empress and cursed this place?" Madeline asked.

Little Emerson nodded, clutching her pond water samples to her chest.

"It's been following us since Shinigami's," the older Emerson said. "How did it get here? Did it come through the gate?"

"The oni doesn't need a gate. It can go anywhere in Meido."

Owen grimaced. "What's it want?"

Little Dax pointed to the backpack Emerson was hugging against her chest. She paused in the middle of the move, her lips parting.

"The stones," Madeline realized.

Owen felt like he'd swallowed nails. The oni had torn apart the empress and hidden the parts. Of course it didn't want anyone to take them back to her.

"And if we don't hand them over?" Dax asked.

"I don't think we want to know the answer to that," Owen told him.

The howl came again, this time close enough to make him jerk. A twist of pain shot up his back. Emerson stepped to Madeline's side, grasping her arm.

"Let go of me." Madeline tried to shake free.

"What's wrong with you?" Emerson asked. When she tried to reach for her again, Madeline shoved her back.

"What's wrong with *me*?" Madeline scoffed. Across the circle, Maddy and Little Emerson held fast to each other's sides, watching them and whispering.

"Take it easy," Dax told her, his knife blade gleaming as he lifted it before him. "She's just scared."

"We're all scared," Owen told him. "Look at us!"

"We need to stick together," Emerson said, her head bobbing. "We can figure this out. We're a team."

"You haven't spoken to me in four years!" Madeline said.

"What?" Emerson blinked, as if confused. "That doesn't mean we aren't friends."

"That's exactly what it means," Madeline told her. "We aren't friends. We were *never* friends."

Owen cried out in pain as the card in his hand flashed with blue, a small explosion that had him dropping it on the ground.

When they looked down, the card was gone, and what remained was a gleaming silver rock, flat and round on one end, and lined with tiny pockmarks.

"It's a tongue," Dax said.

A shrunken, silver tongue.

The fourth stone.

"How . . ." Emerson started, then her face twisted with pain. She looked to Madeline. "So that's the truth? We were never friends? It must be. We can't get the stone without solving the card."

"What do you care?" Owen asked her. "You hated Madeline up until five minutes ago."

"Bigger problems right now, guys," Dax told them. "Does anyone see a gate?"

Owen bent to retrieve the stone just as a crash came from the bushes to their left.

"Run!" his younger self screamed.

Madeline hurried through the woods to her left after Maddy, but the kid was so fast she had to double back for her older, shuffling self. The younger Emerson was dragging the seventy-year-old Emerson the opposite direction. Dax followed the Madelines.

"Don't split the party!" Emerson yelled.

"Wait!" Owen hurried after her, but he was slow, each step unsteady. The shadows spread over the ground like a raven wave. His breath seared his throat as he hurried around a tree. One step at a time, he shuffled through the fallen leaves until the howl quieted behind him, until the only sound was the crunch of twigs and gravel beneath his footsteps and the roar of his own breath in his ears.

When he glanced back, there was no one behind him.

His steps slowed.

His gaze shot forward, but Emerson was gone.

"Dax!" he called, but his voice was weak. Around him, the trees had grown tall and thick, the path behind him obscured in the branches. "Madeline!"

No one answered.

"Emerson!"

He was an old man, alone, with a silver tongue in his fist.

MADELINE

Urgency pounded through Madeline's weakened veins as another howl cracked through the air. An old playground came into view through the trees, and Little Maddy dashed toward it, skirting around a metal slide, aged with rust and jagged punctures, and a decrepit swing set. As Madeline gingerly followed, her elbow clipped one of the heavy black chains, sending a jolt up her arm. The swing groaned, full of menace and grim promise.

"Faster!" Maddy yelled.

Tears burned Madeline's eyes. *Hurry,* she urged her unfamiliar body. But she was slow and feeble.

The footsteps behind Madeline drew closer, a thundering gallop too quick to be human.

"There!" Maddy shouted, pointing to an arching set of monkey bars ahead. Moss grew at the top of it, vines climbed up the sides, but through the center, the green fire shimmered, contrasting with the shadows on either side.

The gate to the next level.

Panic took control of her body. Without glancing back for the others, she threw herself forward, stumbling toward their exit. A cry sounded behind her, low and angry. It shook the trees and the ground, and vibrated Madeline's vision.

"The oni!" Maddy screeched, just behind her.

Madeline fell through the arching bars, rolling across the ground beneath. A rock jammed into her shoulder. Rough dirt scraped her knees. She lunged up, dodging behind a stout tree trunk to hide.

The movement of her body caught her by surprise. Her legs were strong. When she glanced down, tight skin covered her muscled thighs. Her back was straight, her hair, back to smooth box braids. She reached for her face, finding no wrinkles.

She was young again.

Relief was fleeting.

The woods stayed silent, but her heartbeat was thunder.

"Dax?" she called as loudly as she dared. "Owen! Emerson!"

No response.

Her breath came in a shudder. She couldn't go back; the oni was that way. Had he gotten them? Had he killed them?

She wrapped her hands over her mouth to stifle her scream. She was alone. The trees were dead here, the giant's eye half open in the black sky. Each rock and bush looked like any other, skeletal and sharp.

A dry branch cracked beside her and she spun to face a tall figure in bloused pants and a sage green tunic fastened by a tie around the waist. A featureless leather mask covered the bottom half of his face, hiding his nose, mouth, and chin, and his dark eyes gleamed over top of it, bright with excitement.

"Aha," he whispered through the mask. "I found you."

Madeline dropped to a crouch, picking up a rock in her shaking hand.

"Stay back," she told the man, her voice too high. "My friends will be here any second."

"Come, my love." The man ignored her warning. He lifted his arms, drawing closer. "You have nothing to fear."

"Stay back!" Madeline ordered, still crouched low.

"Don't be that way," he pouted. "It's me! Kuchisake!"

Cold sweat prickled her brow. "I don't know you."

A hesitation, and then he laughed. At the flick of his hand, two dark shadows formed behind him. Black, bulging creatures, coated with bristly hair that gleamed in the moonlight, and long legs that ended in spear points.

Spiders.

They were as big as boulders, and with a short scream she jolted backward, cold bark imprinting on the damp skin of her back. She sobbed. The challenges stuttered through her mind. Fear, cowardice, lies . . . What came next in Emerson's list? She couldn't think. If this was the next task, she didn't want to face it alone.

"Why do you cry?" Kuchisake whispered. "Don't you think I'm handsome? Do I not please you?"

He came closer, but she couldn't move. On a breath, she caught his scent: jasmine and rot. Two more massive spiders hung down from the trees, blocking her path on either side.

"Stop there," she whispered, trying to summon bravery.

Where were the others?

"So beautiful," he murmured, his eyes trailing down her throat, her chest, her legs. She tried to cover herself but there was too much of her on display. "Look how happy you make me." He pulled back to remove the leather mask over his mouth, revealing a jagged, bloody smile cut from ear to ear.

Madeline froze in horror.

"I could make you happy, too," he said.

"N-no."

"Why not?"

"Because," came a low voice from behind her. "She's with me."

Dax stepped around the tree, his shoulders back, his fists ready.

Madeline staggered at the sight of him—she'd never been so re-lieved to see anyone in her life. But there was a strange light in his eyes that sent wariness ringing through her brain. A softness to his steps that was predatory. Even the shadows seemed too thin to cling to him, slipping off the gleam of his skin and the cut of each muscle.

There were more massive spiders tracking him from behind. Though they stayed out of sight, she could hear them, a quiet scuttle on the ground, a rustle in the trees. It wasn't Owen and Emerson—their footsteps made a more predictable pattern.

Dax didn't look at her. He never took his eyes off Kuchisake.

"She's with you?" Kuchisake said, his giant, slit mouth curving unnaturally into a frown.

"That's right," Dax said evenly. "Your minions didn't mention it?"

He motioned toward Little Dax and Maddy, now half hid-den behind a rock, giggling. Though they were part of this game,

Madeline couldn't help feeling a stab of betrayal. Had she been led this way deliberately? Were they even in the right place?

Where were Owen and Emerson?

The man snapped his fingers, and the two kids disappeared. She blinked at the spot where they'd been standing, the terrible thought sliding through her that Kuchisake might be able to make her vanish just as easily as her younger self.

He stepped back from the tree, his gaze hard. "Prove it."

"What?" she whispered.

His eyes smiled. "If he is your love, he can have you, but you must prove it." With a tilt of his chin, the spiders crowding her scurried away.

He wanted her to show him they were together? Fine. On shaking legs, she hurried to Dax. Tentatively, she wrapped her arms around his waist, feeling like a doll, bent for a perverted stranger's entertainment. Her head rested against Dax's chest.

"See?" she said, shivering as Dax's warm hand found her waist.

"No, no, no." Kuchisake began spinning his mask in the palm of one hand. "Show me you're in *love*." He grinned again, the split of his skin revealing a flash of molars at the back of his mouth. "I adore a good love story."

"Kiss me," Dax whispered.

"What?"

She looked up at him, brown eyes round and frightened.

"Kiss me."

Her heart kicked against her ribs. Lightning shot through her mind, memories of other times she'd thought about kissing him. When she was ten, and he could land a flip off the swings. When she was twelve, and he'd made her a crown from a paper plate after beating Ian at his own video game. When she was fourteen, and fifteen, and sixteen, watching couples kiss in the halls at school, wondering if anyone would ever look at her the way Dax had.

He leaned down to press his lips to hers.

They bumped noses. She kept her eyes open, watching Kuchisake in her peripheral vision. Her arm got smashed against Dax's chest.

Her cheeks flamed.

The man began to laugh. "I knew it!" he cried. "You tried to trick Kuchisake!"

Worry flared through her.

"No," she said. "We're together. I swear—"

Dax grabbed Madeline's face in his hands and *kissed her.*

She closed her eyes, tasting the salt on his lips, hearing her own surprised intake of breath and the thrum of blood in her ears. His fingers speared through her hair, dragging her closer, and when her hands spread over his chest, something shifted inside her, taking her fear and twisting it until it frayed and broke, spilling warmth throughout her body.

She kissed him back—gently at first, but then she was leaning into him, her hips against his, her hands spreading over his bare chest.

A mist fell over her mind.

Her fingers went numb, then her feet. The soothing sensation crawled up her legs and arms and down her neck, until she was floating in a warm cloud.

"We can't tell anyone."

They were under the bleachers in the gym, where she'd told them to meet after eighth-grade math. She looked again for Dax, but he wasn't coming. He hadn't been at school for three days. Ever since it happened.

"He's missing," Owen said. "He could still be in that cave!"

"You want to go in there and find him?" Maddy asked, pulling anxiously at the twists in her hair.

"The police could," Owen said.

"The police will think we're responsible!" she told him, Ian's bright blue eyes staring back from her memory in horror. "They'll think we did something to him. You want to go to jail?"

Owen buried his face in his hands. "No. But his parents . . . they could look for him—"

"They could tell our *parents. My mom and dad would kill me if they knew I was there!"*

"We don't have a choice," Emerson agreed. *"What happened . . . it wasn't normal. No one will believe it."*

"Then it's settled," Maddy told him. *"We were at The Bean all afternoon. Then we went home. That's the story."*

That's the story.

The words faded in her mind as the memory dimmed.

Emerson and Owen melted.

The bleachers blended with the woods. The past became the present.

And finally, the boy with the blue eyes was gone.

She let out a breath as Dax pulled back, his thumb skimming across her cheek. The cool air glided down her throat, loosening all the tiny knots tied in the muscles between her ribs. As he pulled back, her eyelids fluttered open. She felt as if the entire world had shifted two steps to the right, and she was finally where she was supposed to be.

"Dax?" She smiled, but it faded as her gaze moved from his pinched brows to his Adam's apple, bobbing as he tried to swallow.

Then a blindfold dropped over her eyes, and as her arms were bound to her sides, she screamed.

———•+•———

She was shoved down into what felt like a box. A covering came over the top, the slide of wood on wood harsh in her ears. She fought against her arm bindings but they held fast. That guy in the mask and his spider friends were in for it when she got free.

"Madeline?" Dax's voice was close.

"I'm here." She reached out for him with her leg but it was a tight fit, and her foot immediately found the wall. Her back pressed against the wood behind her. She and Dax were being moved, dragged across the ground on some kind of sled. Her wrists were still bound tightly against her back, the rope sticking to her skin. Her fingertips pressed against the boards behind her tailbone as she flexed them to fight off the numbness.

Something brushed her bare thigh, and she jerked her knee

sideways, smashing it against something firm and warm—Dax's chest. He grunted as their prison tilted again.

"It's me," he said. "Don't move."

She didn't have much of a choice.

"Where is he taking us?" she asked.

"I don't know," Dax grumbled. "There we go. *Finally*."

She wasn't sure what he meant until his fingers slid under her blindfold and peeled it aside. It clung to her hair and skin, fine wisps of pale, white webbing.

She blinked in the dim light and found Dax's dark eyes staring back at her. He was holding the pocketknife in his hand, and she turned so he could reach her bound wrists. Her gaze shot around the small space—a wooden cage the size of a trunk, with paper-thin spacing between its bars. It was enough to let slivers of lantern light in, but not enough to see more than black moving shapes outside.

The spiders, she remembered with a shiver. She could hear their feet, clicking across the ground. They must have been dragging the box behind them.

"Are you all right?" he asked, his urgency speeding her pulse. "Are you hurt?"

A groan slipped through her lips as he cut her arms free. She rolled her shoulders, massaging the feeling back into them. How long had they been moving? Her head felt cloudy. Through the boards on the floor, she could see the dirt sliding by.

"Where are Owen and Emerson?" she asked. Emerson would have a field day with Kuchisake when she learned what he'd done to her.

He shook his head.

"They'll find us."

He snorted. She didn't know why. Maybe Owen was more tentative, but Emerson would never let him leave them behind.

"Sure they will." He raised an arm to motion to their moving box, but smacked his wrist against the wall. Pulling it to his chest, he rubbed it, the pale scars on his palms reminding her of Keneō and his hunger for their skin.

She had a feeling Kuchisake wasn't going to be any better.

She shifted and twisted until she got her knees beneath her. The low ceiling made her hunch; the tight walls forced her elbows close. She reached into the shadowed corners, feeling around the walls for any weaknesses in the wooden slats.

"What are you doing?" he asked.

"Looking for a way out of here."

He huffed, as if in disbelief, and she glanced over. He was like a lion in a kitten's crate. His head was bent forward, his cheek against his knee. The only way he fit at all was to hug his legs against his chest.

"Hope you're not claustrophobic," she said.

"Me too."

The crate tilted again as they were dragged around a turn, and she rocked against his bent leg. His thigh flexed, hard muscle under cool skin. When they were righted, she went back to her search, crawling over him to press against the boards, her fingertips feeling for loose nails or bindings.

As she reached overhead, they came face-to-face. His gaze dipped down to her throat, then up to the ceiling. It made her think of how his chest had felt against hers when they'd kissed in the woods. How his hand had curled around her rib cage.

It had started for show—to convince Kuchisake they were in love—but it hadn't ended that way.

Emerson was going to die when she heard about it.

"Ha *ha*!" Her fingernails tucked under a split board on the wall across from Dax and peeled it back with crack. A long sliver of wood came free, like a dagger, and she gripped it in her fist.

"Careful," he said.

"Worried I'm going to give you a splinter?"

He snorted. "Something like that."

She went back to working on the wood, but couldn't get another slice free, or break a big enough hole in the siding to reach through.

"What do you think he wants?" she asked. "Kuchisake."

"If I had to guess, I'd say a new girlfriend."

The word made her face warm.

"Well, good luck to him," she muttered. "Because if he tries to come at me again . . ." She jabbed the stick forward, like she'd do into his gut. It hit the wall as they jostled.

"Okay, Madeline," he said. "Why don't you have a seat. I don't think you're getting enough oxygen."

"Maddy," she said.

He lifted a brow. "Sorry?"

"Maddy," she said again. "You called me Madeline again."

He gave her a puzzled look. "Are you all right? Did something happen before I found you two in the woods?"

"Like what?"

"I don't know, a rock falling on your head?"

She rolled her eyes. Of course he was making jokes at the wrong times.

"Pothole," she muttered.

He stared at her, his face paling.

"Are *you* all right?" she asked him.

When he didn't answer, she sat beside him, holding the stick between them. "Is this about . . . you know."

"What?" he asked, his voice a little rough.

"The kiss."

He shifted down until he could lift his head straight. "What about it?"

"I don't know." She moved closer, so their hips and shoulders were touching. As the carriage lurched, her knee bumped against his. "You're acting weird."

"*I'm* acting weird."

"Yeah. A little," she said, in a way that meant, *completely.*

He was quiet for a moment. "It just caught me off guard."

Now she knew he was lying. "You're the one who kissed *me.*"

"Because we had to."

Irritation had her feet flexing. "Don't act like you didn't want to. You did say you had a crush on me."

He balked, hands raking his hair forward. "That was a dare."

"But you agreed it was true!"

"A long time ago!"

"Didn't seem like it," she said, recalling the feel of his teeth nipping her bottom lip, and how his whole body had seemed to melt closer to hers.

"We haven't seen each other in four years," he said.

"And whose fault is that?" she threw back.

"How about Ian?" He lifted his hands, exasperated.

"Who?" she asked.

Dax laughed, a sharp-edged, angry sound. "Hilarious." Silence dropped between them, accented by the crunch and grind of their cage being dragged over the dry ground.

"I don't know what you're talking about."

"I'm talking about Ian disappearing and us never speaking again!"

"Who's Ian?"

"Who's . . ." He banged his shins against the cage as he pushed up. "Oh, I get it. Dax is crazy. Dax went to the psych ward. Stupid me for thinking you, of all people, would be above making strait-jacket jokes."

She leaned to the side to meet his gaze. "I wasn't making any jokes. I'd never make fun of you about that."

"And yet," he said.

She shook her head. "Look, I don't know what got into you, or who this Ian is, but we need to figure out a plan for how we're going to get out of this."

Dax was staring at her. There was something wrong with him. She could see it now—shadows under his eyes that hadn't been there since she'd seen him at Traverse after Owen's play. The way his jaw worked back and forth as if chewing his words before he said them. Every one of his muscles was tense.

She placed her hand on his forearm, and he jerked beneath her touch.

"Dax, what is it?" she said. "It's me. You can talk to me."

He released a slow breath.

"Where do you think Ian is?" he asked.

She groaned. "I told you, I don't even know who that is."

"*Ian,*" he said again, as if that would make her understand. "Our friend, Ian Spencer."

"I don't know an Ian Spencer," she said, a pit forming in her gut. Why was he being like this? It felt cruel, but there was pity in his eyes, and that didn't make sense either.

"Yes, you do."

"No," she said slowly, sympathy filling the well inside her. Maybe Dax really did see things besides yōkai. Maybe he did need help.

"We just saw him. Back with the other kids. He played Truth or Dare."

Her forehead scrunched. "Dax, those were kid versions of us. You, me, Owen, and Emerson. There was no one else."

His hand covered his mouth, dragged slowly down his chin. Dread pooled in her gut. She was starting to think that Dax knew something she didn't.

"Madeline, why do you think we're here?" he asked slowly.

"Maddy," she said again. Why did she keep having to remind him of that? "We played a game. It brought us here." Shinigami flashed in her mind. Was this a test? Or did Dax really not remember?

"Why did we play it? We haven't spoken in four years."

"Because . . ." Wait. Why had they started playing? She couldn't recall. As she searched her mind for answers, there was nothing but the same gentle fog that had rolled in when Dax had kissed her. "Because that's what we do. We mess around. We hang out."

Even as she said the words, she knew they were wrong. She hadn't seen Dax in a long time, but why? She didn't know.

It didn't make sense.

"Who brought us back together?" he asked.

She shook her head. Her mouth was dry. "Emerson texted?"

"What about how we met," Dax said. "As kids, do you remember?"

"You came to my house," she said, but that wasn't right. Why would he just show up at her house one day? Something was missing. They hadn't known each other, and then, somehow, they were friends.

"Maddy," he said when she scooted away from him. "It's all right."

"How is this all right?" Her blood was too warm, pumping

too fast. The walls around her were so close. "Is this one of your pranks?"

He shook his head.

Her breath hitched. She gripped the splintered piece of wood harder.

Dax reached for her hands, pulling her back beside him. "Do you remember that day at the cave?"

She nodded, but the well was growing wider inside her. A black hole, sucking in her ribs and organs. "We said we were going to The Bean, but we went to the river."

"What about the game?"

"The card game," she said. "We have the same cards now. Lies and cowardice and fear . . ."

"What happened when we played back then?"

Her breath was coming faster. "Owen said the cards were like Karuta, and then . . ." She shook her head, feeling the same soft velvet glove reach through her mind. "We went home."

He gripped her hands tighter. "That isn't what happened."

"What do you mean?"

"We played a game with the cards. We started . . . this." He spread out his hands as far as their enclosure would allow. "Then *we* went home, but Ian didn't."

She bit the inside of her cheek, bringing a bright spark of pain to her senses. How could what he was saying be true? But when she tried to recall the rest of that day, her memories came back empty. She knew she'd gone back to her house, but she couldn't remember leaving the cave, or saying goodbye to her friends, or why they hadn't spoken after.

Ian.

Her heart tripped. The name was so familiar, but she didn't know anyone named Ian. She was sure of it.

Wasn't she?

"Ian's been in Meido?" she whispered.

Dax nodded. His thumbs moved over her knuckles. Soft. Re-assuring. When he exhaled, his breath was cool on the top of her shoulder.

"No," she said, tears burning her eyes. "If he was our friend, we would have looked for him. We wouldn't have left him in the cave. Why would we wait so long to come here?"

"I was busy fighting ghosts and trying out different medication cocktails," he said. "And you . . ."

"I what?"

"You were scared, I think."

She scoffed. "I was *scared*? One of my best friends was stuck here with monsters and I was too scared to help him?"

She ripped her hands out of Dax's, rising to her knees. Her head hit the ceiling, and she punched it in frustration. Then her knuckles hurt. She dropped the spike of wood, rubbing them.

"That isn't me," she said. "I'd never do that. You're lying. You're making this up."

"I promise I'm not."

"How do I know?" Her voice was shaking. "If I forgot a person—someone who was apparently important enough to me to come *here*—how do I know I'm not forgetting things about you? How can I trust anything you say?" Her heart was galloping. Sweat dewed on her brow.

His gaze met hers and held, dark and unyielding.

"Because it's us, Maddy. You and me. I've got your back, and you've got mine. If you can't trust anything else, you can trust that."

Her breath came out in a shudder.

"Anyway," he said, glancing away. "I don't think you knew where he went, or if there were monsters there."

"That's no excuse." She fell back on her heels, flattening her hands over the floor. "Why didn't you tell me we had to go back?"

After a moment, she felt his hand on her back. She rounded into it, feeling his fingers spread over her spine. The box may have trapped them, but it was his touch that held her in place.

"I tried to call you," he said. "Your parents screened your calls."

She blinked in disbelief. "They wouldn't do that."

His palm shifted slowly up between her shoulder blades. "Did you also forget that they hate me?"

"They don't hate you," she said, but she scowled, because this wasn't entirely true. They'd never said it, but they'd always found a way to politely leave Dax out of the equation. They never asked how he was when they knew she was with him, or if he would be at a party or gathering she, Owen, and Emerson were attending. Dax was never included, which she suspected had something to do with his no-rules lifestyle, but she had never asked, because if she had, they might have told her she couldn't see him.

Sometimes silence was better. But not when it came to a friend.

"Were we close?" she asked. "Ian and I?"

"As close as any of us," Dax answered. "Close enough for us to walk through hell to find him."

She shifted back, her knee now against his shoulder, his bent leg against the side of her ribs. She felt ill. How could she forget the reason they were here? This wasn't a game played for fun. They'd come to Meido for a purpose. And that reason was a friend named Ian.

She didn't even know what he looked like.

Panic swelled inside her. Her vision tunneled. All those laps in the pool seemed like such a waste of time now. She couldn't even remember how her mom had talked her into joining the team. A hundred lunches filled her mind, perfect calorie-counted portions consumed with so-called friends she barely talked to, or in the privacy of her own car. For four years she'd been alone, while someone who mattered enough to her to risk her life for was stranded in this game.

The box jiggled and rocked.

"What's happening to me?" she asked.

He took her hand and held it against his collarbones, resting his chin atop their folded fingers as her mind frantically struggled to wrap around this new reality.

"This must be what happened to Emerson," Dax said.

Her head shot up, fear clenching her throat. "What do you mean? Is she all right?"

Dax's brows crinkled. "She was acting strangely. Remember? Clingy and nice and stuff."

"She *is* nice." Though when she thought about it, Maddy remembered pushing Emerson back when she'd held her hand. Her stomach gave a sharp twist. She couldn't think of why she would have done that now.

Dax gave her a look that suggested otherwise, then scratched his head. "You forget Ian. She changes personalities. It's like . . ."

"What?"

He frowned. "I don't know. Like someone's messing with us."

"You think it was that last game we played with the kids?" She shivered, thinking of how old she'd felt in a matter of minutes. "They said Meido is trying to help us."

"If we do the challenges right," he said. "But I think if we don't do what Meido wants, we get in trouble."

"The punishment," she whispered. "Shinigami said the game would punish us if we broke the rules. But we didn't, did we?"

"Kind of hard to tell when we don't know what the rules are."

He was right. All that was clearly defined was that they complete each challenge and bring the stones to Izanami. Now they didn't even have the stones, or the cards, or their friends.

They could have broken a rule without knowing it.

"Maybe we weren't supposed to kiss," she said.

"I think that was fine," he said quickly. "I mean, same thing happened to Emerson, and she didn't kiss anyone."

Maddy glanced to him, her shoulders dropping. "Fine, huh?"

He cleared his throat. "Slightly above average."

A tiny grin lifted the corner of her mouth. "Six out of ten."

She watched his lips, remembering the soft feel of them. He unfolded their fingers to reach for her cheek and she leaned into it, letting her eyes close just for a moment.

It's us, Maddy. You and me.

"Maybe seven," he said.

She smiled, and when he smiled back, her heart thumped in her chest.

"Maddy, it's going to be okay. I promise. I . . ."

The box stopped.

Maddy jerked back as the top of their prison was cracked open.

She blinked, frantically trying to take in her surroundings as her eyes adjusted to the night sky and the white moon. Had the eye been that open before? It taunted her now, a bright, glowing crescent in the dark. They had to finish this before it opened completely.

Two people, guards in black robes, stood over them, their eyes lifeless and gray as they peeked over the leather face masks they wore to cover their mouths and noses. Maddy's muscles coiled, ready to spring, and she grabbed the wooden stake, tucking it against her forearm.

"Get up," one man growled. "You're coming with us."

<hr />

They were heaved out of the box into a walled-in courtyard, hard gray stone under their feet.

"Where are you taking us?" Dax demanded.

He reached for Maddy as she reached for him, but one of the guards had gotten between them. When Dax struggled, he was struck in the gut, and with a grunt he fell to his side. The guard wheeled back to kick him in the face, his sandaled foot appearing beneath his robe.

"Dax!" Maddy twisted the splintered wood in her wrist and stabbed it into the guard's shoulder.

He turned slowly, his eyes eerily blank. Maddy clenched her fists, ready to fight, but the man didn't attack. He didn't even seem hurt. Slowly, he pulled the wood free, revealing the black pointed end that had stuck into his body. It dripped ink to the ground as he lifted it, and he snapped it in one fist.

"What are you?" Maddy whispered.

"Let's go," the man spat as the other guard twisted her arm behind her back and shoved her forward.

"It's okay," Dax told her on a cough. He was jerked up, as if he weighed no more than a doll.

They were marched alongside a high stone wall cracked with black ivy and long spindles of spiderweb. The groan of the river came from somewhere behind it, taunting her, as if their freedom were just out of sight. Beneath them, the ground was paved with cracked stones, frigid against her bare feet, vines and prickly weeds shooting up in the gaps. The foliage thickened to the right, where a dirty white building with a black tiled roof jutted crookedly three stories into the air. It was bigger, more sophisticated, than Shinigami's shack, though just as ancient, and dread filled her at the thought of what might wait inside. She glanced back to their wooden cage in the corner of the dingy courtyard.

There was no second box for Emerson and Owen.

The guard in front of them pulled back a paper screen door like the one at Shinigami's house and walked inside, dragging Maddy by the arm after him.

Her eyes darted around the sparse hallway. The wooden floors were dark and glossy, the walls, white plaster. Paintings were hung at equal intervals—dirty sketches of naked women with women, and men with men, and even men and women in more than single pairs. All genders engaged in every possible configuration.

She felt a flush rise in her cheeks, but it cooled as she moved closer and saw the red, jagged smiles cut across their faces.

Kuchisake's voice whispered in her ear: *I can make you so happy.* She shivered.

The hall turned and opened into a large, shadowy room, filled with people in moth-eaten kimonos and reeking of rotten food. Readiness coiled in her muscles. Were these players, like the people they'd seen fighting the tengu? They weren't braced in defense, but frozen, like wax figures with dead eyes.

She would have taken fighters any day over the creepy stillness in this room.

Her eyes shot from what looked like a band in the near corner— two men with wooden flutes and a woman with a long-necked guitar—to the long tables against the side wall. Mountains of rice crawled with maggots. Flies buzzed around the splintered bones of fish. Flaking eels were draped over a pot of cloudy pond-scum broth. Maddy fought the urge to gag.

Every face turned to look at them as one.

Maddy's breath caught in her throat at the sudden movement.

She recalled what Shinigami had said about the yōkai—ghosts in their world, but flesh and blood in Meido. Dax, making her tell herself it wasn't real. She'd seen worse things in Meido than the pink severed flesh of a person's inner cheeks, but she couldn't think of what at the moment.

The room was lit by thick candles, dripping with wax. The flames cast jerky shadows over the paper sliding doors that lined the hall, and at the far end of the room, on a raised platform, was a large, wooden throne, intricately carved with tangled, naked bodies.

On that throne lounged Kuchisake.

His right leg hung over one of the chair's arms, the other stretched before him to the floor. He'd changed into an emerald kimono, fastened around the waist by a large black sash, and he flicked one wooden sandal against the bottom of his foot with his toes, as if bored.

Adjusting the leather mask over his mouth, he crooked a finger their direction, and Maddy and Dax were shoved through the parting crowd toward him.

For a moment, he appraised Maddy with a narrow gaze, then he lifted a clay bottle off the ground. "Sake?"

"What do you want from us?" Maddy asked.

Kuchisake took a swig, then sat up, planting his feet on the floor. "I give them food. I give them clothes. I make them smile, and still, they aren't happy." He jabbed a hand toward the crowd. Their bodies were still holding the same position, while their faces tracked Maddy and Dax's movements.

She swallowed dryly, recalling the man Keneō had been cutting up for dinner. Were these people stuck here, or did they belong, like Kuchisake?

Was this the next challenge?

"Some people are hard to please," Dax muttered.

"Are you hard to please?" Kuchisake asked. "Smile for me."

"Not really in a smiling mood," Dax told him.

Kuchisake lunged toward him, and in an instant had one arm around his back, as if he might dip Dax in some elegant ballroom dance. His other hand lifted over Dax's face, the long, spear-pointed fingernail of his index finger digging into the corner of Dax's mouth.

"Wait!" Maddy shouted, hands outstretched, envisioning how easy it would be for Kuchisake to slice Dax the way he must have done to all these people. "You don't have to do that."

Kuchisake's stare burrowed into her, warped with confusion.

"But he is unhappy."

"You don't need to cut him to make him happy," she said quickly. "There are other ways."

"Such as?" Kuchisake sounded genuinely interested.

Her mind shot to the stones. That would make them both happy, but she didn't have the cards to exchange one for—the last she'd seen, Emerson was carrying the backpack.

"You could let us go," she suggested.

Kuchisake's brows flattened. He turned back to Dax. "Tricks."

Dax's hands scraped over Kuchisake's wrist as the man began to slice a wider smile on Dax's face. He yelled out as his legs kicked in vain.

"No tricks!" Maddy said, jumping toward them, her hands outstretched.

Kuchisake paused, a crimson bead of blood forming at the corner of Dax's mouth.

"No tricks," she said again. "That was a joke! We don't really want to leave. We love your, um, party." Her skin prickled under the dead gazes of the room.

The line of Kuchisake's spine softened. "I used to throw the best parties. But they've grown so dull."

"You just need some more food."

"I have food." He tilted his chin to the tables, where the flies were buzzing.

"Right. I meant music." She glanced again to the band, but the players didn't seem to know what to do with the instruments. They held them awkwardly, staring straight ahead like puppets.

"Yes," Kuchisake said. "These musicians are no good."

"Dax plays guitar," she said, remembering how he'd been carrying a case when she first saw him.

Kuchisake pulled his nail from Dax's mouth and set him upright.

"This is true?"

Maddy swallowed as Dax wiped the blood from the corner of his mouth. If it wasn't, they were in serious trouble.

"Sure," Dax said tightly. "I play."

"Wonderful!" Kuchisake clapped his hands. "Bring him the shamisen!"

A man with pale blue eyes approached carrying the strange, long-necked guitar. He might have been a few years older than them, but his hair had gone white at the roots, and his thin moustache touched the edges of his carved smile. Again, Maddy thought of the players she'd seen before, and wondered, with a slash of pity, if he was one of them.

"Choose something lively," Kuchisake told them, then went to sit on his throne.

Maddy hurried to Dax's side as he took the instrument.

"Can you play that?" she whispered.

Dax frowned as he flipped it in his hand and pressed his fingers to the strings. "It's got three less strings than I'm used to, but I'm not sure anyone here will know the difference."

"It might be part of the challenge," she said, pulling up Emerson's strategy. "Live Fast, Cry Loud, Heal Hate . . . It's the first H. Hearts."

"Wounded hearts," Dax said with a nod. "But we don't have the card."

"I lost the card," the man said.

Maddy and Dax both turned to him, still standing like a statue in front of them.

"You're a player," Dax said.

Maddy glanced outside as a shadow passed behind the paper doors. The fateful tap of eight legs against the floorboards followed, sending chills over her scalp.

"We are very happy here," the man said. "You will be very happy, too."

"How long have you been here?" Maddy asked him, a drop of cold sweat sliding down her back.

The man's chin lifted. He blinked, as if confused. "We have to find the stone."

Maddy and Dax shared a worried glance.

"What do you have to do to find it?" she asked.

"We had to be happy."

Fear tumbled down Maddy's back like cold water. "Being happy would solve a wounded heart card," she said. "We're not letting that monster cut us."

"I'd rather not," Dax agreed. "There has to be another way to play the game. This obviously didn't work for them." He winced. "No offense, man."

A line creased between the man's brows.

"This is no game." He began to shake. "This is *no game*. Don't you know what this place is?"

"Shh!" Maddy told him, stepping closer to block Kuchisake's gaze.

The man's gaze focused on Dax. "You were there. You told Jolene to follow you."

Dax shook his head. "I don't know Jolene."

"We have to finish this together. We can't leave unless we finish it *together*." The man's eyes went wide. "It was you."

Anxiety tightened Maddy's stomach as the man repeated his claim, louder this time. He was lost, in the way Maddy had been lost in the carriage when Dax had told her about Ian. How could he possibly know Dax? But there was a certainty radiating through him that put her on edge.

What did this place do to people? She'd forgotten a friend—Ian—her reason for playing this game. Would she lose other memories too? She didn't want to stay a moment longer than she had to.

Kuchisake stood.

"Okay," Dax told him quickly. "Yep. I was there. You, me, and Jolene. You called it."

"Are we ready for the show?" Kuchisake asked.

At his words, the man grew still. Docile. His brows spread. His mouth went slack.

"You will be very happy here," he said with a wretched smile, then he turned and stepped back into the crowd, leaving Dax and Maddy near Kuchisake and his throne.

"That wasn't at all uncomfortable," Dax said under his breath.

"I'm sure this won't be either," she said, then stepped to the side to present Dax to the crowd with a wave of her arm.

He strummed a chord, cringing at the dissonant tone the shamisen's strings made. "Any requests?"

Kuchisake surveyed the crowd, then clapped his hands. "Something that will make them dance."

Maddy wove her fingers together before her, remembering suddenly that she was standing in front of a crowd of people without any clothes on. No one seemed to notice—it was by far the least offensive thing in the room—but the cool night air was whispering over her skin and bringing goose bumps to her arms and legs. She wished she had something to cover herself.

Dax cleared his throat, his ears turning faintly pink. He played a few notes, then started to sing a Green Day song, "Basket Case," that Maddy remembered immediately from how much he'd hummed it when they were kids.

She gaped at him as his voice filled the room, deep and gritty and warm.

He was good.

Really good.

She had the sudden urge to laugh. To punch him in the shoulder and say, *Why didn't you tell me you could sing?* As he broke into the chorus, she felt as if she'd put on a new pair of glasses and was finally seeing him clearly for the first time.

When he got to the line, "sometimes I give myself the creeps," Kuchisake sliced his hands through the air, and yelled, "No, no, no!"

Dax stopped.

Maddy stiffened. Her eyes darted around the room. The sliding walls would be easy enough to break through if they had to make a quick exit, but she could see the spiders' hulking shadows beyond them.

"Something with passion," Kuchisake demanded. "Something I can feel in my gut." He punched himself in the stomach to show what he meant.

Dax rolled his shoulders back. "I don't—"

"Something that makes me not want to cut you," Kuchisake added softly.

"All right," Maddy said lightly. "I'm sure he's got something he can dig up." She sent Dax a hard look. "Don't you?"

Dax's gaze dropped. He flicked a finger over one of the strings, like he was plucking one of her nerves.

Seeming to make up his mind suddenly, he set the shamisen against his chest like a guitar, and began to sing.

"Three days ago I saw you, in the grass beside the ocean."

Her breath caught. She didn't recognize the song.

She watched his lips, the curve of his mouth around each word.

"You told me that you loved me, but you'd never take me broken."

His back rounded, the muscles stretching around his shoulders like wings. She was less aware of her own nakedness then than she was of his. The cords of his neck that tensed when he held a note. The tendons behind his knees. The vulnerability of his voice and his skin, out on display for all to see, punched through her.

"I saw you after breakfast, trading stories with your friends. You laugh but now I can't, because I know the way it ends."

This wasn't the boy who joked at the wrong times, or the fighter with the eyes of stone. This was the heart she'd always suspected lay beneath his calloused skin. It was so obvious now, she couldn't believe she'd never seen it until this moment.

"You hold me but don't see me. You never let me go. I hate myself for missing you. I hate that you don't know, that I'm haunted.

"Haunted."

He opened his eyes, and looked to her.

"That's all I ever want, to be haunted."

She met his gaze, her hand pressing to her belly to still the flutter deep inside. His hand curled around the neck of the guitar in a way that made her breath come faster. When his lips parted, she remembered the way they'd felt against her own, soft and yet sturdy. Safe and dangerous.

"Dax," she murmured.

He took a step toward her.

"Yes!" Kuchisake roared, stopping Dax's approach. "That was it! Look at them! Look how they dance!"

Maddy tore her eyes away from Dax's to take in the room. The people were moving now, swaying stiffly, clapping like windup dolls. Kuchisake raised his hands and the candles glowed brighter, bathing the room in a yellow glow. It softened the scars on everyone's faces and made the spots of blood on the floor from their slit mouths glisten.

Dax flinched when Kuchisake slapped him on the back.

"You belong here," he told Dax. "You feel it, don't you?"

Dax gave him a tight smile.

"I see what lies in your heart now," Kuchisake said, then pointed Dax's chin toward Maddy, his long, bladed fingernail catching a flicker of candlelight.

Maddy tensed at his words. Was he talking about the wounded heart? This could be the challenge; maybe Dax had solved it by baring his soul with that song. But the way Kuchisake was staring at her gave her a very bad feeling.

"I know what will make you happy," Kuchisake said, then, with a wave of his hand, the guards appeared again through the crowd. Maddy was dragged away before she could mount a proper struggle. Her last sight of the room was of Dax holding the shamisen, while Kuchisake whispered in his ear.

—•—

She was taken down a dank, mossy stairway, to a cave with a stone spring. Two women with cut faces appeared through the thick steam, their eyes as dull as the people upstairs. They tried to take what remained of her clothing, getting a little too close for comfort when she declined. She only got them to leave her alone by explaining that she could undress by herself. While she did, they wet large sea sponges and poured fragrant jasmine oil into bowls.

"I didn't know prisons had spas," she muttered.

The women did not respond.

Two wooden steps descended into the rocky bath, lit by gently swaying strings of bioluminescent light attached to the low, caverned ceiling. In one of her science classes she'd seen something similar made by glowworms, and as the steam beaded on her bare skin, she couldn't help the wonder that pulled in her belly.

It was dashed as one of the women tossed a bucket of frigid water over her naked body.

She shrieked and tried to step into the bath, but they blocked her. With furious strokes, they scrubbed her body with the sponges. When she guarded her chest, they washed her back. When she twisted away, they moved to her legs. Bending low only gave them access to her hair. She growled in frustration as they cleaned away the mud and muck until her skin felt raw and prickly with goose bumps.

Then they moved aside and motioned her into the pool.

"Oh, now it's okay?" she said through chattering teeth. Without an answer, she sank into the water, expecting heat but overwhelmed by the familiarity of the cool temperature. It welcomed her, even here in this awful place. She knew how it would feel as she spread her fingers and toes, how it would lap over her skin and make her light. It was just like the pool at home, too cold, and then just right, sharpening her mind and readying her muscles for action.

"Where is Dax?" she asked, but the women ignored her. She kept one eye on the entryway, where the guard was posted. She thought of how he'd knocked the wind out of Dax when they'd arrived. That didn't leave her feeling confident about getting past him.

The water beside her shoulder splashed, and Maddy was startled to find one of the women wading into the pool, the bottom of her plain, gray kimono soaking to the ankles. For a moment, she worried this was about to become a group activity, but then the woman sat on the edge and motioned her over.

She didn't speak, and the blank look in her eyes did nothing to comfort Maddy's nerves. Still, she eased closer, and soon the women were rubbing oil into her hands and forearms.

The cool water kept her sharp, but the oils threatened to soothe her senses. She watched the women through narrowed eyes, feeling like a turkey being prepared for Thanksgiving dinner.

"Why are you doing this?" she asked the women.

They didn't respond.

"Are you players?" she asked, quieter.

Nothing.

With a pang, she thought of her conversation with Dax after their capture.

"Have you ever met someone named Ian Spencer?" She stumbled over his last name. It was Spencer, wasn't it? She hated that she wasn't certain.

They didn't even look up.

She crossed her arms over her chest as one of the women used small wooden cups to pour water over her shoulders. Was the same thing happening to Dax? They'd succeeded in appeasing Kuchisake, but that didn't mean either of them were safe. For all she knew, he could be being cut right now. Or forced to entertain that crowd of swaying, blank-eyed players.

She wondered if he was singing again.

Her throat tightened.

If Kuchisake hurt him, she was going to make him regret it.

Splashing through the spring, she planted her feet and rinsed herself off. The ladies barely looked at her as she stood. They patted her dry with towels, then pulled a plain white slip over her shoulders.

"Where's my stuff?" she asked.

They didn't give her clothes back.

One woman reached into a lacquered box near the cavern's wall and removed a dress—not just any dress, but a wedding gown. Maddy recognized it immediately. The scooped white lace neck with its short princess sleeves. Its tight satin bodice, fanning out to layered skirts. She'd seen this dress before, in a magazine. She'd cut out the picture because she'd thought it was so beautiful. Because one day she was going to have one just like it.

She'd made a collage around it, with pictures of other things she wanted in her life. A house with a big yard. Three dogs. A soft-serve frozen-yogurt maker, and an array of hiking equipment for when she became an explorer, and a black belt in karate.

Dax had seen it and teased her relentlessly, but she hadn't cared. She was going to have all of it.

Looking at this exact dress now, she felt as if someone had tunneled inside her and put her most private dreams on display.

"Where'd you get that?" she asked.

Silence.

The women dressed her roughly, pulling the gown over her head and fastening the seemingly hundreds of buttons. The bodice was constricting, the skirts heavy. They didn't allow her to twist or run if she needed to. Stiff white heels were crammed onto her feet. Her hair was twisted into a thick bun at the nape of her neck. The women pulled her braids so tight she thought they were going to yank them out.

"Ow," she said, but as her lips formed the word, one of her attendants used a thin brush to paint her lips red. She twisted away. "Okay, that's fine. Thank you." Anxiety fizzled in her chest as one of the women lifted a mirror from the box to show her her reflection.

She sucked in a breath. The girl before her was graceful. Elegant. She looked like a princess—like she belonged on a throne beside Kuchisake.

Her stomach sank. She did not belong here. She had to get home.

She was trying to strip out of her costume when the sound of approaching footsteps had the women scurrying away. Maddy stiffened, wishing she had her sneakers, not these ridiculous heels. Her gaze darted around for anything she could use to defend herself, and landed on the handheld mirror.

She snatched it out of the box where the woman had left it and braced it before her like a sword.

The man approaching was tall and slender, and as he slid through the shadows with ethereal grace, her heart began to pound.

Kuchisake.

He was not wearing his mask, and the jagged edge of his wounded mouth made her shiver. It was worse than the scars on the women's faces, partially because it looked fresher, gaping open at the corners. Partially because when he stepped into the light and looked at her, he smiled.

She gripped the mirror tighter.

"There she is," he said. "Beautiful."

"Where's Dax?" She sidestepped, trying to put herself between him and the door.

He stepped closer.

"He's close, don't worry." Kuchisake's grin stretched as he placed a hand on the breast of his jade kimono. "He and I are very good friends now."

"I doubt that."

Kuchisake's tongue pressed through the gaping wound in his cheek, then retreated. "You make him very happy. I can see it. Does that please you?"

"Where is he?" she asked again.

Kuchisake giggled, high and excited. "So nervous! I understand. I once had a love I could not bear to part with." His smile faded. "His joy was my joy, and his pain . . ." Kuchisake smiled again, screwing one finger into the open slab of his cheek. "Well, that was my joy, too."

Maddy looked down at her satin gown, dread bearing down on her courage. Kuchisake had already confessed his love in the forest. He was clearly unhinged. It was not a stretch to think he wanted more than just casual conversation.

"This gown," he said with a pleased sigh. "It is as fine as a lace cloud. Is it as you wanted?"

"How'd you know about this?" she asked.

"I hear many whispers." He tapped his ear, and in response, the inside of her own began to itch. Releasing the mirror with one hand, she scratched at the underside of her jaw, feeling the quick scuttle of an insect over her knuckles. When she drew back, a spider the size of a bottle cap was climbing up her wrist.

With a cry, she shook it off.

Had that been in her ear? In her *head*?

Sickness burned through her as she dropped the mirror. It crashed against the rough floor, splintering into gleaming shards. With a gasp, she scratched at both ears, but no more spiders emerged.

"I have to go," she said with a dry gulp. "Thank you for the party. But I have to find my friends."

"But I am your friend." Kuchisake looked aghast, or maybe that was just the awful pucker of his bloody cheeks. "No, you cannot leave now. It is not safe out there. Here, behind my walls, I can protect you."

"Protect us from what?" she asked, trying to keep him talking so he wouldn't see her slide to the right and creep slowly toward the exit.

"There are far more dangerous creatures than me in these woods, young love." The chill in his voice made her tremble.

The oni.

Shinigami had told them that the demon was the most feared of all yokai. Maddy remembered how it had hunted them in the woods when they'd played with their younger selves. She could feel its presence around them now like a low-hanging fog.

Kuchisake tilted his head. "Did you really think it wise to steal what had already been stolen?"

Maddy froze on her path to the door. He knew about the game—the cards, the challenges, the small stones Emerson carried in the bag. Maddy could feel it in his pointed stare.

"The creature wants the stones back, you know. He will never stop hunting you. Empress Izanami calls to him, even in pieces." Kuchisake grinned. "Much like love, yes?"

"I wouldn't know about that kind of love," she said carefully.

"Stay long enough and you will," he promised grimly. "After all, Meido was built on a broken heart." He moved closer, gliding like a snake through the steam.

She didn't plan on staying any longer than she had to. Ian had given them until dawn to finish this. They had to wrap up these challenges, deliver the stones to Izanami, and get to Ian before the giant opened his eye.

"It was different before. Not so cold. Not so sad," Kuchisake continued, the drop in his voice making him sound older than he had before. "I threw the very best parties."

"I bet you did." If she could keep him talking, maybe he would be distracted long enough that she could escape. Then she could find Dax and they could get out of here.

"Then he had to go and ruin it." Kuchisaki sighed.

"The oni," Maddy said.

"The oni?" Kuchisake barked a laugh. "No, we were cursed long before any demon. It was Izanagi who ruined us."

She paused as Kuchisake crossed in front of her to the pool.

"Is Izanagi any relation to Izanami?" she asked.

"Any relation?" Kuchisake sputtered. "Does the moon have any relation to the sun? The water to the earth? *Any relation.* Izanami and Izanagi were the first. The empress and her brother lover."

"Brother lover. How nice." Maddy cleared her throat, hiding the judgment from her face. Her world's history was fraught with consanguineous royal relationships, why would this place be any different?

"What do you mean, the first?" she asked.

"The first *everything,*" he said, gesturing wildly. "Before Izanami and Izanagi there was nothing. An empty space. A blank palette. They dreamed the very ground you stand on. The trees. The sky. The stars and moon and sun and rain. Izanami painted the mountains with her fingertips. Izanagi's piss filled an ocean." His nostrils flared, and Maddy could feel the contempt rolling off of him. "Everything you see, they made from chaos."

"Exactly how old are these people?"

"Are you not listening?" Kuchisake asked. "They were here before time. They *made* time."

She thought of what Emerson had said on the bridge about pocket worlds and how they could have fallen into an alternate dimension, a place built from Japanese mythology that diverged to become a game, a hell.

"What did Izanagi do?" she asked, taking another slow step toward the door.

"He betrayed us," Kuchisake said. "Not at first. At the start, all was well. Every moment held new wonder—a day. A night. Fire. A child's cry. The empress and her emperor ruled with honor, and their people were happy. *I* was happy." He sighed. "Izanami trusted me, her most loyal advisor, with her secrets. I kept my lips sealed, of course." He tapped the center of his lips with one finger, and Maddy was reminded of the kids in the woods who'd worked for him, and their game of secrets.

"My empress had concocted something new. She called it 'the passage.' A green fire that would carve a path between two lands. The carrier had only to hold the flames and whisper where she wanted to go, and . . ." He snapped his fingers. "She would arrive in that spot."

"I've seen that fire," she said. "In the woods when we came here. And in the gates between challenges." Her memory sparked with green flames.

"She asked me to plan a celebration to show her love and her people what she'd made," Kuchisake continued. "It was a spectacle. Fresh fish and tsukemono. Mochi with sweet azuki paste. And music. Oh, our Dax would be proud!"

Maddy's teeth clenched at the mention of him and the assumption that he was theirs to share.

"They all came to the empress's palace. The great silk weaver. The midwife. The empress's mighty warrior—they call him Aka Manto now, though then, he was known as Jizo. They were all there for Izanami to unveil her secrets." Kuchisake's smile faded, pulling at his cheeks. "She showed us the passage, and we were in awe. But the flames grew unruly, and destroyed the palace and all within. Only one escaped."

From Kuchisake's tone, Maddy could guess who.

"The empress's lover."

He nodded. "The passage worked. It took us to another place. Yomi no kuni."

Maddy stilled. The kids had mentioned Yomi no kuni—that's where the empress was.

Kuchisake's gaze grew hard. "Izanagi searched for his bride— for all of us. He travelled through the dark lands of Meido, but when he finally reached Yomi, he found Izanami changed. She was no longer his beloved empress. She was burned and broken. Beginning to . . . *decompose*."

Maddy's breath came faster. She thought of the boy Dax had mentioned—their friend—Ian. He had been here four years. Was he changed, too? Burned, and decomposing?

They couldn't waste another minute. They needed to find him now.

Kuchisake sighed. "For all the love Izanagi claimed, he could not look at her. She was unclean. Dangerous. Corrupted by kegare."

"I know that word," Maddy said. Shinigami had used it when they'd first arrived. "The oni spread it when he . . ." She hesitated, remembering the steam over the teacups in the shack.

"When he tore her apart?" Kuchisake winced. "To commit violence and bathe in blood—especially the blood of one already . . . *altered* by this place—taints all those it touches. But how could you expect anything else from a child born from a rotting womb? A child abandoned in this place by his bastard father?"

A thrust of pity took Maddy by surprise.

"Wait," she said. "The oni is Izanami and Izanagi's kid?"

Kuchisake nodded. "Empress Izanami was pregnant when she came to Meido, but this place changed her. Izanami and Izanagi's child was born a monster, its mother's scars tattooed over every inch of its body, its father's betrayal in its heart. It was no wonder she hated him."

He loved Empress Izanami, as so many did. But she would not return his love. They say it drove him mad.

"Now we are all cursed," he said. "The lords of wanderers and ruins. The midwife welcomes the dead. The weaver clothes trees in skin."

Maddy shivered. "Keneō." Her hands ran down the embroidery of her lace collar, her thoughts shifting from the man in the suit of flesh to their first contact in Meido, an old woman with a toothless smile. "Shinigami."

Kuchisake cocked a brow. "She still loves her children, though they are different now. A tunnel in the earth is their birth into the land of the living."

"A tunnel," Maddy whispered, thinking of the tunnel they'd entered to come here. She swallowed, a cold terror brushing across the base of her neck. "What do you mean she welcomes the dead? We didn't die." Her chin pulled inward. "If I were dead, I'd know it."

But even as she said it, doubt wormed through her.

"Surely," agreed Kuchisake, in a way that did not feel encouraging. "It's always easy to spot the dead. They're so boring at my parties."

She lifted one hand from the mirror to touch her face, finding it warm. Her fingers ran down to her neck, where she felt the firm, rapid beat of her pulse.

She wasn't dead.

This was a game. A twisted, psychotic game, that most importantly had an exit. If they completed the tasks, they could go home. You didn't come back alive after you died.

When she shuddered, he gave a wet cluck of his tongue. "I have worried you. That was not my intent. If your Dax carves out your organs, you can be sure that he will carry them in a satchel close to his heart, all the days of his life."

She gave a pained wince.

Kuchisake clapped his hands. "Now, join me, my beautiful bride. We have much to celebrate."

He turned on his heel, disappearing through the steam, and leaving her gaping after him.

"I'm not marrying you," she said. She'd known that he was unhinged, but now that his purpose was clear, she felt ill.

The two women appeared at her sides, pushing her forward.

"Did you hear me?" she called, then looked at the women. "I'm not doing this."

They said nothing.

Before she could fight further, she caught movement at the back of the cave, just beyond the pool. Through the mist, a glowing red eye blinked at her. Then another.

And another.

Eight, she counted. Eight eyes. Eight long, black legs unfurling from the far corner of the room, right over where she'd been bathing.

Something crossed over her foot, and when she glanced down, she saw a spider the size of her fist. With a cry, she stepped back, feeling something squash beneath her sandal.

Wafting away the steam, she saw that the cavern's rocky floor was covered with small spiders. Coffee black and fanged, they rolled over one another in small waves, making overlapping rings around her feet and Kuchisake's, like they were stones dropped in a pool.

And the largest was slowly approaching across the ceiling.

She rushed toward the front of the room, smashing spiders with each step. The guard moved out before her, apathetic to the crunching beneath his feet and the growing slickness on the soles of her sandals. She wrapped her arms around herself, trying to keep from brushing the walls where the creatures climbed, and shrieked when she could feel the feather-soft legs dancing up the back of her calf beneath her wedding gown.

Finally, they reached the main floor, but the room where Dax had sung was now empty. The paper walls to the courtyard had been opened, and the crowd had been moved outside, to the dead grass below the steps to Kuchisake's house. Her breath came faster as she searched for Dax, finally settling when he appeared at the front of the group. He had been dressed as well, and was wearing loose black pants and a kimono jacket.

When he saw her he stepped toward her, but Kuchisake blocked his approach with a swing of his arm.

She rushed past the guard to meet him.

"Look how she runs to us," Kuchisake told Dax, his eyes twinkling. "She is perfect, is she not?"

Dax's stare darted from her eyes, to her mouth, to the thick skirts around her legs. He shuddered a sigh of relief.

"Are you all right?" he said quietly, as she moved close.

"I'm fine. You?"

He nodded.

"What's going on?" she asked.

"At last!" Kuchisake stood before them, addressing the crowd. "My friends, even in a place like this, we are fated for joy and healing."

Maddy glanced from him to the crowd before them, staring mindlessly toward the palace. The man with the shamisen who'd claimed that he'd known Dax was amongst them, dead-eyed and grinning, and a growing horror pulled through Maddy's chest as she realized the mutilation this ceremony might entail.

She was about to tell Dax they needed to run when someone slid through the crowd, placing herself directly in front of the man. She was wearing a faded red kimono and a leather mask, and Maddy's eyes widened as she registered her light, buzzed hair.

"Emerson," she breathed.

Her eyes were clear now—no longer clouded with age. Her posture was tall, and her skin youthful. Relief filled Maddy. Her friend was back to normal.

"The binding of souls is a sacred tradition," Kuchisake continued, like a pastor at the head of a church—like the pictures of her parents' wedding on the stairway wall at her house. "One of heart, and spirit, and blood."

There was a lump on Emerson's back—Maddy could see it as she turned slightly to make room for Owen. She must have been wearing the backpack beneath her robe. Owen, back to his cocky teenage self, had managed to find a mask as well, and his eyes darted between her and Dax.

In one of the wide sleeves of his gray tunic, she spotted a yellow corner of paper.

The wounded hearts card.

"It is a promise that cannot be undone," Kuchisake said. "Even in death your souls will belong to each other."

Maddy met his black eyes, fear whispering through her.

"Smile, my love," he said, his breath sending a cloud of incense over her that made her eyes water. "Your heart is healed. You will never be lonely again."

Your heart is healed. The words resounded in her head.

Wounded hearts.

She flinched as Kuchisake reached for her hand. She couldn't marry him. She refused.

Did she have a choice?

"Hey!" Dax tried to cut in, but Kuchisake held him back with his other arm. Maddy was no match for his strength. In a quick, efficient movement, he sliced open an inch of Maddy's inner wrist, just above her veins, with one sweep of his bladed nail.

Maddy's lungs hollowed on a surprised gasp. Pain sang up through her shoulder. She tried to jerk away, but Kuchisake held fast, giving a terrible giggle. He lifted his finger to his mouth and licked off the blood.

His eyes rolled back in pleasure.

"Such sweet filth," he groaned. "So vile. So pure. Once, this ke-gare would be abhorrent, but now . . . it hardly matters, does it? We're all monsters here."

When Maddy glanced to the side, she saw that Emerson had climbed two steps toward them. As much as Maddy longed to run, she held out her other hand to stop her.

They had to finish the challenge.

"Now you," Kuchisake whispered to Dax.

"Just get it over with," he said.

"What every lover wants to hear, isn't that right, my sweet?" Kuchisake laughed again, then cut Dax at the same place.

Maddy winced, feeling a spark shoot up her arm a second time, as if the pain had been her own.

Kuchisake bound their arms together with a silk belt that had hung from his sash. Then he raised their hands high overhead.

"To love, the greatest weapon. May it destroy you both."

The crowd clapped politely, then at Kuchisake's sneer, roared with enthusiastic shouts and praise.

"Dax," Maddy said, eyes round. "I think we just got married."

Dax blinked at her. At their bound wrists. She could feel the warm slickness of blood against their skin, more intimate than any exchange of rings, and was glad—glad that it was him and not Kuchisake.

Their host elbowed Dax in the side. "Kiss her, you happy fool!"

She glanced again to Owen, the card still in his fist. It hadn't changed yet. Maybe they needed to kiss again.

She leaned forward, but Dax hesitated.

"It's okay," she whispered. "We have to."

He shook his head quickly, sweat beading on his forehead. "What if you forget more?"

Her mind shot to the kiss in the woods. To the buzz in her ears and the fog in her brain.

To a boy named Ian who she hadn't even known to miss.

Worry had her biting the inside of her cheek, but they didn't have a choice. To get out of here, they needed to advance to the next level. They needed to solve the wounded heart card, and the test was right before them.

They had to get married.

"If I forget," she whispered fiercely, "make me remember." She pulled him closer, their wrists still bound by the silk tie. "And if you forget, I'll make you remember, and we'll get out of this to-gether, just like we started."

It's us, Maddy. You and me.

She pulled him down to her and kissed him.

Her head went quiet. She pressed closer, an ache as definite and promising as faraway thunder rolling through her. He trembled at her quiet gasp. She knew this union wasn't real, that they were just acting, doing what they had to do to get out of this, but it felt like more, like something sacred, and when she opened her eyes, she realized that all the years liking him, missing him, even being mad at him, had been practice for now.

She pulled back, feeling like she was shaking from the inside out. She became aware of the crowd before them. The clapping. Kuchisake's laughter. When Dax looked down at her, his eyes were filled with such genuine longing, she could barely catch her breath.

She looked over to Emerson and Owen, then frowned, because the card was still a thick rectangle of paper in her friend's hand.

Maybe Emerson was confused too, because she leaned over and said something to Owen. Maddy couldn't make out what it was, but it must not have been about the ceremony, because Owen clenched the card in his fist. His brows drew together as his shoulders slumped forward. He looked as if she'd struck him—worse, that she'd gutted him—but she didn't notice at all.

A moment later Owen jolted, his eyebrows arched in surprise, as the card in his fist dripped away like molasses, revealing a long, white, curved rib.

Maddy's breath caught.

The fifth stone. They'd won the challenge.

She turned to Dax, but before she could tell him, a wail split the night, and the gate of the palace exploded inward in a spray of wood and shattered rock. She fell, the belt binding her wrist to Dax's ripping free. Coughing on a mouthful of dust, she hugged her knees to her body as a stampede of people began charging into the house. A foot caught her in the side, making her gasp in pain. Someone tripped over her dress. Screams cut through the roar of blood in her ears.

"Maddy!" Dax called from somewhere through the running legs. The terror in his voice blended with her own, needling through her skin.

"Dax?" she called. "Emerson!"

She shoved herself to a stand and squinted toward the gate. There'd been a blast of some kind. A bomb. She couldn't see what had done it, but the gaping hole where the gate had been was black as the night beyond.

"Dax!" she shouted again. She scanned for Emerson and Owen but couldn't see them through the charging crowd. Between the screams came the rapid clicks of the spiders' pointed feet.

She spun toward the palace, but it was only chaos—dozens of people charging up the steps to get inside. Another guttural howl filled the night, scraping across Maddy's nerves. Then something came flying through the air, a woman, tossed as if she were a rag doll. Her arms and legs flapped uselessly; her clothes rippled in the wind.

She slammed against one of the pillars of the palace and fell in a pile at its base.

"Oni!" a man screamed.

Maddy's blood ran cold. A child's voice ripped through her mind: *The oni doesn't need a gate. It can go anywhere in Meido.*

The demon had found them again.

"Maddy!" Dax reached her, his hand, still slick with their blood, gripping hers. "We have to go. Look!" He pointed through the night to where the wooden box had brought them, at the side of the house. There, stretching nearly to the coifed tile roof, a spider was frozen in place, its long, hairy legs spread, four on one side, four on the other.

From beneath it came a shimmering pale green glow.

Their exit.

She started to run toward it but was quickly caught around the back of the collar. When she spun, Kuchisake was grimacing down at her.

"Where are you off to?"

"Let go of me!" she hollered, twisting in his grasp.

Dax shoved him back, but Kuchisake, moving with grace and inhuman strength, threw him into the roof's overhang. Dax landed on the stone floor with a thud as a new layer of dust rained down over them.

"Dax!" Madeline screamed as Dax rolled across the deck.

"You don't want to stay?" the man roared, his split mouth opening fully to reveal his yellow molars at the back of his jaw. The foundation of his palace shook with his rage, bits of tile roofing sliding off into the crowd. Around him, his army of spiders had gathered, keeping anyone who tried to pass into the safety of the palace at bay.

"Let go of her!"

A blast of flames caught Kuchisake on the side. He staggered back, slapping at his burning kimono. Maddy shoved away from the heat, guarding her eyes against the bright flash. Terror stuttered through her. No one had mentioned that the oni breathed fire.

But as the flames cleared, she saw that it wasn't the oni. It was Emerson, holding what looked like an iron rifle, a tank attached by tubes to its base slung lopsidedly over her shoulder. Instead of bullets, flames erupted from the end of the barrel, throwing a slash of light over her glistening face.

"Go!" Emerson shouted. "Owen's got the stone!"

Maddy ran, but Kuchisake tripped her and she fell to her hands and knees, one white heeled shoe flying free.

Emerson grabbed her arm, trying to haul her up, while Kuchisake, still aflame, fisted the back of her wedding dress. His shoulder bubbled and melted, but he didn't stop.

"No, no, no . . ." Kuchisake chanted, but his words were cut off by a blade to the neck.

Dax stood over him, pocketknife in his hand, his teeth bared. Black blood bubbled from the wound and as Kuchisake touched it tenderly, he looked at his ink-smeared hand in surprise.

"An engimono?" he murmured.

Maddy didn't wait for him to say more. Kicking off her remaining shoe, she grabbed Dax's arm and dragged him toward the spider gate. Emerson yelped beside her as a black spear sliced through the air—a spider leg, embedding in a man's chest before them. She bathed the monster in fire from her flamethrower. It let out a piercing scream and scuttled away.

"Come on!" Owen was just beside the gate, the long stone in his fist. "Hurry up!"

They sprinted away from Kuchisake and his house, Dax on their heels. They'd nearly reached Owen when she heard a crash behind them, followed by thud against the ground hard enough to make her stumble.

She looked back to find a creature twice the size of a human galloping toward them on its hands and feet. At first, Maddy thought it was a spider, but its skin was waxy and red, and the hair on its skull was matted down to its massive shoulders. The creature pounced, but before Maddy could react, she was shoved from behind by Dax. She tumbled forward, rolling across the dead grass to Owen's feet.

In horror, she looked back just in time to see the monster grab Dax by the throat and ram him into the ground.

"Dax!" Maddy screamed.

"What is that?" Emerson notched the flamethrower against her hip and pulled the trigger, shooting an orange stream of fire at the creature's side. With a snarl, it turned on her, its red claws cutting through the air to knock the weapon from her hands. It flew into the side of Kuchisake's house, breaking with a crack as it set the outer wall ablaze.

The creature refocused on Dax, striking him with a massive fist. Its nails glinted as it scratched him. Its teeth gnashed as it bit him in the side.

The oni. Maddy knew it from the fear echoing in her chest.

"No!" she screamed, charging toward them.

The oni turned with a hiss. Black eyes were sunk into his protruding skull. Horns twisted from its temples. His skin wasn't just red, but knotted and scored from head to toe.

A demon. She could see now why he was called that. If there was any creature that belonged in hell, this was it.

The knife had fallen out of Dax's hand and she swept it up, jabbing the point into the oni's thick thigh. It broke through the skin with a crunch, embedding two inches of steel into its pulsing muscle.

The oni hissed again. Its head swung back as if in pain. Then it sprang into the shadows.

Dax wasn't moving.

Before them, the spider that made the gate began to flick its legs.

"We have to go," Emerson was saying. "Pick him up! We have to move!"

Still gripping the knife, Maddy grabbed Dax under one arm.

Owen took the other. Dax's head dropped forward. His feet dragged behind.

They charged through the gate, the spider's red eyes glaring at them from above, the green flames reaching up from below. As they went under, cold from the barren ground lanced up Maddy's legs under her dress. The scent of mildew blasted away the blood and death behind her. She glanced up at the spider's segmented body and the tufts of black hair, vibrating as a slow line of webbing began to drool down.

She twisted around it, and they landed in a heap on the other side of the gate.

"Dax?" she said as Owen and Emerson flipped him over. She gasped at his battered face and the bloody bite marks on his chest and throat.

"He isn't breathing!" Emerson said, one hand hovering over his mouth.

"Dax!" Owen shouted. "Can you hear me?"

Maddy didn't think before pushing him aside. She knelt at Dax's ribs, feeling his sternum. She was a swimmer. She'd had to take CPR every year since she'd joined the team. She'd never done it on a real person before, but that didn't matter now.

Dropping Dax's knife in the dirt, she layered her hands one over the other on his slippery chest and began compressions.

She counted to thirty, then tilted Dax's chin up and gave him two long breaths. His lips were still. His skin like ice.

In her mind she saw the oni slamming him to the ground.

She saw it biting his side.

Dax didn't move.

"Oh god," Emerson said, covering her mouth as Maddy switched to compressions again.

Tears stung her eyes.

It's us, Maddy. You and me.

"No," she said out loud, wiping them aside on the shoulder of her wedding gown. "Wake up, Dax!"

It went on forever. The seconds stretched to days and years.

Dax's eyes stayed closed, his lips gently parted. His rib cage rose and fell only when she breathed into his lungs.

After a while, Owen's arm crossed around her chest. He squeezed tightly, then pulled her back. She shoved him away.

Dax lay still on the ground.

"Stop it," she sobbed. "This isn't funny."

Say something rude, she wanted to shout at him. *Jump up to scare me.* Anything would be better than this.

She shook his arm. "Please wake up."

Emerson crawled to Maddy. For one long, painful moment, they clung to each other, their tears soaking their borrowed robes, their hands balling into fists. Maddy wanted to hit something, but her arms were too weak. She wanted to scream, but she couldn't find the air.

This wasn't supposed to happen. She had lost Ian, a friend she couldn't even remember; she couldn't lose Dax, too. Not after everything they'd been through. Not after Kuchisake had cut their wrists and tied them together. *A promise that cannot be undone,* he had said. *Even in death.*

Her stomach twisted. If Dax could die in front of her, so could Emerson and Owen. So could she. She'd been so confident that they could succeed when they'd gotten the last stone, but now that hope was gone, ashes in the wind, and she felt like they'd already lost.

"What's wrong?"

Maddy spun to find Dax sitting up behind them. With a cry, she launched herself at him, throwing her arms around his neck. His skin was still icy, and so she squeezed him tighter, her hot tears wetting his neck.

But Dax did not hug her back.

He's hurt, she realized. "Sorry. I'm just . . ." As she pulled back, she met his eyes, and a shiver passed through her. There was something strange about them—his pupils were too large, his lids open too wide.

He smiled, all teeth.

"Dax?"

He frowned.

"You dropped your knife, pal," said Owen, his voice cracking. He held out the blue knife and dropped it into Dax's open palm.

Dax stared at it as if confused. Then he shuddered.

He turned back to Maddy. His stare warped with worry. He grabbed her and held her close. "You're okay?"

"Yes," she whispered. His throat was warm against her forehead. "Are you?"

He nodded.

She let herself melt into his arms. He was all right now. She had saved him, and they were going to finish this, and find someone named Ian, and go home.

EMERSON

They needed to rest to replenish their health for the next challenge, but they didn't have much time. They'd wounded the oni, but he'd be back, and without the flamethrower Emerson had found during the attack, all they had to defend themselves was Dax's knife. Above, the fingernail sliver was now a half moon, flat on top, round beneath. The last time she'd looked, it had been a fat crescent. If the giant's eye continued to open more with each challenge, it would be a bright, full circle by the time they solved the final card.

They picked their way along the riverbank, taking turns helping Dax, until the shale cliffs on either side cut their path down to a narrow strip of gravel. The cold needled through her kimono—from the way Owen was pinching the collar of his closed, she guessed he was freezing as well. At least they weren't wearing the tattered pants and shredded jacket Dax had on, or worse, Maddy's wedding dress. The spider gate had returned them to the woods, but the trees were all dead now, their branches stark and naked, and the air smelled of ash and burned hair.

It was a wasteland. A place for dead things.

It was exactly where they were meant to be.

Finally, they reached shelter—a hole punched in the cliff, big enough to hide them.

While Maddy and Owen made a fire, Emerson set up a perimeter of dried brush around the cave's entrance. It wasn't enough to protect them, but it would crackle with warning should an intruder come. Dax gripped his knife, staring through bruised eyes into the dark. The memory of his stillness clung to her nerves, knotting the muscles behind her neck. He seemed all right, but how could he be? He'd nearly died.

He *had* died.

Maddy was watching him, one hand circling her opposite wrist where a pale blue, silk belt was tied. Emerson could feel her worry as if it were her own. She had always been that way. When Maddy was happy, Emerson couldn't help but grin. When Maddy was hurting, Emerson withdrew alongside her.

A piece of her had been missing when Maddy was absent.

She crept up beside her friend, offering a gentle nudge with her shoulder.

"He's all right, you know."

Maddy worried her lip between her teeth. They'd gotten a small fire going, and Owen was kneeling beside it, warming his hands.

"I hope so," she said.

"You saved him. That was pretty incredible."

Emerson thought again of how Dax hadn't moved for long moments after Maddy had stopped CPR.

She frowned, catching a glimmer as the small blade he flicked in and out reflected the fire. An "engimono," that man with the split face had called it. Keneō had said that word too. Owen had thought it meant "good luck," but Emerson wasn't sure about that. There was a difference between luck and magic. That blade was scarcely big enough to cut open a box, yet Kuchisake had been afraid of it, and it had actually hurt the oni when Maddy had stabbed him.

There was more to that knife than luck.

"You shooting that flamethrower like a badass—*that* was incredible." Maddy pulled on the scarf around her forearm.

Emerson sighed. It had been like playing *Assassin 0* but a million times better.

"How's your wrist? I saw that guy cut you." She leaned closer, then cringed as Maddy pulled down the scarf to reveal an angry red wound that ran across her veins.

"Turns out getting married is a lot like donating blood."

"Like everything else here." Emerson snorted. "Congratulations, by the way. That was quite a kiss."

"We had some practice before the ceremony." Maddy wiggled her eyebrows.

Emerson gaped, then gave her a high five. "Does this mean you'll be sharing milkshakes and wearing matching outfits?"

"I already got his initials tattooed above my heart." She batted her eyes.

"Gross."

"Wait until you see where he inked mine."

"Vomit."

Maddy giggled.

"Well, thanks for taking one for the team." Emerson knelt by the backpack where she'd stowed the last stone, and held it up for closer examination. It was as thin as a finger, curved, and twice the length of any of the others. "You two got us stone number five. I think it's a rib."

Maddy frowned. "Actually, I don't think we did."

"What do you mean?"

Maddy took the rib, her fingertips sliding over its smooth length. "During the wedding, Dax and I kissed, but the wounded hearts card didn't change right away."

"Okay," Emerson said, following Maddy's gaze to Owen.

"You said something to Owen. Remember? It looked like it hurt his feelings."

A jab of guilt made Emerson scowl. "I just asked if he thought he'd ever get married."

Maddy nodded slowly, as if she'd just pieced something together. She lowered her hands, tucking the bone back into the bag, then pulled Emerson down to sit beside her on the sandy cave floor.

"Does the name Ian ring any bells?" she asked, flickering shadows dancing across her face.

A buzz filled Emerson's ears, like bees on faraway flowers.

"Did you see another kid in the lies challenge?" Maddy's brow scrunched. "Not the younger versions of you, me, Dax, and Owen, but someone else?"

"Yeah." Emerson lifted her chin toward the guys. "I think Owen knew him. You and Dax seemed like you did, too."

Maddy slouched. "Here's the thing—I don't remember him."

"From before?"

"From anytime. I don't remember him *at all*."

Emerson turned to face her fully. "What do you mean?"

"It's like that person, he's just wiped completely from my mind."

"How?"

"Dax thinks the game is punishing me. Because I broke the rules."

"What rule did you break?" Emerson's mouth was dry as she spoke the words. The fog was back in her mind, as if she should know the answer to this question.

"I don't know." Maddy shrugged. "But that's not all. Apparently you also knew Ian. Before. When we were all kids."

Emerson quirked a brow. "I think I'd remember that."

"Yeah, I thought I would have too." Maddy leaned closer, taking her hand. "Dax said we were all friends, and that day at the cave, Ian never came home. That we're here now to find him."

Emerson's brows knit together. Her stomach began to churn.

"That's impossible. We're here because of the game."

"Which we're playing because . . ."

Her lips parted, but she couldn't think of an answer. Why were they playing this game? Why did they have to finish before the giant's eye opened? She knew that they were here, and that they had to complete the challenges, but the reasons behind it were unclear.

Her heels dug into the sandy cave floor.

"That kid from the lies challenge brought us here?" she asked.

"That kid has been living here for the last four years," Maddy said. "Well, the seventeen-year-old version of him, anyway."

A slow grip was tightening around Emerson's throat. She didn't understand what Maddy was saying, but the more she searched her memories for this boy, this Ian, the more confused she became. It was as if he'd only started to exist the moment she'd met him in the woods.

But Owen had known him. Dax and Maddy had too, even if she didn't remember.

Emerson recalled now how strange she'd felt when the boy had looked at her. As if he recognized her.

As if *she* should have recognized *him*.

Emerson pulled her knees to her chest, the old robe she'd taken off some shuffling, cut-mouth woman outside the wedding drooping over her bare thighs.

"I forgot him?" she murmured. A person. *The* person behind their very reason for being here.

It seemed impossible.

"More like the game took him from us." Maddy moved closer, until their knees bumped. "Dax says Ian going missing is why we all split up. It makes sense. Why else would you and I not see each other for four years? Why would you drop out of school?"

"I . . ." Emerson swallowed. "I don't know."

"It's the game," said Maddy, pointing at the bag with the cards and the stones. "It's screwing with us."

"But why him?" Emerson felt like she was holding sand but it was falling through her fingers. "Why take a person away? This Ian isn't some random acquaintance if we came here searching for him, and the fact that both of us lost him makes it even more, I don't know, *deliberate*."

If it was truly a punishment to forget someone, why take away the person that had led them into this nightmare? Wouldn't Meido want them to remember who was behind their suffering?

"I think it's *because* we came here to find him," Maddy said. "If we can't remember who we're looking for . . ." She shivered.

They would wander around forever.

Emerson's blood chilled.

"At least we don't remember losing him," Maddy added bleakly. "That sounds pretty traumatic."

She was right. And as much as Emerson wanted to find the fault in Maddy's claim, she couldn't. There was simply no logical reason why any of them would stop being friends unless something catastrophic had happened.

Even if she didn't know Ian, she could feel the weight of his absence bearing down on her shoulders, tugging at her control. Without her memories, she didn't know who she was. She was a body without a mind, like those brainless creatures outside the house where Maddy and Dax had been taken.

Emerson glanced to the fire, where Owen was warming his hands and Dax was staring warily into the night. "Why haven't they forgotten?"

"I'm not sure," Maddy said. "Maybe it's something we did. Or didn't do."

Emerson ran her nails over her short hair. "When we were with Keneō, right before the card changed to a stone, there was a moment where everything kind of went fuzzy, then crystal clear. It was like . . . I don't know, waking up."

"You felt lighter." Maddy nodded.

She nodded. "Like I'd been underwater, and could finally breathe."

"But that was when we got the eyeball for the cowardice card," Maddy said. "You were brave then. You're the reason why we passed that level."

Emerson flicked her tongue over the thin band of metal around her lip. It was like staring at a puzzle where several pieces were missing.

"I was brave and solved the cowardice challenge, but I was punished," she said. "You kissed Dax during the wounded heart challenge, and were also punished."

A piece slid into place.

"At the wedding, I asked Owen if he'd ever get married, and that hurt him somehow," she said, her thoughts a snowball starting to roll downhill. "I must have wounded his heart, and the card changed to a rib."

Maddy glanced to her wrist. "It wasn't the wedding that solved it."

"It was wounding a heart," she said. "The card didn't change when you kissed Dax. It was what I'd said to Owen." Frantically, she grabbed the bag, and dumped the pieces on the ground. Her movement caught the attention of Dax and Owen, who came over.

"And when you kissed Dax, you healed your heart, and so you acted deliberately against the challenge. That's why you were punished."

"Owen, do you remember Ian?" Maddy asked.

"Cute guy, blue eyes? Haunted the shit out of us until we came to this place?" He stared at her. "No, who's that?"

"I'm serious." Maddy waited.

"Yes," Owen said slowly. "Of course I remember Ian. What does that have to do with being punished?"

"We thought we were supposed to do the opposite of the cards," Emerson said, her words coming faster. "But we were wrong. Remember with Keneō? I was brave, and I forgot Ian because the card was a test of cowardice, which *you* demonstrated"—she pointed the rib at Owen—"by telling me I was insane and should shut up before I got us all murdered."

"I stand by it," Owen said, narrowing his gaze behind his old wire-rimmed frames. "What do you mean, you forgot Ian?"

"The game punished us," Maddy said. "We don't know who he is."

Owen sputtered. "You don't . . . It's Ian. *Ian Spencer.*"

"I tried that," Dax told him. "Doesn't help."

"Don't you see?" Emerson went on. "We're not supposed to solve the cards. It's a *matching* game—that's what you always said, Owen. We're supposed to do what the cards say!"

Owen ran a thumb over his lips, his brows furrowed. "It *is* a matching game. In Karuta, one card always goes with another. That . . . that day in the cave . . ." His hand dropped to his side. "Ian acted out loyalty without even thinking about it."

"How?" Maddy asked.

Owen blinked at her. "He pulled me free from the rocks in the cave-in. He . . . he said he wouldn't leave me."

"And you got the stone," Emerson said.

Maddy was nodding. "I was terrified in the arena when that lady stuck in the bushes took the card from me. That's when it turned to a tooth."

"It wasn't Dax killing the bird and being brave, it was your fear that got us the stone," Emerson said.

"But she was looking right at him," Maddy said.

"It doesn't matter. You solved the card," Emerson said.

"Then why didn't I lose my memory of Ian?" Dax asked, moving gingerly to the ground to sit across from them. His tongue darted out across his split lip. Emerson had a hard time looking at his face. It was a kaleidoscope of bruises. At least the wounds on his sides were hidden beneath his ripped-up kimono jacket.

"Maybe Maddy showed her fear before you could be brave," Emerson said.

"You still did a really good job," Maddy whispered to him. She scooted closer and patted his thigh. He snorted.

"It holds for the lies challenge, too," Owen said. "The card didn't turn until Madeline said she and Emerson weren't friends."

"It's Maddy," Maddy said with a wince. "I didn't mean that."

"Exactly," Emerson said. "That was the lie! We're best friends!"

"Adorable," muttered Owen.

"So what do we have next?" Dax asked.

"Live Fast, Cry Loud, Heal Hate and Breathe," Owen said. "The second H. Honor."

Emerson gaped at him.

Maddy raised an invisible microphone. "Ladies and gentlemen, let's give him a hand. He finally figured it out."

"I can memorize lines if given the opportunity," Owen said, but his cheeks were pink.

"So we need to be honorable," Dax said.

"Yes," Emerson said. "And when the bravery challenge is up, we can't show any weakness."

"Why do I feel like that's directed at me?" Owen muttered.

She focused on the ceiling. "No reason."

"The failed players don't know this," Dax said, clearing his throat as Maddy pulled his hand onto her thigh. "They keep trying to solve the cards, not match them."

"There was that guy at Kuchisake's party," Maddy said to him. "Remember? He thought he knew you. He was clearly confused. Maybe the game took more memories every time he screwed up. Kept punishing him for getting the challenge wrong."

"The way it punished us by taking away Ian," said Emerson.

Owen shook his head at the ground, where he was tracing a half circle with a small stick. "I can't believe you don't remember Ian."

"You think that's what happened to Keneō and Kuchisake?" Dax asked. When Owen quirked a brow, he drew a line with his finger along the curve of his cheek.

"Kuchisake and Keneō aren't failed players," said Maddy. "And neither is the oni, or Shinigami. They were here from the beginning."

"What do you mean?" Emerson asked.

"The oni is Izanami's kid," Maddy said. "When I was getting a father-of-the-bride speech from Kuchisake, he told me."

Emerson's train of thought stopped cold.

"Explain," she said.

As Maddy detailed what Kuchisake had said about the empress and the emperor, a hard knot of worry balled in Emerson's stomach. Abandoning your kid because your heart was broken was one thing, but the kid slicing his mom up in retaliation took it to another level. This was family drama at its worst, and they did not need to be stepping in the middle of it.

"Kuchisake said Izanami had burned down the palace making this portal fire. The passage. It was supposed to take you places, like ruby slippers, I guess. It didn't work out—they all ended up in Yomi no kuni," said Maddy. "That's the place where the kids said the empress still is."

"What else did Kuchisake say about it?" Emerson asked, mentally logging every bit of information. They needed all the details if they were going to be prepared, and she felt a dozen steps behind thanks to her recent bout of amnesia.

"Just that the emperor betrayed them," said Maddy. "He couldn't stand the sight of Empress Izanami, all burned up and wasting away."

Emerson thought of the oni and his terrible scarred skin. "How horribly poetic. The emperor can't stand his wife's burns and decay, and now his son is a demon who looks even worse."

"What are we going to do if that thing comes back?" Owen asked.

"When," said Emerson grimly. "I don't know how it gets from challenge to challenge without a gate, but since it can, I think it's safe to assume it will come after us again."

"The engimono," said Maddy. At this, Dax removed the pocket-knife from the pocket of his dirt-stained pants. "Kuchisake said you had one. He was almost scared of it, did you see that?" she said, excitement lighting her eyes.

"Yōkai don't like it," Dax said, scratching a hand over the back of his neck. "I always knew it was lucky."

Emerson bit her lip ring. "When Maddy stuck the oni, he seemed really hurt."

"You didn't get older in the game when we did," Owen said to Dax. "It's that knife! Remember, the kids said he had good luck, that's why he wasn't changing!"

"They also said the game wants us to win." Emerson pulled on her lip ring. "It's growing like we were."

"What does that mean?" asked Dax.

She shook her head. "I don't know. But it's strange how it's following a gaming pattern when I know games," she said. "That flamethrower, that's my weapon—my *exact* weapon—the one I always choose when I play online. And it was just leaning against the house during the wedding like . . . like it wanted me to take it." She opened her hands, remembering the weight of it, how it had fit perfectly in her hands. "We played Karuta in that cave our own way four years ago. We acted out the cards, and here we are, acting them out again. Even the language everyone is speaking . . . it's being translated for us so we can understand." Her stomach tightened at the thought of this living world shaping around them.

"My dress," said Maddy, smoothing down the tattered skirts of her wedding gown. "This was my dress. The one I picked out of a magazine when I was a kid."

"I knew it," Dax said, with a shy grin. "I thought maybe I was making that up."

"The ceremony wasn't exactly straight out of a shrine either," Owen said.

"It looked like my parents' wedding," Maddy said with a scowl. "But with a lot more blood."

"How does the game know all this stuff about us?" Dax asked.

Maddy sucked in a breath. "There was a spider in my ear. Possibly my brain. I don't want to talk about it."

Emerson cringed. "I don't know. But it doesn't make sense why Meido would want us to win, when everything it puts us through is so awful."

"Maybe that's the curse," Maddy said. "It wants its empress back, right? But it's cursed, so it's just trying to make the best of a bad situation." She looked to Dax. "If we all had engimonos, it might not be so bad. How did you make that knife lucky? Can we make more?"

Owen shrugged. "I don't remember my mom talking about it, but usually charms are blessed objects, right? They're really rare and revered."

"Who blessed it?" Maddy asked.

"Ian gave it to me," Dax said, rolling it over in his hand. "Maybe he made it lucky."

Emerson's stomach hollowed. Mystery surrounded the image of the dark-haired boy from the lies challenge. He was two-dimensional in her mind, depthless. The fact that she couldn't recall anything about him from before they'd met in the woods had her digging her heels into the ground in frustration.

"What was he like?" she asked. "Ian."

She and Maddy looked up at Owen and Dax, who glanced at each other, and after a long moment smiled.

"Remember Foxtail Five?" Owen asked.

Dax coughed into his shoulder, wariness flashing in his eyes. When Emerson looked down, she found the knife gripped in his fist.

"Three thousand years from now, in a land of honey and starlight . . ." Maddy started, and Emerson laughed.

It had been the first line of their short-lived comic series in the sixth grade, about four warriors fighting to rid the world of evil, named for the street they lived on.

"Why honey?" Dax grunted.

"I don't know, *sweetheart*," said Emerson, with a wink. Dax laughed, his shoulders relaxing.

"I was Queen Kickass, captain of the army," Maddy said. "Emerson was Captain Carroway, head of military intelligence. Dax was . . ."

"A talking toad who could read minds," said Dax.

Emerson grinned. "And Owen was Dr. Radcliffe."

"Dark Underlord's private physician," Owen said.

"Dark who?" Emerson asked, and Maddy shrugged.

"Dark Underlord," Owen said, finally looking up from his dirt horseshoe. "You didn't honestly think we'd write a comic called Foxtail Five with only four heroes, right?"

Maddy narrowed her gaze at him. "That does seem suspicious."

Owen scoffed. "Dark Underlord was the leader. Ian used to draw these pictures of him, that were . . . anatomically correct."

"Huge package," said Dax.

"Got that," said Emerson.

"That's where he hid the gold," Dax explained. "He kept stealing it from RichMan Bank, except his spandex suit wasn't exactly designed with pockets, so he hid it in his pants."

Memories unfolded in Emerson's mind, spreading warmth through her chest. She and Owen arguing about the plot while Maddy and Dax blocked out the fight scenes, but when she tried to picture Ian there, she couldn't.

"He's been gone almost as long as I knew him," Owen admitted with a frown. "How is that possible?"

Emerson felt like a box was around her memories, blocking her from seeing the truth. "How did we know him? School?"

"You and I met him on the Lego robotics team," Owen said. "He wore a tie to the final competition so I wouldn't be the only one."

"I met him in fifth grade," said Dax. "Right after Mom and I moved to town. He saw me trying to break down boxes by the dumpster and gave me his knife." Dax flicked open the blade Maddy had jammed into the oni's side. "Told me to keep it."

It had been hard for Dax when he'd first moved to Cincinnati. At first, all he'd talked about was how much better Denver was. Then, after a while, the truth started leaking through. The kids at his old school had been mean. His mom couldn't afford to fix her car when it had broken down. He'd never met his dad, but he knew his mom was afraid he'd take Dax away from her.

"Maddy met Ian in Ms. Abbott's class in second grade," said Dax. "He picked her for assistant line leader and got teased by everyone that they were boyfriend and girlfriend."

The quiet that spread across the fire was softer than before.

"Were we?" Maddy asked, brows scrunched. "Boyfriend and girlfriend?"

Dax shook his head.

"He shouldn't be here," said Owen. He swore, then wiped a tear away with the back of his hand. "How did it even happen, you know? He should have run. Why didn't he just run?"

Emerson pictured the cave, trying to imagine Ian not coming out of it with the rest of them. She couldn't remember any of them leaving.

"Maybe a yōkai got him," said Dax.

Owen paled. "That's all you can say? Maybe a yōkai got him?"

Dax winced as he shifted positions. "I've been over it in my head a million times. He was on cross-country. He was faster than any of us. The only way he got stuck in that cave is if something caught him."

Emerson blew out a stiff breath. Maddy was right. Maybe it was better that they didn't remember what had happened that day in the cave.

"I should have gone back for him," Owen said, leaning over his knees, his hands in his dark, dusty hair.

"We all should have," said Maddy. "If he was that important, we shouldn't have left him."

"But he trusted me," said Owen. "He . . ."

"Yeah," said Dax quietly. "He did."

Owen stared at him for a full beat, as if trying to see if a joke would follow. When it didn't, his head fell forward.

"I don't think he'd blame you for any of this." Emerson touched Owen's back gently. She could practically feel the misery clinging to him like a sopping coat. A moment later, he shook her off.

"Yeah, well you don't know, do you? You don't even remember him." His jaw flexed as he rose, turned away from the group, and sat on the opposite side of the fire. "We should get some rest before the eye opens any more." After a moment, he lay down and rolled onto his side, away from them.

"He's right," Emerson said, pity warring with reason. She didn't have to long for physical romance to see the emotional devastation it caused. Ian's disappearance had changed Owen. It had changed all of them, even if she couldn't remember how.

This boy had been their glue, and without him, they had broken apart.

Dax and Maddy were talking in hushed tones, and when Maddy touched Dax's cheek, Emerson felt like she was intruding. Awkwardness prickled over her skin as she turned away. Checking the cards in the bag and then the stones one more time, she settled by the fire, her head on the back of her arm. As she stared at jutting rocks above her, her thoughts returned to Ian. They had seen horrible things since their arrival in Meido. How he had managed to survive on his own here, she didn't know.

A dull pain prodded beneath her ribs, and she rubbed it absently.

How could she have lived with herself for four years, knowing he was missing? It wasn't right. It wasn't her, or Maddy. Any of them.

A piece of the puzzle was still missing.

A shadow came over her, and then Maddy plopped down in the sand beside her. Shifting around a few rocks, she lay down so their shoulders were touching.

"I thought you'd be on your honeymoon tonight," said Emerson quietly as the fire crackled, warming her other side.

"And miss the first sleepover with my best friend in four years?" Maddy snuggled closer. "I don't think so."

Emerson grinned.

"Dax wants to keep watch. I think it'll make him feel better if he's doing something, you know?" Maddy said, her worry cleared by a short cough. "So what's first? Should we paint our nails or smash the patriarchy?"

"Do you even have to ask?"

"Great," Maddy said. "I picked Pink Sparkle Bubblegum just for you."

Emerson elbowed her in the side, making her giggle. Then she pulled the bag under both their heads, a shared pillow. "You nervous about later?"

"The part where we all might die getting more petrified body parts? Or the part where we find out if someone named Ian hates us for stranding him here for four years?"

"All of the above."

"Nah. Sounds fun."

Emerson didn't have to look over to know Maddy was smiling. Hooking her pinky around Maddy's, she sighed. Ian or not, it seemed impossible that they would have spent the last four years apart. Maddy was as much a part of her as her family, and her love for games, and the yearning inside her to learn.

Without her, Emerson had walked away from school. Walked away from her parents. Walked away from the marches she used to do with her dad in Washington Park. She could see herself sitting alone in her room now, but it seemed wrong. That wasn't her.

This was her.

She rolled over on her side to face her friend.

"Whatever happens tomorrow, promise me we won't drift apart again."

Maddy faced her, steel in her eyes.

"They'll have to pry me off with a crowbar."

Emerson leaned her cheek against Maddy's shoulder.

"Good night, Captain Carroway."

"Good night, Queen Kickass."

Three breaths later, Emerson was asleep.

—·—

They rested for what felt like the blink of an eye, then they were on the move again.

Emerson led the way, guided downriver by a magnetic pull deep in her marrow. The air had turned electric, tasting like tinfoil and bringing static shocks to every rock and branch she touched. As the sky grew lighter, the clouds above the horizon bruised to black, sparking with bolts of pale green lightning that sizzled through her nerves. She kept her chin down and her thoughts on the task ahead.

Five cards down. Two remaining. Honor and Bravery.

Reluctance pushed against her; time quickened her steps. The giant's eye hadn't changed, but it still mocked her, half-open and glaring, lighting the path before them with a bruised, grainy hue. If they didn't complete the final challenges before dawn, Ian was lost.

The cliff beside them flattened. The sand beneath their feet turned gray. They kept to the river as long as they could, but it split into a thousand veins, each sinking into the scorched earth. Soon the weighted clouds began to spit snow, but it tasted like ash and smeared soot on their faces and clothes.

Restlessness spread within her. Dax limped in front of her, carrying the pack with the stones and the last two cards. He was marked by the oni, his jaw and throat yellow and purple. A scabbed bite mark peeked out from the ripped side of his jacket, but he seemed otherwise all right. Behind her, Owen stumbled along, his eyes on the ground. He hadn't said a word to any of them since they'd stopped to rest in the cave.

She slowed down to walk beside him.

"You know, odds of getting four of a kind in poker are four thousand one hundred sixty-nine to one."

He glanced over to her, a divot still in his bottom lip from where he'd been biting it.

"The odds of winning the lottery are one hundred and seventy-five million to one," she went on.

"And you're telling me this because . . ."

"You're more likely to get eaten by an alligator than die in a plane crash, which is twenty-nine million to one, by the way."

"More statistics. Perfect."

"And you're more likely to do that than find true love."

Owen blinked at her, then looked away.

"I don't have to remember him to see how you felt about him," she said. "The fact that you two found each other is pretty rare. Even if it didn't last."

"Yeah. Well, thanks." He looked away, then added, "I wish it had never happened."

"No, you don't."

He tightened the belt around his robe. "No, I don't."

She bumped him with her hip. "I missed your ugly face."

"I missed your useless facts."

"Full disclosure, I made up the last one. But it was a great point, wasn't it?"

He stopped, then tilted back his head and groaned while she laughed.

"What's so funny?" Maddy, just behind them, drew closer, Dax following.

"Owen was just talking about how much he missed us," Emerson said.

"I was not," he objected.

"I think he really wants to hold our hands but he's afraid to ask."

Owen groaned again.

"I'll hold your hand," said Maddy.

"I'll hold *your* hand," said Dax, weaving their fingers together.

"So this is officially a thing?" Owen said to them. "Wow. It only took a decade."

Maddy grinned, leaning into Dax's shoulder. Emerson smiled. Owen was right—this had been brewing for a long time.

But just as easily as the lightness in her chest had gathered, it popped.

Before them, glowing in the light of the half moon, was a palace.

The shadowed fortress was carved into the side of a mountain, half hidden by a landslide of rock and charred wood. The entrance was a black torii guarded by two stone samurai, one with the head of a horse, the other with that of an ox. She stared at them for a beat, and when they didn't move, released a breath.

"Beware the demon within," read Owen in the figures carved at the top of the gate.

An eerie moan, like an old door blowing open and closed on a creaking hinge, came from the palace. Owen stepped closer to Emerson's side.

"The oni," Maddy said, snagging a stick off the ground. "It must be in there."

They crossed beneath the gate, eyeing the gruesome masks and intricate crossed swords of the stone soldiers on either side. Each step left a footprint on the ashy ground, a record of their presence for anyone following. A gravel walkway led to two broken doors, and as they approached, Dax pointed to words scratched into the wood on the right side.

"I am Ian Spencer," he read, his voice a sandpaper whisper. An address followed, a street off Foxtail Avenue, near her house. A birthday.

Then, Owen Walker.

Maddy Lyons.

Emerson Bell.

Dax Perkins.

A lump rose in Emerson's throat. Beneath this, the words "Don't forget" had been carved a hundred times, maybe more. The scratches looked old.

He'd tried to remember her, even when she had forgotten him.

"He's here," Dax said.

But so was something else. She could feel it breathing over them, a cold rush down her spine.

Maddy gripped her stick like a bat. Owen grabbed a handful of gravel as Emerson reached for a stone the size of her fist.

Dax pulled the straps of the pack tighter around his shoulders.

Slipping through a hole gouged in the door, they walked into a wide foyer. Half the roof had been burned away, letting in the bursts of lightning from the swirling storm above. In flashes, the charred walls and floor were revealed. Bits of singed cloth hung from the bent arms of old folding screens and broken tables. The floor was coated with ash, but footsteps led toward the back of the room.

"Ian," Dax whispered. The word laced the bands around Emerson's ribs tighter.

As they followed the footsteps toward the back of the room, their path grew darker. Maddy tripped over something on the floor and pointed to a slender white bone half wrapped in threadbare silk. It wasn't like the smaller, petrified rib in the pack, but looked as if it had once belonged in a human body.

Emerson's breath caught. She leaned closer, finding another bone just off the path from the footsteps, then an unhinged jaw, and a spray of what looked like teeth. All were pushed aside, as if swept out of the way.

"What happened here?" she asked, her voice low.

"I don't think we want to know," said Dax.

"Kuchisake said there was a party the night Meido was cursed," Maddy said. "Maybe this is from the fire. This is where the passage came from."

The passage, Emerson remembered Maddy saying. The green flames that had transported them here, and from one level to the next.

Owen went still, cueing Emerson's freeze.

"Do you hear that?" he whispered.

She held her breath, which was too loud in her ears. The ragged sounds of crying came from somewhere deep in the palace.

Dax charged forward, but Maddy caught him, her fist in the back of his sleeve.

"Wait," she said. "Just wait."

The cries were overlapped by a high, pained wail from behind them. Then a sound of choking. Then a child's scream. They seemed to come from all around—from the floor and the walls and the air itself.

"What's going on?" Owen pulled on his earlobes, as if fighting the urge to cover them entirely and block out the sound.

A dozen voices had joined the chorus. Pained shouts. Screams. A gargling moan.

Emerson jolted back. The floor beneath her feet gave way with a loud crack, and she fell, tumbling down through the floorboards in a spray of dust and ash and bone. Before she could scream, she landed on her back, the air expelling from her lungs.

The ground beneath her slipped, and she slid forward into the darkness on a landslide of bones. Something crashed hard into her side, and she looked up to see Maddy scrambling toward her, lit by a dim glow somewhere behind them.

"Emerson?" Maddy looked down at the blood and dust on Emerson's cut hands, then pulled her into a tight embrace. "You okay?"

Emerson nodded.

The bones beneath them shuddered again, and then Dax and Owen came sliding down the heap. They landed in a tangle— Dax's knee in Emerson's face, Owen's hands on Maddy's chest. He pulled back quickly with a muttered apology.

Dax stood. Dust and small fragments of bone clung to his robe and hair, and when he shook, they came off in a cloud.

"How do we get back upstairs?" Owen was eyeing the hole in the ceiling above them with a worried frown.

The room they'd fallen into reminded Emerson of the dens where animals left the carcasses of their prey. There were no windows, no doors. Just bones sloping away from the front of the building. Based on the sound of their voices, the walls were close. This room couldn't have been larger than a single-car garage.

"Maybe we don't have to," Maddy said. She pointed over Emerson's shoulder to a small, flickering light—a candle, burning low in the distance.

With a shared look of caution, they joined Dax in standing. Maddy moved forward, feet quiet on the stone floor. Carefully, they picked their way over the bones and approached the light—a dull glow that split into two torches on slender iron stands as they drew closer to the source. A hall opened before them, the floor dusty marble, the walls and ceiling glossy black, like obsidian.

Green fire flickered on the two closest panels, their reflections staring back at them through the flames. The cold made Emerson shudder, and Owen squeezed her shoulder.

"We have to go that way," Dax said. "Everywhere else is blocked."

She swallowed thickly. "That probably means it's a trap."

"Or a challenge," Maddy said.

She took Emerson's hand, and together they stepped into the hall.

—◆—

As they left the room of bones behind, the air cooled, breathing across Emerson's throat, sneaking beneath her tattered kimono. The black hallway was gleaming, despite the palace's state of abandonment. Flickering green flames ran along the bottom of the walls. It lit their steps and cast a sickly glow over their faces.

"Don't get too close," Maddy said. "We don't want it sending us somewhere before we finish the challenge."

Emerson stepped closer to the middle, glaring at the fire. It had only shown up before when they'd arrived in Meido, and then when they'd leveled up. Did this mean they were close to the challenge? Or was this another test, meant to lure them away from their goal?

"Watch out!" Owen jumped, and Maddy let out a gasp of surprise. Emerson braced for what might be coming, but instead caught movement on one of the wall panels to their right.

Silence buzzed in her ears.

"Is that you?" Dax asked, squinting at Owen's reflection.

"I think so," Owen said. The boy staring back at him from behind the glass was definitely *him*, but a different version. His hair was a little shorter, his clothes different. As Owen lifted one arm, his reflection mirrored the move.

Then the reflection smiled.

"That's definitely not creepy," Maddy muttered.

The dark reflection swirled into a brightly lit stage, where Owen was dancing with an ensemble in blue shirts and gray pants.

"That was *West Side Story*," Owen said. "I did it sophomore year."

"You were good," Dax said, impressed.

"Why do you sound surprised?" Owen asked, still staring at his image, now dance-fighting another crew. As they watched, Owen tripped a boy with red hair, then kept dancing as if he'd done nothing.

"That's Tyson Starling." Owen frowned. "He twisted his ankle before opening night. I was his understudy."

"Twisted it all on his own, huh?" Emerson crossed her arms over her chest.

With a scowl, Owen shrugged. "I might have helped."

Emerson turned to the opposite side, lit by a line of green flames along the floor, where she saw herself taking her dad's car keys while he watched TV in the other room.

"What is this?" she asked.

"Look," Maddy said, pointing to Dax playing his guitar in the back of a dark coffee shop. His eyes were closed as he silently sang.

When he finished, he walked to the door, snagging a man's wallet from his back pocket on the way.

"There's you," Dax told her, pointing to where she dove off the starting block, gliding through the water. Her arms churned in powerful strokes. Gleaming droplets slid off her glistening skin, running in rivulets between her flexing shoulders. Her suit rode high on her toned hips.

"Stop drooling, Dax," Owen said.

Dax coughed into his fist.

In the lane beside Maddy, the girl she was racing twisted suddenly in the water, then stopped, grasping her chest as she clung to a lane line.

Maddy's cheeks turned red. "I um . . . used a seam ripper on Angela's suit before the race. Her strap broke in the first twenty-five meters."

"A seam ripper?" Dax sucked in a breath. "You're truly terrifying."

"Like you can talk, pothole."

"Is it wrong that I kind of like it?"

"Yes," she said, but still reached for his hand.

"So these are things that have happened in the past." Owen stepped forward to watch himself lean over to cheat off his neighbor's test in a geography class. "Our less than honorable moments."

In another reflection, Emerson kicked her bedroom door shut in her mom's face. She recalled doing that, but felt sick about it now. Why had she acted that way? "The challenge isn't about the past though; the rest have all happened in real time. This is going to test our honor now."

They moved forward between the emerald lines of fire. The hall went on and on, into the black. She couldn't see the end of it.

"Back for more wallets?" Owen motioned to Dax in the mirror behind him. He was younger by a few years—his face was fuller, his hair shorter, but still messy. He was wearing his Green Day T-shirt. It was baggier then, not quite as threadbare.

His smile faded as the wall behind him came into view—dark, crumbling stone, lined with cracks and layered with graffiti.

"That's the cave," Maddy said.

"That's the day Ian disappeared," Owen added, when the Emerson from four years ago came into view, grasping Maddy's hand. They shouted for Dax.

Emerson crept forward, a dark intrigue dragging her toward the glass. She remembered walking with Maddy. She remembered the cold in the air, and the sound of the water dripping. It came back to her as if it had been yesterday, but when she tried to fast-forward the memory in her mind, her vision turned murky.

"You were trying to scare us," Maddy said, looking to Dax. "It was a prank. I remember."

Dax nodded. Behind the glass, his younger self was hiding in the shadows. Emerson remembered that now. How he'd whispered in a spooky voice, and jumped out to surprise them.

She hadn't seen him then, but she could now, and as she watched, he removed something from his back pocket.

"What are you doing?" Owen's voice thinned as Dax's reflection scattered a handful of playing cards on the ground, kicking dirt over them.

When he was done, he jumped out to scare Maddy.

"That isn't . . ." Dax's throat clicked as he tried to swallow. "This isn't right."

"Shinigami said the cards weren't hers," Owen said.

They belong to the one who begins the game.

That wasn't Dax.

It couldn't be Dax.

Horror chilled Emerson's blood as a boy with messy hair leapt onto Dax in the mirror and they fell the ground, laughing and wrestling. *Ian.* Emerson knew him from Truth or Dare, but though she waited for some deeper pang of recognition, it never came.

When Ian pulled a card from the ground below them, Mirror Dax's eyes lit with excitement.

"They were yours?" Maddy asked him, her hand sliding from his.

"Of course not," he assured her. In the mirror, the kids played a game Ian directed. Worry built in Emerson's chest, water freezing to ice. This was a lie. A trick of Meido. Minutes passed, and soon they watched as the walls of the cave started shaking, and the younger Emerson and Maddy took off down the tunnel, a flashlight bobbing before them in the dark.

Ian dragged Owen free from the rubble.

The card flashed and turned to a withered stone.

"Half a heart," Owen muttered as the Owen from the past jumped up and ran for the exit. Dax ran after him, then stopped.

Ian wasn't moving.

The ground around him churned.

"He's sinking," Emerson whispered, her throat growing tight.

"No," Maddy said, her hands rising over her mouth.

Sliding through the shadows of the cave, Dax moved behind Ian. He stood still as clumps of dirt fell from the ceiling. He watched as Ian clawed at the ground, his mouth gaping as he screamed for help.

Emerson couldn't look away.

"Help him," Owen said, as if the real Dax had any ability to do so. "What are you doing? Help him!"

But the Dax in the mirror only smiled, his white teeth cutting a sickle moon in the dark.

"That's not what happened," Dax said, his words clipped and anxious. "Maybe this is a test. To pick what's true and what's not."

"This is honor, not lies," Owen said.

Tears streamed from Ian's eyes as his legs sank into the ground. Emerson's stomach twisted. Behind him, Dax watched, swaying gently from side to side.

"That isn't me," Dax said.

"It looks like you," Owen said.

Maddy glanced at Dax, her eyes round with fear.

Emerson didn't remember this. She frantically searched for something familiar to latch onto, but every part of the scene in front of her felt slippery and wrong.

Before them, Dax finally reached for Ian. But instead of taking his hand, he grabbed a fistful of his hair and shoved him down.

Maddy gasped.

"Wait." Dax forced a laugh. "You don't honestly think . . . That isn't me. You believe me, right?"

Maddy's thumb pressed to the wound on her opposite wrist, circled by the silk belt.

"Of course I do," she said, but her voice was too soft for it to be true.

"All the other things we saw were real," Emerson said.

"That doesn't mean all of it is," Dax told her, hands outstretched. "This is crazy. I can't believe we're having this conversation."

In the mirror, the younger Ian disappeared into the earth, and Dax stood, wiping his hands off on the sides of his jeans. In the hall, Dax's breath came out in a whoosh. Beside him, Owen and Maddy stared in his direction, a cross between worry and horror creasing their faces.

"Earlier, I said I didn't know how Ian didn't make it out of that cave," Owen told Dax, "and you said, 'Maybe a yōkai got him.' Why would you say that?"

Emerson glanced back at the wall, to where Dax was flicking the blue knife open and closed in his hand. After a moment, he turned and walked into the dark, without a light to guide him.

"I was just talking," Dax said, his voice louder. "It didn't mean anything." He jabbed a hand at the wall. "I swear, this isn't real!"

"I don't know," Owen said. "People seem to forget a lot of things around here."

Dax looked to Maddy. "I didn't do this."

She nodded. "If he says he didn't, he didn't. This is the honor challenge. We need to stand together."

"Unless the whole point is that we shouldn't," Owen said pointedly. "You don't even remember what happened that day."

Tension sizzled between them. Emerson's fingers began to drum against her thigh.

"Do you?" she asked Owen.

"I remember Ian saving my life," he said, his voice rising. "I remember running out of there. I remember calling him a dozen times that night but he didn't answer, and then"—Owen stepped closer to Maddy, his hard gaze whipping between her and Emerson as he raised an accusing finger—"I remember you two telling me we could never say a word about it."

"We wouldn't do that," Emerson said.

"And I wouldn't bury our friend alive!" Dax threw back.

"Everybody calm down," Maddy said. "We need to think this through."

"What we need is some clarity," Owen said. "What happened to you after that day at the cave, Dax?"

"He saw a ghost and went to a hospital," Emerson said, her hands fisting.

"Ever think there's a reason why that happened?" Owen threw back, his cheeks red. "None of us saw ghosts but him before last night."

Dax paled.

"It's coincidence," Maddy said, her gaze flicking back to the mirrors, now dark.

"Is it?" Owen asked. "Or did Dax drag us into this? First with the cards, then with Ian."

Doubt swirled inside Emerson. The walls seemed to pull closer, the fire to burn brighter.

"How would I do that?" Dax asked. "I didn't walk around pretending to be Ian to scare you back here."

"You came to Owen's play to find us," Emerson said. "How did you know we'd be there? Maddy, did you call him?"

She shook her head.

"Well?" Owen asked.

"It was good luck, that's all," Dax said. "Showing up at some play doesn't make me a bad guy."

"No." Owen's face twisted with pain. "Sending Ian here does."

Dax pressed his thumbs against his temples. "Stop."

"Dax," Maddy said. "How'd you know we'd be at school last night?"

"I don't . . ."

"Were the cards yours?" Emerson asked, her pulse pounding in her ears. Around them, the walls were flickering to different images. Places she recognized—Keneō's dining table, lined with skin napkins. A tengu, circling the arena. The woods, where they'd all grown old.

Everyone but Dax.

"Please." Sweat was beading on Dax's forehead. "This is ridiculous."

"Ridiculous is letting you carry around our ticket out of here." Owen lunged at Dax, grabbing the strap of the backpack. Dax twisted away, shoving him to the side.

"What are you doing?" Emerson rushed toward them but was bumped aside by Dax into Owen.

"Dax!" Maddy cried as Dax ripped the small knife from his pocket. With a practiced flip, he opened the blade. Green light from the flames sliced across his face as the mirror beside him changed to Kuchisake's house, where a monstrous spider was skuttling across the wall.

"No, I . . ." Dax said, his hand trembling as he backed down the hall. "Just listen to me."

"What the hell?" Emerson said.

"He's lying," Owen said.

"I didn't do this," Dax told them. He turned toward Maddy. "You know me. You trust me."

Maddy's reached for Dax, the scarf hanging from her wrist. "Put the knife down."

He looked down at it as if he were surprised to find it in his hand.

The river they'd fallen into twisted in a mirror behind Owen as Maddy stepped closer to Dax.

"You want me to be brave?" Owen asked, squaring his shoulders. "This is what it looks like."

"Owen," Maddy warned.

"Ian was my best friend." Owen's back rose and fell with quick breaths. "I should have been there for him."

"Owen, stop," Maddy said.

"You're not thinking this through," Dax said. "You know me."

"I haven't seen you in *four years*," Owen spat. "And as far as thinking things through, I'm not the one holding a knife, pal."

Dax's jaw flexed. He closed the knife and tucked it into his pocket. As he raised his hands in surrender, Owen tackled him. Rage flew from him as he swung his fists at Dax's bruised face. Dax lifted his arms to stop the blows, but he didn't fight back. Around them, the mirrors flickered, showing every place they'd been in Meido.

"Stop!" Emerson cried. This was wrong. They were friends; they had to finish this together.

But Owen's words cut through the screaming in her brain. If the walls showed the truth, then they had to act honorably, didn't they? To defend their friend. That had to be how they would pass the challenge.

But which friend? Dax, who might have been lying? Or Ian, who she couldn't remember?

Maddy leapt onto them, trying to pull Owen back, but he twisted away from her. Grabbing the bag, he yanked open the zipper. The cards spilled free, clattering against the hard ground. Dax turned and tackled Owen, a spray of dust rising around them. They rolled into Emerson, knocking her backward toward the wall of mirrors.

"Emerson!" Maddy screamed, but it was too late. Emerson's heel burned with a sudden shock of ice. Panic jolted her heart as she gasped.

Then her vision was consumed by green flames.

———

Emerson tumbled backward through the mirror. Maddy's scream followed her, fading as she fell. She landed with a hard thud.

Silence.

She swallowed a quaking breath, chilled air searing her throat as she took in her surroundings. She was in a dark, familiar room, a dry mat crinkling beneath her heels as she scrambled up. Candlelight pulsed in the center of the room on a low table, its halo glow lighting circles of old, melted wax on the wood, the faint scent of brewing tea.

"Hello?" Her voice quivered. She turned, but there was only darkness. She looked up, but shadows had swallowed the ceiling. "Maddy?" she whispered. "Owen!"

"Oh, my. Have you lost your friends?"

Emerson froze. She knew that low, graveled voice. She knew this place.

"Shinigami?"

The darkness before her shifted and took the form of a small person shrouded in tattered black linen. As she moved past the candlelight, her face became visible, the shadow on the wall behind her stretching as broad and distorted as the oni.

"First there were five. Then there were four. Now, only one." The lines around the old woman's eyes deepened as she smiled.

Relief exhaled in Emerson's sigh even as readiness coiled in her muscles. Shinigami had helped them before. But even if she was an NPC, that didn't make Emerson feel safe.

"Why am I back here?" she asked. "Where are the others?"

"Where you left them, I imagine," Shinigami said. "As for why you are here, I do not know. You came to me, after all."

"I didn't mean to," Emerson said, turning again to look at the wall she'd just tumbled through. She reached out, her hands grazing splintering wood. She shoved it, hoping it would give way, but the shack only creaked.

Her breath came faster.

"I was just in the palace. I need to get back. Maddy needs me. Owen, and . . ."

Dax.

She knew him. She could hardly remember a time without him in her life. Even if he'd been absent four years, he wouldn't have done anything to hurt them.

But the mirrors had looked so real.

She could still see the cards that he'd spread on the ground.

The knife in his hand before Owen had attacked.

"To face another's darkness is no easy task," Shinigami said as Emerson spun back to face her. "Izanagi himself, emperor of all, fled when he saw that Meido had changed his love to a creature of death. The passage may have brought us here, but it was him who abandoned us." She glided closer, cueing Emerson's heart to skip. "Can you trust your friend knowing that he is rotten and burned inside? Or will you shun him, the way Izanagi shunned Empress Izanami? The way she shunned the child that returned to tear her apart?"

"Are you saying Dax is rotten inside? All that back there in the mirrors with the cards and the cave and . . . and pushing Ian down. That was true?"

Shinigami dipped her chin. "The reflections in the halls of Yomi no kuni never lie."

Betrayal sliced through Emerson's ribs. How could Dax have done that? They'd trusted him. He'd been their friend.

Hadn't he?

He said he'd called her over the past four years, but she couldn't prove it—she'd never gotten a message. He said he'd been in a facility, but that could have been a lie. It wasn't like she could ask his family—she'd never even seen where he lived.

He'd been the first one to find the cave, and he took them all to it four years ago. The night they'd gone back, he'd found them at Owen's play at Traverse High, without being told where to meet. Had he been following them? Stalking them? Waiting for a chance to get them all back?

Cold filled her, and soon her teeth were chattering.

What part did Dax play in this?

A sound came as if from far away. Her name, shouted on the wind.

"Maddy?" She ran across the cabin, ripping back the sliding door. "Maddy!"

The night was silent. Overhead, the giant's eye gleamed back at her, nearly open.

"Owen!" she shouted. But there was no response.

She charged back into the hut, hearing her name again, faint, but clearer than it had been outside. It was as if the sound was coming from the wall itself.

"How do I get back?"

Shinigami tilted her head. "You choose to honor the game, despite the ugliness it reveals?"

Honor. The word had Emerson rocking forward on the balls of her feet. That was how they solved the challenge. Not by fighting one another in a hallway over what happened to Ian. By returning to face the music.

"I can't go home if I don't," she said.

"Can't you?" Shinigami waved a hand, and where the front of her shack stood, a cave appeared. Not just any cave—*their* cave, the one where they had played the game and gotten sucked into this terrible place. Only as she stared at it, the dark recess shifted, giving a view of the outside. This wasn't the view into Meido, but out of it.

Home.

Her heart stuttered.

"Go ahead," said Shinigami. "You have worked so hard. You deserve to rest."

"But Maddy . . ." Emerson swallowed, glancing back toward the wall she'd fallen through. "My friends."

"They'll follow."

A breath heaved from Emerson's throat. The exit was right there. She could hear the river beyond it—the heavy rush of the Ohio, the quiet lap of it against the rocky shore. The clean scent of the night air reached toward her, drawing her closer.

Her feet had taken a step before she registered what she was doing.

She planted them, and turned to meet Shinigami's deep, black gaze. "We have to leave together." Her voice was hollow. The pull toward the cave's exit was so sharp, she could feel it in her bones. It called her. Tempted her. She could be in her own room in the next hour, safe in her bed beneath the covers.

"Where is she?" Maddy's voice whispered through the wall behind Emerson. "Find her!"

Emerson shook her head to clear it, but the pull toward the cave remained. She fought it. Maddy was looking for her. Her friends would not abandon her. She would not abandon them either.

"I can't go home without them."

"Why is that?"

"Because they're my friends." She pressed her teeth together and backed away from the exit, until her back was flush with the cold wall behind her. She dug her heels into the splintered floorboards. "I won't leave without them."

"Then we are the same. I will not leave my empress here either." Shinigami waved her hand, and the cave was gone. Emerson tilted forward, the air pulled from her lungs.

A test. Was it part of the challenge?

She hated Shinigami for taunting her.

"What does that mean?" Emerson asked slowly. "Empress Izanami's already home. I thought she was in the palace."

"Yomi no kuni is as much her home as it is yours. It is a prison, and she is trapped there, even in death, until she is freed of the curse." Shinigami smiled, her mouth a curved crevice, her eyes glossy black. "When the empress rises, so will the final passage—a gate of green fire to the land Izanagi took from her. The land of the living. And when she crosses through, the yōkai will reign."

Shinigami lifted her hands, a joyful move accented by the crack and pop of her joints.

For a moment, Emerson said nothing, wracked with a new terror.

"If we finish the game, we trigger the end of the world?" she finally asked.

"Your end is our new beginning," said Shinigami.

Emerson was certain she had missed something. She knew that Izanami and Izanagi hadn't ended on good terms, but she hadn't realized that returning the stones to the empress would mean the destruction of life as they knew it.

"Why didn't you tell us that before?" Emerson demanded. But she already knew. Shinigami had been cursed by Izanagi, too. If Empress Izanami left Meido, Shinigami would be free as well.

Dread seeped through Emerson's skin. That's what this had been about the whole time. They'd thought it was a game to gain their freedom and find their friend, but it was so much more than that. While they'd been saving their own lives, Meido had been using them to bring back the banished empress.

The game *had* been trying to help them, she just hadn't considered what winning would cost.

"There has to be another way," said Emerson. "What if we destroy the stones? Then Izanami won't rise and cross over, right?"

Shinigami's eyes narrowed. "She will not. But neither will you. You will stay in Meido and wander like those before you, playing, playing, playing."

The words wrapped around Emerson like bindings pulled so tight she could barely breathe.

"So that's it," she said. "We finish this, we lose. We do nothing, we lose."

She refused to believe it. There was always a way to win. A restart. Another checkpoint to go back to. No game was unbeatable. She pressed the heels of her hands to her temples as the rotten scent of Meido's air filled her nostrils.

"The passage," she murmured.

Shinigami's smile hardened.

"Emerson!" Maddy screamed, louder now.

Emerson flinched, torn between needing to find her friends and hearing what Shinigami would say.

"The flames brought Izanami here," Emerson said. "It brought me back to this shack. It's how the oni gets around Meido, isn't it?"

Shinigami narrowed her gaze. "You cannot outsmart Meido. It was made long before you and will last long after you are dust."

"You said a gate of flames will open to the land of the living," Emerson said pointedly. "Can we get out before the empress?"

Shinigami's mouth tightened to a sneer. "That is not your purpose."

"Can we get home?"

Shinigami couldn't answer, because at that moment a hand pressed through the wall and grabbed Emerson's shoulder. She was jerked backward, dragged through ice and green fire that singed her nerves. She opened her mouth to scream, but gasped instead as her back slammed against Maddy's chest. Her friend gripped her close.

"Are you all right?" Maddy asked.

Owen was behind her, his arm still linked around hers in a chain. "What happened?"

"I . . ."

Dax had been holding Owen's arm but drew back quickly, his mouth pulled tight, his face pale. The backpack was still on the floor beside his feet.

It was true? What the mirrors showed?

The reflections in the halls of Yomi no kuni never lie.

"You did it," she whispered. "You're the reason we're all here."

Hearing Shinigami confirm it had been a stab to the gut, but it was nothing compared to facing Dax and knowing the truth.

He opened his mouth to object, but any words were swallowed by a sudden crash of thunder. Chaos overtook the glass on the walls beside them. A storm whipped gray, brittle branches and gravel from one frame to the next. Chills crawled up Emerson's neck as the ground in the mirrors began to rumble and split, the green flames surging with a burst of icy wind.

"What's going on?" Maddy asked as Dax dropped to gather the scattered cards back into the bag, which he slung over his shoulder.

"We have to get out of here," said Owen gravely.

There were things Emerson needed to tell them, things they needed to know. But now wasn't the time.

"The flames," Emerson said, feet already pedaling past a mirror flashing from the storm to a wall of thorns, littered with human corpses. "They'll take us where the mirror shows."

They ran. The grim sky pulsed with other images. Woods of wandering souls, their faces sliced into permanent smiles. Children playing a game between the trees. Behind her, footsteps slapped against the floor. Dax was right on her heels.

Maddy screamed as a mirror suddenly split from the wall and crashed forward across their path. The thick glass spit fire as she collected herself, then leapt over it to the other side.

"Come on, come on!" she shouted, holding her hands out for Emerson to jump. She did, feeling a slash of ice across her shin as she made the leap. Owen followed, Dax on his heels.

They ran again, but the walls were rumbling inside now, breaking and shattering against the pressure of the storm behind them. Glass exploded into their path, shards of it embedding in Emerson's clothes and scratching her cheek.

"Emerson!" Maddy screamed as the walls of glass blocked her in, her reflection flung back at her from all sides. Emerson reached for her hand, dragging her clear as another mirror fell behind them.

"Stay together!" she ordered them.

"Wait." Owen grabbed Emerson's arm from behind, slowing her down. "What is that?"

"It's a dead end!" Maddy slammed to a halt.

Ahead, the green flames crossed their path, now impeded by a wide, black mirror.

In it, a pedestal stood in a dark room, and on it rested a golden stone.

"Is that . . ." Maddy started.

"It's the honor stone!" Owen stepped closer to the mirror before them, the only one untouched by the growing squall. He turned to Emerson. "You said the mirrors will take us where we need to go, right?"

"Yes," Emerson replied, but wrongness clenched her fists at her sides. She'd seen game scenarios like this. Traps, meant to lure you in. Had they been honorable? Had they earned it? This felt too good to be true.

"What are you waiting for?" Owen shouted over the howling wind.

"Give her a second!" Maddy turned Emerson to face her. "What is it?"

"I-I don't know," Emerson stammered. "Shinigami said the mirrors never lie."

"Then let's get the stone and get out of here!" said Owen.

Emerson met Maddy's dark eyes, pinched with fear. "What if this is a setup?"

Maddy turned back the way they'd come, sweat dripping down her temple. "Where's Dax?"

"Forget Dax!" Owen said. "You saw what he did!"

"He has the stones and the last two cards!" Maddy argued.

Behind them, Emerson's reflection stared back from the mirror, lit from beneath by emerald fire. The hall of onyx mirrors had become a funhouse maze, and they were surrounded.

"We're trapped," she whispered.

To her right, a tree banged against the glass, sending a cracked web shooting out in all directions.

"We can't leave him," Maddy said. "A guy at Kuchisake's house said we had to finish this together. We have to find him! *Dax!*"

"We can't stay here." Owen turned, his back pressed against her side, his hands up and ready for anything that might break through. "This whole place is caving in on itself!"

Emerson focused on the stone before her.

"This is the honor challenge," she said. "The walls have shown us being dishonorable. Taking the stone, it's . . ."

"Don't you dare say *too easy*," said Owen. "Nothing about this is easy."

Emerson closed her eyes. "The game has kept to a pattern. Do the challenge on the card, the card turns to the stone."

"Maddy!" Dax shouted from far down the hall.

"Dax!" She lunged forward toward a fallen mirror.

Owen snatched her wrist. "Don't get too close! You'll fall through like Emerson did!"

Thoughts screamed through Emerson's temples. The mirror before them still held a prize on its pedestal, but grabbing it couldn't be the right path. The images shown here were dishonorable. Taking it didn't follow the rules of the game.

Taking it was cheating.

Cheating was dishonorable.

But they couldn't finish this without Dax—who she'd trusted with her life in Meido. Who had started the game with his own cards and sent Ian here by shoving him into the ground.

A crack cut through the mirrors on either side like lightning, bursting one after another.

They were out of time.

"Come on!" she shouted as the roof overhead cracked and gravel pelted down on their heads. Leaving the prize in the mirror behind, she grabbed Owen and Maddy, and, heaving their weight behind her, dove through the green flames into the last glimpse of a hurricane.

DAX

The mirrors had gone dark, and the green flames of the passage with it.

There were no images playing back at him now. No lies to turn his friends against him. No flickering green fire running the length of the hall to guide his way into the unending gloom. There was only silence. Stillness. Wreckage.

"Where are you?" he shouted, his voice breaking.

The bag heated against his spine. Slinging it over his shoulder, he unzipped the compartment and saw a flash of gold light as one of the cards went up in smoke.

In the bottom of the bag was a stone.

He lifted it, the knot of copper cool in his hand and shorn to a flat edge on one side.

"Half a heart." He recognized it from the piece Owen had given them for loyalty.

"Looks like they're still playing."

Dax spun, and there, reflected back from one of the onyx mirrors, he found Ian.

Dax faced him, sure that his tongue was too thick to speak and his chest was caving in on itself. He braced for anything. Ian had been here a long time; who knew if he remembered the names he'd carved into the palace door. Maddy and Owen had forgotten him; maybe he had forgotten them too.

But it looked like Ian. The boy who'd given him a folding knife, and clothes Dax's mom couldn't afford. Who'd trusted him with his secret about Han Solo, and the guy at the video game store, and, finally, Owen.

He had the same hunched shoulders and sharp blue eyes. A

U-shaped scar on his chin from when he'd fallen off his bike in the sixth grade. His hair was trimmed, and he was dressed nicely— jeans and a button-up shirt. Nothing like the ripped coat and shabby pants Dax had gotten at Kuchisake's.

"Nice tie," Dax finally managed.

Ian looked down, threading his fingers around the peach-print necktie he wore in a loose knot around his neck.

"It was Owen's."

Dax nodded, his guard raising. The clothes, the necktie, they didn't fit.

"Are you real?" Dax asked.

"As real as any of these memories," Ian said, and Dax cringed, recalling the things he'd seen in this hall. "The game made me forget. This place helped me remember."

"You played the game."

Ian shrugged, the move so painfully familiar that Dax winced.

"As long as I could."

"And now?" Dax asked. "Are you a memory?"

"I'm Ian," he said. "Whatever's left of him, anyway."

Dax felt unsteady, too much confusion clouding his mind. Was this what they'd been chasing the whole time? Not the real Ian, but a memory?

"Do you know what happened to Maddy? Or Emerson or Owen? Did they get sucked into that mirror with you?" He placed his hand on the cracked black surface of the glass and Ian mirrored the move, their hands aligning.

It unsettled Dax, and he drew back.

"No," Ian said. "The passage took them."

Panic traced down Dax's spine. "What are you talking about? The fire gate? Where did they go?"

Ian crouched, then shook his head. "I'm not sure."

"But you said they're still playing."

"They must be, otherwise the card wouldn't have turned."

His words pressed through Dax's despair. Somehow, somewhere, Maddy, Owen, and Emerson had succeeded in finishing the honor challenge without him. His heart leapt with hope, while the rest of him felt as if he were sinking into the floor.

From somewhere far away, the wind howled.

"It's getting bad out there," said Ian, looking up. "You must be close to the end."

Dax pictured the giant's eye, fully open. Were they too late?

"Do you remember when we met?" Ian walked out of the frame, freezing Dax's heart until he reappeared in the next panel.

Dax hurried after him. "What does that have to do with anything?" As much as part of him wanted to talk with Ian, he didn't have time for nostalgia. Maddy, Owen, and Emerson were gone. He didn't know if they were okay, or how to find them. "Are they on the next challenge? Are they all right?"

"You had taken all those boxes out to the dumpster for your mom," Ian said, as if he hadn't heard Dax.

"Yeah. So?"

"How long had you been out there?"

Dax's thoughts turned to that day. He couldn't remember the specifics. It was a long time ago. "I don't know. A while, maybe."

Ian walked to the next panel, and Dax fell into step beside him.

"You don't remember what happened before?"

"Mom and I were unpacking," he said, but the words felt wrong as they left his mouth. He couldn't remember doing that.

Panic tumbled through him. He'd sung this song with Maddy after they'd been captured by Kuchisake's spiders. She hadn't remembered what had happened to Ian. Now he couldn't remember what had happened before he and Ian had met.

"Am I being punished?" he asked. "Did the game take my memory?"

"How'd you find the tunnel?" Ian asked.

"I don't know. Who cares! How do I get out of here?"

Ian tilted his head, and Dax turned to find the panel on the other side of the hall glowing with the pale peach light of sunset. As the scene came into focus, he recognized the Roebling Bridge. Automatically, he searched for benches and walkways, but they weren't there.

The entire park looked different. Sparse. The gardens and water fountains weren't where they belonged beside the levee. The grass hadn't even grown in yet.

This must have been before the park was built.

Which didn't explain why he was walking along the water's edge, wearing his old jeans and the Green Day shirt his mom had gotten him for his birthday.

"What is this?" Tension prickled his skin. He didn't want more visions of things he hadn't done.

The Dax on the glass was younger—maybe eleven or twelve. A boy was standing beside him in a grungy flannel shirt with bleach-blond hair.

"Who is that?" he asked.

"Beats me," said Ian.

As they watched, the younger Dax led the boy downriver, toward a dark crevice between the rocks.

"That's the tunnel," said Dax, crossing his arms over his chest. The move did nothing to stave off the cold now filling his chest.

The boy disappeared inside the cave, but before Dax followed, he removed a stack of worn cards from his back pocket, flipping through them as if to make sure they were all accounted for.

Then he disappeared inside.

"No," Dax wanted to shout, but the word was a whisper. "Those cards aren't mine. I don't even know that kid!"

The scene switched immediately to a winter day at dusk. Dax was wearing his same shirt and leading two girls down the same path.

"What is this?" Dax asked. "This never happened."

In silence, they watched him motion the girls through the rugged entrance of the cave.

"I'd never been in that tunnel before we went in it that day. I never saw those cards before we found them."

"Are you sure?" asked Ian. The suspicion in his tone put him on edge.

"I don't know any of these people!"

It was fall. The trees were red and yellow, and the couple following Dax was laughing. When the man glanced back, Dax caught sight of his face—his pale blue eyes and strange, pointed moustache.

He'd seen that man before—at Kuchisake's house. Only then, his mouth had been split clear up to his ears. The woman linked her arm though his and kissed his cheek as the Dax in the mirror motioned her forward.

You were there. You told Jolene to follow you.

Dax balked.

"Are you all right?" Ian asked, still locked on the other side of the glass behind him.

This place was messing with him, just as it had when it had shown him shoving Ian into the ground. This wasn't real. He'd never met the man he'd seen at Kuchisake's. If Dax had, he would have remembered him.

"What is this?" Dax asked. "Why are you showing me this?"

"Because you forgot," Ian said. "Just like you forgot what you did to me."

"No." Dax shook his head. "I didn't do anything to you."

"It's okay," Ian said when Dax spun to face him. "I'm not mad. Not anymore."

"I didn't do it!" Dax shouted, his voice echoing off the ceiling.

Fighting off yōkai was one thing, but he'd never hurt a real person. He wasn't that mindless machine that had pushed Ian into the ground in the movie that had played before them. He knew the difference between friends and enemies. He would have rather cut off his own arm than done anything to cause Maddy or the others harm.

"Relax," said Ian. "You didn't have a choice."

He didn't understand why Ian was saying this.

"How would I forget something like that?" he asked, his voice rough.

"I think the more important question is, how did you remember me?" Ian asked. "Or Maddy? Or Owen and Emerson?"

Dax's brows scrunched in confusion.

"I knew what you were the first time I saw you," Ian said. "I'd passed you outside that field for a week before I finally got up the nerve to talk to you. I actually brought a knife just in case I had to defend myself."

"What are you talking about?"

"You looked different," Ian said. "A little smudgy around the edges. Kind of gray—like an old picture. I'd never seen anything like you."

Dax wasn't entirely certain what Ian was trying to tell him. "Like me?"

"I didn't know if you could talk. I wasn't sure what I'd say to you if you did. But when I saw you in the field with those boxes, I don't know . . . You looked kind of lonely, I guess."

"What field?" Dax was losing track of what Ian was trying to say. Maybe Ian really had forgotten things. "I was at my apartment."

"Those apartments burned down years ago," Ian said. "Before we moved to town."

Dax's jaw clenched as the scent of smoke curled his nostrils. From somewhere deep inside, he heard his mom's voice calling his name—terrified, desperate. His hands suddenly heated, the scars on his palms prickling with pain.

The feeling subsided a moment later.

"I had the knife out in case you, I don't know, attacked me or something." Ian laughed. "I was eleven, so I thought a two-inch blade would do the trick."

Dax reached into his pocket, pulling out the blue pocketknife. "You gave it to me."

"I told you it looked like you could use some help, remember?" Ian asked. "I gave you the knife and you changed. It made you . . . more real, I guess. Not all the way, but enough. After that, the others could see you, too. I told them you'd moved from Denver."

"I *did* move from Denver."

Ian kept walking.

"That knife protected you," he said. "It let you grow up with us. Remember things. Remember us."

"An engimono," Dax whispered, remembering Kuchisake's reverence when Dax had jammed the blade into his neck. Remembering how it had warmed him after the oni had attacked—like a mug of hot cocoa on a cold day.

"A good luck charm." Ian nodded.

Dax's head was throbbing.

"Our parents never saw you," Ian continued. "Most of the time they couldn't even hear us say your name. Kids at school thought we were weird sometimes, but they usually forgot about it when we weren't around. You were only real to us."

Dax looked down at the knife, small and rusted in his quaking hand.

"This is impossible," he said.

"There are a lot of impossible things in this world," Ian said.

Dax shuddered as the stones lit up around him. Movies, playing on a dozen different reels. Memories he had of riding the bus to school, and history class, and the lunchroom, but where he should have sat or stood there was an empty place.

He saw himself standing outside the dumpster breaking down boxes, only the dumpster wasn't there, and neither was the apartment complex. It was an empty field, piled with dirt and trash.

He saw himself in a white room at Tricounty Wellness, only the guitar wasn't on his lap, it was on his mom's.

That's good, Vera. You're getting the hang of it, Raul said as she plucked at the strings, her eyes fixed on some point in the distance.

"Mom?" His voice broke. She wasn't supposed to be there. That's where *he'd* gone after the fire—a fire he'd set after he'd seen Aka Manto for the first time.

He spun and saw Maddy's dad picking up the phone, but in the spaces where he knew he'd asked for her, there was only static.

Whoever this is, if you call this number again, I'm contacting the police, he said, and hung up.

"Stop!" Dax shouted. But it wouldn't stop. The next stone showed a half-empty coffee shop, the patrons ignoring his performance in the corner. The barista wouldn't fill his cup with water, so he reached over the counter and got it himself.

Dax couldn't breathe. His knees gave out and he fell forward, hands slapping against the stone floor.

"Please stop."

The walls changed to a cloudy day when a man with black, greasy hair climbed the steps of an old apartment. At the top the door opened, and Dax's mom stood, her smile bright, her polka-dot dress one Dax had never seen her wear.

When the man reached her, he pulled her close and kissed her with enough passion to hollow Dax's stomach.

"Aka, mata wa ao," he murmured in her ear.

Red or blue.

"Aka Manto," Dax whispered.

"Your dad," said Ian. "Total creep. He's been trying to get you back here for years."

It's time to come with me.

"No," Dax said. "He's not my dad. Aka Manto is a yōkai. I'm . . ."

A yōkai too.

The last time he'd seen Aka Manto in the coffee shop, when he'd said the Foxtail Five were already gathering. It was a name Dax hadn't heard in years. A silly comic named for five kids who lived off Foxtail Avenue, between Washington Park and The Bean Coffeehouse.

"You've been wandering for four years. The engimono's luck must have faded when I changed into the oni," Ian said. "I think it started working again when I came back to find the others."

Dax couldn't hear this.

He was real. He was alive.

It's like a kid. Constantly growing up. Well, maybe not like you. But the rest of us. The kids had told him that. Meido could change, but he couldn't. He'd thought the engimono was protecting him from aging in their game of Truth or Dare, but it was him.

"Don't be so hard on yourself," Ian said, crouching beside Dax on the opposite side of the glass. "You kept them safe as long as you could."

"What are you talking about?" he said, between strained breaths.

"You don't remember The Bean?" he asked. "We used to go there after school sometimes. It's right down the street from where we live."

Again, the coffee shop flashed onto the wall, but now it was vaguely familiar. He could see the corner table where they used to sit and drink smoothies and do their homework. He'd played that coffee shop just a few days ago. How could he have forgotten it was their spot?

"You stayed there to protect them," Ian said. "Owen, Maddy, Emerson. You kept Aka Manto and other ghosts away from them for four years. You should be proud."

Dax didn't feel proud. He felt like he was finally, truly, losing his mind.

"I don't know how you did it," Ian went on. "No yōkai I've ever heard of can fight the call to bring more players back to this place. It must have been pretty cold out there all alone."

It had been cold. He'd been cold as long as he could remember. Thirsty. Tired.

Only once he'd come here had he started to feel alive again.

"If I protected them, why did I do this to you?" Dax asked, desperate for some out, some way to prove Ian wrong.

"I don't know," Ian said. "Maybe you knew I was different because I'd seen you first. Maybe you really did feel like you had to." He gave a jerky shrug.

Dark memories pressed against the border of his thoughts. Things he'd blacked out. Things he never thought he'd do.

The man with the moustache. The girls. Countless others he'd brought to that cave before Ian and his friends.

Beware the demon within.

He'd thought that was about the oni. But it had been about him.

"This isn't a game," he said weakly, remembering what the man had told him at Kuchisake's house.

His chest grew tighter. What had he done to his friends? Where were they now?

"Life is a game," Ian said. "Why wouldn't death be? We're talking about gods. *The* gods. To them, we're nothing but fireflies in a jar."

He was telling the truth. Dax could feel it.

"How did it happen?" he murmured. He didn't have to specify what. Ian knew.

At once, every stone around him lit with orange and yellow flames. Though the room remained cold, his body heated in response, sweat dampening his hair and sliding down his brow. Something obscured the top of his vision, and after a moment he realized it was the underside of his bed.

He was hiding under it.

The sound of breathing filled the room, quick and strained, accented with a hard cough. Across his room, he could see his mom holding a steel pot like a baseball bat.

Stay away from me! she was shouting. *Stay away from my son!*

He remembered now. She'd been acting strangely, staring at the door. Shaking and crying. *It's going to be okay, I promise,* he'd told her desperately. She'd thrown a candle to keep Aka Manto away, but it crashed into a window and lit the curtains on fire. They'd fallen, and he'd burned his hands.

He looked down at the pink scars, now scalding red.

He'd mixed it up in his mind.

She'd been the one to see the ghost—to see Aka Manto, who'd returned for his son. She had started the fire to stop him, and been sent to Tricounty Wellness Center, and he . . .

He'd died.

He gasped, but the air was too thin. His insides were twisting, fraying. He wished Maddy was here, even though he knew it was wrong. He missed her the way he missed his mom. In a final way. In a way that knew he'd never see her again.

I'm sorry, he thought.

He'd wanted more than these few days with her. He'd wanted to take her out on a date. To learn what made her laugh now. To kiss her as much as she'd let him.

A sob choked him.

He saw Emerson, working out the details of their real-life RPG. Owen, furious enough to hit him in Ian's defense.

I'm so sorry.

Dax reached back into the bag and gripped the half-heart stone in his fist. He swiped the back of his wrist across his wet eyes. Pushed himself to stand.

Maybe he hadn't been honorable when he'd faced these mirrors for the sixth challenge, but he was still here. They would need the stones to complete the game. He could still help with that. He could do what he hadn't done for Ian.

And when the bravery challenge came, he would be ready.

"If I finish this, what happens to our friends?" he asked. "Will they be all right? Will *you* be all right?"

"I don't know about the future," Ian said, pulling absently at his tie. "Just the past."

Dax knew he wasn't real—that this Ian was just a memory—but he still didn't want to say goodbye.

"I'm sorry I did this to you," Dax said. "You were my best friend."

Ian gave him a sad smile, then he stepped aside, and the panel went black.

"Ian?" Anxiety rose in Dax's chest as he rushed forward, but the mirror where Ian had stood was now missing, a gap in the dark wall.

Straightening, Dax stepped through the hole. A staircase ascended before him, and he climbed it. It seemed to stretch halfway up the mountain. By the time he reached the dim room at the top, he was breathing hard. The splintering wooden walls on either side were bowed from the weight of the high ceiling. The long, dusty floor led to a coffin-sized gray stone slab, on top of which a withered body rested. Clothes hung loosely off the bony wrist that draped over the side of the stone. The neck was too thin, the face grotesque. Sandpaper skin, stretched over the bone. Lips, black and curled back over missing teeth. A hole where there'd once been an eye.

Empress Izanami.

Fear pitted Dax's stomach.

He set the pack on the ground and removed the bravery card and the six stones they'd collected. Two halves of a heart. An eyeball. A tooth. A tongue. A rib. They were gold and black, white and copper. Pieces of a shriveled body that had been torn apart. The glinting light reflected off them across the dusty plank floor. He looked up the slanted walls, lined by lamps with black-wicked candles, to the high ceiling, and flinched. A hundred of the tengu from the forest hung upside down like bats from the beams.

Dax nearly dropped the stones.

The birds didn't move, their leathery eyelids closed in sleep.

He forced himself to look back at Izanami's body. At the empty cavity of her chest, the ribs broken out like they'd been pried back, the bloodstained robe torn open.

This had to be the final challenge—to be brave, even as he stood alone with six stones. Maybe, when he gave them to the empress, the last card would finally turn, and he could send his friends home.

He would not let them down again.

At the slab he paused, one last breath before the plunge. Then he leaned forward and carefully placed the eyeball in an empty socket. It softened, then glistened, then swelled, fitting the notch. He placed the tongue and tooth in her gaping mouth, and they grew wet, beading with moisture. One by one, he slid the pieces of her heart into place, watching in horror as they fused together and wept blood. He covered them with a rib.

Breathing hard, he stumbled back, but nothing happened. The final card, gripped in his fist, did not change.

"Come on," he said. "Please."

A low hum filled the room, emanating from the stone slab. Dax pulled the blue knife from his pocket, flicking open the blade.

The hum grew louder, raising a torrent of wind that whipped at Dax's clothes and hair. Above him, the tengu stirred. One unfurled from its cocoon, flexing its murky wings. It hit another, which burst from slumber with a furious screech.

Dax stood his ground, gritting his teeth, holding Maddy in his mind. He would remember her the way she'd been the day they'd married. A fierce grin tilting her lips, a reckless glint in her brown eyes. The dress he'd sometimes secretly imagined she'd wear one day for him.

He would be brave for her.

He would fight for her.

Harder, the wind blew, circling the room until the walls began to clatter and the beams on the ceiling lifted off their moorings. Dax ducked low, bracing himself against Izanami's stone slab. More birds woke, their cries drowning out the sound of the storm. It became so loud that Dax didn't hear the creature climbing the stairs behind him until it was too late.

The oni hulked in the door of the room, his muscled back rounded, his chin jutting forward. One of his horns must have scraped the ceiling, because chips of wood were tangled in his nest of raven hair. Black blood wept from a dozen wounds—his face, his shoulders, his massive chest and thighs.

Every scar on the demon's red body seemed to heave and thicken as he met Dax's stare. Rage and violence burned in his eyes. Fear tempted Dax, but he swallowed it down. This was no time to falter. He had to be brave.

He sprang up, ready to charge, but something grabbed his wrist. When he looked down, delicate, skeletal fingers had closed around his arm, their grip unyielding.

He was so surprised, he dropped his knife. It hit the ground with a hard *thunk,* with the weight of a thousand stones. His last defense, just out of reach on the dusty floor.

Cold worked up his fingertips, his arm, branching across his chest. He swallowed a gulp of air, but his lungs were frozen, unable to stretch. His vision grayed, a world of color compressing to shadows and light.

His last sight was the oni snagging the final card off the floor and barreling down the stairs.

The creature slipped from his mind. Emerson and Owen followed. Then Ian. He held on to Maddy as long as he could, but soon she too was gone.

As the last of his humanity was torn from his grasp, he fell into darkness, the cold shadows welcoming him home.

OWEN

Owen gagged on a mouthful of dirt, the metallic grit crunching between his teeth. They'd fallen straight into the thrashing storm outside the palace gates. A rancid wind tore at his clothes. Freezing rain pelted his face. Pebbles and sticks slashed at his bare arms and the back of his neck. He pushed off the ground into a crouch, finding the dead woods that had surrounded the mountain blocked by a wall of dust. It churned around the eye of the storm—the house of Izanami.

"Owen!"

Maddy was behind him, her tattered dress streaked with soil and blood from the wound that had reopened in her shoulder. Determination set her jaw as the wind slapped her hair across her face. The howl of it cut through the pounding in Owen's temples.

"Emerson?" he shouted, fixing his wire-rim glasses on his nose.

"I'm here," she groaned from behind a dam of dead branches. "I guess a soft landing was too much to ask."

Sprinting around the branches, he reached to help Emerson up. As she stood, another gust pelted them with dirt.

"Is this the next level?" Maddy asked, closing in to make a tight circle.

His gaze shot skyward, to the three-quarter moon on the horizon. It was glaring and bright, a spotlight shining down on the palace.

"The eye is almost open," he croaked. "The honor card must have changed!"

"But we don't have it," Emerson said. "Dax does."

Maddy grimaced up at the sky, gritting her teeth. "Does it matter? The game moved forward either way."

"Then let's finish the bravery challenge before this place falls apart!" Owen told them.

Dawn, Ian's haunting voice cut through his mind. If the giant's eye opened fully, they would lose.

"Look!" Emerson pointed behind them to the empress's palace. The sky around it was dark and rippling, like oil swirling around a drain. Owen squinted at it, realizing the dark cloud wasn't a cloud at all, but a thousand giant black birds.

"Tengu," Maddy said, biting down on the word.

Emerson yelped in surprise as the ground began to quake. Maddy gripped her arm to keep from falling over. Shadows began shifting behind the wall of dust—an eerie wave stretching from one side of the horizon to the other.

"What is that?" Owen asked, his voice rising.

"I'm not sure I want to find out," Emerson told him. "When I saw Shinigami, she shared some details she may have forgotten before."

"Such as?" Owen asked.

"If we win, Izanami comes back to life."

"Isn't that the point?" Maddy asked.

"And crosses over to our world with all her yōkai friends," Emerson added, her lip pale around the ring that pierced it.

"What?" said Owen. "That's some fine-print bullshit!"

"I think we can still get home," Emerson said quickly. "The green flames got us here. When we finish the game, a gate of fire will open back to our world to let the empress through. We just need to beat her there."

"We just need to . . . Have you *completely* lost touch with reality?" Owen said. "Look around! Time isn't exactly on our side!"

"We don't have a choice," said Maddy. "Empress Izanami's in the palace. Dax was there too. We need to find him, get the last card, and finish this before it's too late."

The last challenge shook through Owen like a warning. This was the bravery challenge, he was sure of it. He knew because he didn't feel brave at all.

The dust shadows at the tree line were taking shape now, filling out into a horde of bodies that shuffled toward the empress's palace. As they drew closer, Owen could make out their ragged clothes and slit mouths.

They weren't wearing masks anymore.

"You've got to be kidding me," Owen breathed.

Emerson grabbed his shirt. "Go! *Go!*"

They ran toward the gate, toward the giant stone statues, but the ground had begun moving in waves, like a sheet flicked over a mattress, and they could hardly keep their footing. Veins split the earth, cutting across the ground at lightning speed. Owen's foot caught in one of the cracks and he spilled forward. The gravel bit at his skin, and blood beaded on the heels of his hands and stained the knees of his pants.

He rose just as one of the spiders from Kuchisake's house climbed through the divide before him. Fear clenching his throat, he threw himself backward, scrambling to get away from its glistening, bulbous body and snapping jaws.

"Watch out!" Maddy jabbed a stick into the creature's side. With a hiss, it pitched sideways, then darted into the dust storm.

"You have to be brave," Maddy said, shoving the stick into Owen's hands. The end was dripping with purple blood.

His breath came out in a shudder. He gripped the stick and nodded.

Through the roar of the wind came a familiar howl. An animalistic scream of rage.

The oni was coming.

Owen stopped, turning back toward the horde advancing steadily toward them. He searched frantically for the demon, but couldn't see past the dust and bodies.

"Owen!" Emerson shouted. "We have to move!"

He felt like each step was weighted with bricks as he stumbled after her.

More spiders were emerging from the cracks, moving fast toward them over the rising ground on their eight legs. The horde had gained speed, rushing toward the palace.

Running as hard as he could, Owen leapt over another crack in the ground, this one bubbling with brown river water. The wind shoved him into Maddy, but she pushed him upright and pressed on toward the torii gate and the stone samurai.

They were close. Twenty yards, then fifteen. As they cleared ten, the statues guarding either side of the palace entrance began to move, their rock bodies contorting with a spray of dust. The one on the right with the horse head looked down upon them with a carved gaze, then raised the sword in its hand.

"We can't stop," Maddy said, but as she barreled forward, the ox-head statue cracked its stone whip, striking the ground just before her. With a cry, she threw herself back into Emerson.

Where Maddy had stood, a divot now pressed into the ground, as long as she was tall.

Owen turned at Emerson's shout, finding her wrestling with one of the spiders. Maddy twisted, kicking out two of its legs. She threw it off-balance just enough for Emerson to jam a sharp rock into its cheek. Sticky liquid exploded from the wound, painting Emerson's arms and chest. Bile climbed Owen's throat as he pedaled backward.

Three more spiders had climbed onto the ox-head samurai statue's back, but it didn't seem to notice. Its stone gaze was still fixed on Emerson, Owen, and Maddy, as if its only purpose was to block them from entering.

"How do we get through?" Maddy called over the wind. The ground on either side of the torii gate was sinking, water rising through the cracks. At the surface, shiny black creatures slithered over one another, a pulsing knot of eels like the ones they'd seen in the river.

Above them, the giant's eye was almost completely open. They could try to go around—reach the palace from the side of the mountain, or over the back—but they didn't have time. Two spiders were now attacking Maddy, and Emerson was helping to fend them off. In horror, Owen watched as the first of the people with split faces reached them, trudging straight into the water or bouncing off the sides of the spiders that stabbed at them with their clawed legs. In the sky above, the tengu were beginning to swoop down, picking off loners to carry them skyward.

Be brave be brave be brave.

His feet pedaled through the churning ground. Sweat dripped down into his eyes. The horse-head samurai statue's sword swung down, but as Owen jumped out of the way, it snapped the whip in its hand, the weapon's gray tail singing through the air in his direction. Before it crushed him, it clashed with the ox samurai statue's sword, swinging the opposite way toward a cluster of spiders. Gravel rained down from above.

Framed beneath them stood the oni.

Owen's chest seized. The demon stared at him with black eyes, its gaping mouth filled with yellow, pointed fangs. His hulking back rounded, twisted scars stretching over each mountain of muscle. The tattered pants he wore were torn at the bottom, and his bare feet looked like a horse's, cloven, with hocks that stuck out like lumps over his ankles.

In his fist he gripped a card.

"No," Owen whispered.

It was their card—the bravery card. Owen could see the edge of the kanji sticking out from within the creature's red, gnarled fist. If the oni had it, that meant he had killed Dax and taken the stones.

They would never get that bag back from the creature. Owen had seen what it had done to Dax before, and he was the strongest fighter of all of them. How were they supposed to beat him with all of Meido breaking apart around them?

They were finished.

Owen took one step back, then another, toward the dead woods and the mutilated players with their awful faces. His heart throbbed, defeat sinking its teeth into his bones.

They had already lost.

"Owen!" Maddy screamed, but it was too late. He'd already turned away. He wasn't stupid. He knew a losing battle when he saw one.

"I can't!" he yelled as he started to run away. Two steps were all it took. His head filled with fog, the pounding in his skull turning to a gentle buzz.

"He's back!" A young Dax leapt up from their booth at the corner of The Bean to throw an arm around Owen's shoulder. He'd been gone for three weeks to see his grandparents in Kyoto, but from the way Maddy was cheering, you would have thought it had been months.

"What'd you see?" Emerson asked.

"Tons of places. The Imperial Palace. Nijo Castle." He puffed up his chest. That was just the start. He had tons of pictures, and even more stories, but felt a sudden grip in his chest as Ian slid out of the booth, extending one hand like he meant to shake.

His dusty brown hair was longer, hanging over his ears and brows. His eyes bright blue. When Owen took his hand, he felt a jolt up his arm. It was such an adult thing to do, shaking hands, and he had the sudden feeling that he'd left for summer vacation a boy and returned a man.

He stood straighter, his eyes dipping to the scar on Ian's chin.

"Welcome back," Ian said.

His voice was lower, wasn't it? They'd talked on the phone a dozen times while he'd been gone, but he hadn't noticed it until now.

"You're taller," he said, lowering his voice too. His face lit like wild-fire. He looked away.

"A little," Ian said, and then, "You seem different."

Owen swallowed. He wanted to know if it was good different or bad different. To say that Ian seemed different too. Like Owen wasn't the only one who'd changed.

His stare fell over Ian's T-shirt, to his chest. His knees peeked out from the bottom of his ragged shorts. His ankle bones were sharp. Owen lifted his gaze, drawn to Ian's dark lashes. Were they always so thick? It was as if Owen had never seen him before that moment.

Emerson and Maddy giggled, and Owen immediately released Ian's hand, shoving both of his in his pockets. "So what happened while I was gone?"

Ian grinned, but as he went to slide into the booth, he faded, like a watercolor under a faucet. Emerson and Maddy kept laughing. Dax sat on the opposite side of the booth.

You seem different.

The words echoed in his head, and then silenced.

Owen stopped running. He rolled back his shoulders, standing tall. He felt different somehow, like a hollow pipe being filled with warm water. There was no more emptiness, no pain.

As the fog in his head cleared, he looked down, cringing at the scrapes on his hands that were smeared with dirt. He needed some sanitizer in a bad way.

A roar behind him made him made him duck and spin toward the sound. His knees turned to jelly at the sight of the giant spiders and mutilated players attacking one another, rolling in waves over the broken ground past the two stone guards of the palace. The dim sky was filled with dust and growing brighter by the moment, revealing hundreds of tengu diving for their prey. Emerson and Maddy had crouched behind the body of a dead spider, but they couldn't get closer to the palace gates—the way was blocked by a bubbling pool of rising water, filling the cracks in the ground.

And between them and the palace was the oni.

Red and scarred, fanged and horned, it threw its head back in an angry snarl as a spider leapt off the horse-head statue and landed on his back. The way the demon twisted, Owen caught a glimpse of his face, exposed to the sky, and felt as if he'd stepped off a cliff.

A scar cut across the base of the oni's chin, pale pink amid the red ropes of raised skin. It was the shape of a horseshoe, and though it had been stretched across the demon's broad face, Owen recognized it.

He'd seen it in the giant's sleepy eye.

Traced it in the ground.

That shape was everywhere in his life—the sky, the stage, his home, his dreams.

He felt like he was in a dream now.

"I know you," he whispered, even while fear trembled through him.

He'd touched that mark. Felt the smooth curve of skin.

The oni snarled, snapping its jaws as three of Kuchisake's grinning players used the spiders' attack to wrestle the oni to the ground.

"Hey!" Owen shouted, anger narrowing his vision. "Leave him alone!"

The water was still rising. It dragged at Owen's ankles as he sloshed toward the pile of bodies. Self-preservation clenched his muscles, slowing him down, but he fought it. This was a sign. This was the challenge. He had to see it through.

The oni howled, tearing panic loose inside him.

Owen moved faster, drawn by the scar he'd seen. By the knowing in his heart.

"Hold on!" Owen shouted. "I'm coming!"

He didn't know if the creature could hear him. He could barely hear himself over the ringing in his ears. Spiders the size of small cars had crawled up the body of the horse-head samurai, but it didn't stop the statue from launching toward Owen, its dull sword raised. He threw himself to the right as the sword came down, a sharp bite of pain lighting up his hip as he landed on debris from the ox-head's leg. Frigid water soaked his clothes and splashed on his face. When he reached down to push himself up he felt something slither over his hand.

He cried out in surprise, throwing himself back, searching the water with his heart in his throat. Whatever lurked beneath was moving again, making a yellow froth on the surface. Gleaming black eels broke through, a pile of them slithering over one another, hissing as their sliced mouths snapped.

Owen pushed on.

"Hang on!" he shouted. "I'm almost there!"

With a roar, the oni burst free from the pile, tossing a man against the black gate with a bone-snapping crack. He'd torn off a spider's leg and was holding it in one hand like a weapon. As a woman with a gruesome smile and blank eyes threw herself upon the oni, he twisted, taking a chunk out of her arm with his teeth.

When he lifted his head, his mouth was circled with blood.

Owen's stomach twisted.

"Hey," he said, suddenly realizing this might be a bad idea. He lifted his hands in surrender. "It's okay. I won't hurt you."

The oni snarled, crimson-stained teeth jutting from his mouth.

Owen focused on the horseshoe scar embedded in the red, inflamed skin that covered the oni's body.

"Looks like you've got a pretty nasty infection going there. Must . . ." He gulped down panic as the oni glared at him. "Must really itch."

The demon looked down, a growl bursting from his painted lips as the water rose over his calloused knees. He turned, trying to escape the opposite way, but the horde was too thick, now backed by more people with black eyes. A mixture of faces with dead eyes, all scrambling, with no mind to their bodies or safety, toward the gates of Empress Izanami's palace.

"Don't worry," Owen said quickly, taking a step closer through the water. "It's nothing a dose of antibiotics can't fix. I mean, they'll probably have to start an IV just to get things going, but—"

The oni snapped at him.

Owen stumbled back, but caught himself. Heat was rising up his throat, choking him, but he swallowed it down.

"Hey," Owen said, softer now. "You're all right. I'm one of the good guys."

The demon swung the spider leg at him. Owen dodged out of the way, water splashing over his shirt.

He planted his feet in the trembling ground.

"You've got our card," he said. "That's good. We've got to keep it away from the empress, though, right? Turns out she's bad news."

The oni narrowed his eyes, but his mistrust only brought another wave of ferocity. This horrible, monstrous demon needed him. He had to protect it. Protect *Ian*.

"You understand me," Owen said, glancing to where he'd seen the creature try to escape.

A growl rumbled from the oni's throat.

Owen stepped closer.

"I know you're scared. Trust me, I get it. But we're going to fix this. You and me and Maddy and Emerson. They're just over there."

The demon snorted. Snarled. But he dropped the spider leg.

"And when it's done," Owen said, "and after you have a visit with the nice doctor and, okay, probably a few specialists, you're going to feel better and everything will go back to normal."

The spiders were fleeing from the water—searching for higher ground on the statues and the torii gate. Only the people remained, though they too were struggling with the rising tide. Emerson's warnings flew through Owen's mind. If Izanami was brought back, she would cross to their world. The yōkai would reign.

Were he, Maddy, and Emerson too late?

Owen took another step closer to the oni. He was within his reach now; if the creature wanted to grab him, to rip him apart, he could. Owen's eyes darted down to the card in his fist.

Owen sipped a quick breath and stepped beneath the oni's hulking shadow.

"Don't be scared," Owen said softly. "It's just me."

The river climbed up to his hips. Eels curled around his legs, but he kicked them free. With one shaking hand, he reached up and pressed his finger to the scar on the demon's chin.

The oni jerked, then went still. His black eyes closed.

For a moment, Meido silenced. The groans and screams and flapping wings of the birds stilled. There was only the curve of that scar and the pounding of Owen's heart.

Then Owen looked up and saw the horse-head samurai's stone fist cutting through the air, right at them.

"Look out!" Owen yelled, and with more strength than he'd ever summoned, he shoved the oni backward out of the way. They splashed into the water together, the fist cutting through the sky just over Owen's head. When they fell, they landed on a boulder half raised out of the water. Though Owen was half his size, he blocked the giant demon's body with his own.

The horse-head's swing hit the ox samurai statue, which exploded the stone with a violent crash. As the horse-head fell, the other statue sent its last blow, cutting it off at the knees with its axe. They both fell into the water, crushing a line of blank-eyed players and blocking the rest from their approach.

Rocks and stones pelted Owen's back, but he spread himself as wide as he could, taking every punishing hit as he guarded the oni's chest. When the storm stilled, he heaved a breath and looked into the demon's eyes, now rimmed with blue.

Owen felt something tear inside of him, loosing beams of blinding light into the shadows of his mind. He knew those eyes—blue and gleaming. He knew the shape of his jaw, hidden beneath this red, knotted skin, and the exact color of his hair, and the way his voice dipped when he was nervous.

I will not lose you again.

I will not let you go.

Owen fought back the fog, clinging to his slippery memories. They were eight, building Legos together in his room. Ten, playing flashlight hide-and-seek. Owen was cheering for him to cross the finish line in track, shouting louder than anyone there. Laughing at a joke he told. Sharing popcorn during a Friday night movie marathon.

"Ian," Owen whispered, the name snatched from the fog in an iron grip of will.

Lines etched across the oni's red forehead.

"*Ian,*" he said again, this time with more certainty.

Emotion seared through Owen's chest, but before he could answer, Ian jerked the card up to his side. It was burning, the heavy paper eaten by orange embers.

Before it fell into the water, Owen snagged the knotted lump of bone the card had become.

A piece of a spine—a single vertebra.

"The last stone," Owen said in awe. "We did it."

From overhead came a loud, sky-quaking groan, loud enough to pop Owen's ears and shake his vision. When he looked up, his lips parted in horror.

The giant's eye was slowly widening into a full white circle.

"Get away from him, you monster!" Maddy, lit by the purple light of the coming dawn, came charging toward them, a stick in her hand. Before she could use it, Owen leapt off of Ian and held the stone before him.

"It's okay!" he shouted. "It's him—the oni is Ian! We got the last stone!"

Maddy paused. Her brows pulled inward as she fixed her grip on her weapon. "Owen, that's not . . ." But as she took a step closer, she squinted at his face, and recognition arched her brows. "Ian?"

Ian snapped at her.

"We have to hurry. Look at the sky!" Owen pointed up, and Maddy cringed.

"How is this possible?" Emerson asked, trudging up behind Maddy into the shadow of a stone samurai's broken chest. "How'd Ian become . . . this?" She motioned to him.

"The oni is supposed to be Izanami's son," said Maddy. "Ian wasn't born here."

Owen frowned, looking again to the thin circle of blue around Ian's black pupils. He'd come here for Ian, he remembered that now. He'd done each of these challenges to find him. But now that he had—now that he knew what Ian had become—a new fear rooted in his gut.

Had they been too late to save him from Meido?

He shook his head. He refused to believe it.

"'It becomes something different every time it's played,'" he murmured. "The kids told us that, remember? The game changes for us. The oni became someone we know. Or rather, Ian became someone we don't know."

Emerson blew out a harsh breath. "Okay. So how do we get him out of that role? We're running out of time."

"How do we get any of us out?" Maddy asked. "We need the rest of the stones to finish the game. Then we look for the final passage."

Owen glanced down to Ian's broad hands.

"Did you take the stones?"

Ian gave a small shake of his head.

"They would have looked like body parts," Emerson tried. "A rib. An eyeball. There was a tongue."

Ian growled.

"The stones are gone," Owen said.

"Where are they?" Emerson asked.

"Dax," Maddy murmured, eyes closing as if his name alone hurt her.

A high whistle cut through the air and embedded in Ian's chest, throwing him backward into the water with a splash. A spear as tall as Owen protruded from the corner of his chest, pinning him to the quaking ground beneath.

Panic lodged in Owen's throat. His gaze whipped back in the direction from which the attack had come and locked on a shirtless figure, leaping from the cracked calf of one statue to the remains of a shattered stone arm.

Dax.

⁂

Ian's head disappeared under the rising water with a spray of bubbles. Pulse tripping, Owen shoved the final stone into his robe's pocket and reached for the spear, but Ian's thrashing arms and legs made it impossible to get close enough to grab it.

"The demon has the final card!" Dax called, keeping to the broken stone islands above water. The sky behind him was growing brighter, the giant's eye continuing to widen.

Struggle played over Maddy's face as she gripped the branch over her shoulder tighter. "Stay there, Dax."

"What are you doing?" He looked down at her weapon, at her fighting stance. His tattered black jacket from the wedding was gone now, and his wet pants hung low on his hips, stretching to his bare feet.

"Help me!" Owen threw himself out of the way of Ian's long, lethal fingernails. Emerson jumped onto Ian's flailing arm so Owen could grab the spear, but was flung to the side with a splash.

"Ian!" Owen screamed, as water gurgled over his own waist. He turned to Dax. "What did you do?"

"What do you mean? It was attacking you!"

"It's Ian!" Emerson screamed at him.

Dax's chin pulled inward. "That's not Ian. I saw Ian. He's in the palace!"

Emerson's angry stare met Owen's. "He's lying. Don't listen to him. You saw what he did to Ian before!"

A soft hissing filled Owen's ears. Another memory slid into

view, grainy and hard to hold. They were in the cave. Dax stayed behind when Ian shouted for help.

"You left him there," Owen remembered, fury hardening his tone. "You sent him here."

"I didn't do anything," Dax said. "The mirrors lied." Crouching on the broken statue, he reached down for Maddy's hand. "The demon stole the final card. We need to get it back so we can finish the challenges."

"We already finished it!" Owen shouted at him. Was that all he cared about? "Forget the game—Ian's going to drown if we don't help him!"

"The final card changed?" Dax asked, his brows arching. Overhead, in the bruised sky, the black cloud shifted. The tengu were moving closer, blotting out the giant's opening eye.

Maddy's knuckles whitened around the branch. "What'd you do with the other stones, Dax?"

"They're in the palace," Dax said. "In a safe place."

"Same place you left Ian?" Emerson asked, fire in her stare.

Dax smiled. "The empress is very pleased with our service."

Chills crawled down Owen's back.

"You gave the other six stones to the empress?" His head was pounding. It all made sense now—the spiders, the mutilated horde, the way Meido was shattering all around them. Shinigami had said that Izanami would bring her army of yōkai to their world if the seven stones were returned. The entire kingdom had been called here to cross over with her.

With a screech, a bird dived toward Dax, but he jumped out of the way, landing in the water beside them. Something was wrong with him. His eyes were too round, too excited, and as he glided through the water, he barely seemed to move his legs at all. The world was caving in around them, and yet Dax barely seemed to notice.

Owen didn't have time to process it. Ian's arms were slowing. The tips of his curved horns were now completely submerged. If they didn't bring him up soon, he would die.

"Help me," Owen begged. "Please."

"Give me the stone," Dax said.

"Don't do it, Owen." Emerson reached for him, but was intercepted by Dax, who shoved her back. In shock, Owen watched as she flew ten feet through the air, hitting the ankle of the broken statue. She crumpled into the water, her body limp.

"Emerson!" Maddy screamed, rushing to her aid.

"What did you . . ." Owen stared in horror at Dax. "*How* did you . . ."

"The final prize." Dax extended his hand toward Owen. "I can fix this. All of it. You just have to give me the stone."

Owen stomach plunged. He stared at Dax, a face he knew. A person he'd called friend. He'd never thought him capable of hurting Emerson.

He never thought it possible that Dax would hurt any of them.

Below Owen, the water barely rippled with Ian's struggles.

"I don't know who you are, but you're not Dax." Maddy had pulled Emerson upright, and with a roar, turned back on Dax. He didn't spare her a glance. With a careless hand, he slapped the surface of the water, and made a wave forceful enough to knock them both back.

Owen gaped at Dax.

"What are you?" His voice trembled.

Dax smiled, a sudden movement so horrifying and sharp, Owen's heart leapt into his throat.

"Give me the stone," Dax said. "When the empress crosses over, she will remember who helped her. Would you like that, Owen? To be famous?"

Temptation whispered at the back of Owen's mind. He saw himself on a stage, the audience rising to their feet in applause. A film where he was given the lead. Magazine shoots and press junkets and social media posts with a million likes apiece.

He'd wanted fame since the high of the curtain call after his first show.

He shook the thoughts free from his head.

"You'll never be alone again," Dax said.

Owen's breath staggered, his fear pressing out of his pores

to the top of his skin. But he didn't want fame if it didn't come with Ian.

Inside, he felt as if his bones were separating. As if he were being torn in two. The stone, or Ian. The world, or his best friend. What would Dax do to him if he refused to hand it over? What would Dax do to Ian if Owen did?

"You want it?" Owen pulled the vertebra from his pocket, and with a shaking hand chucked it into the shuffling stampede. "Go get it."

Dax sneered, bulging eyes and curled lips. Then, with a burst of speed, he leapt into the air to chase the stone. Owen didn't know how he moved so fast, but he was past caring. He turned back to the spear end protruding from the water and grabbed ahold. His feet found Ian's broad chest under the murky surface. Using his friend's body as leverage, Owen pulled with all his might, but the spear stayed firmly planted.

"Owen!" Maddy cried, swimming back toward them.

"Help!" he shouted, desperation seizing him. "It's stuck!"

Maddy reached him, her hands surrounding the spear below his. Emerson joined them, a cut on her forehead painting her cheek red. With a collective groan, they pulled, finally dragging the spear free from the ground beneath.

Ian burst from the water with a gasp and a dazed look in his black eyes, the length of the spear still protruding from his side. He turned to Owen, all glimmer of humanity gone. Owen's hands shot up as water sluiced from Ian's massive shoulders.

"It's okay," Owen said, fear icing his gut. "You're okay."

Ian grabbed the handle of the spear, and dragged it free, the slurp of wood sliding out of flesh tingling Owen's gag reflex. When it was out, Ian hurled it to the sky, stabbing a tengu through the wing. With a screech, it fell, snapping against the broken samurai stones.

Then he turned back to Owen, Emerson, and Maddy, and snorted a mist of hot air.

"We need to stop Dax," Owen told him. "We need to get the stones."

Ian tilted his head back and howled, then shoved them aside and charged into the chaos.

—•—

The empress's palace was breaking apart.

Owen, Maddy, and Emerson trudged as fast as they could through the water, following the path Ian had carved through the horde of split faces. The quake had travelled up the mountain and now was shaking the foundation of the black fortress. Beams fell from the walls, tiles from the roof. On the front steps, the thunderous groan of the stampede was punctuated by the screaming wind.

Owen broke through the front door, climbing over a pile of bodies Ian had left behind. He searched for his friend, for a flash of red skin and horns, but the spiders and bodies were so tightly packed, it was impossible to see where he'd gone.

"There!" Emerson shouted, yanking Maddy and Owen toward the hole in the floor where they'd fallen through before. He was prepared to jump, to face the same daunting bone slide from before, but water had already filled the lower level, and was bubbling up over the broken planks.

"How do we get down?" Maddy called, desperation pulling the muscles of her neck tight.

Owen didn't know. The army of failed players had broken through the front door and were spilling inside, climbing over others who'd become trapped in the wide room. Soon, there was a wave of bodies falling over one another. They began pressing tighter to Owen's sides, pinning his arms down. Their foul breath and rotting cheeks filled his nostrils, bringing a surge of bile up his throat.

The space around him was suddenly cleared by the swipe of a giant, red arm. But as soon as Ian arrived he was overrun, dozens of people climbing him like insects.

"Ian!" Owen shouted, trying to dig him out.

Ian's blue-rimmed eyes flashed with panic as they met Owen's.

"I'm not going to leave you," Owen said, trying to reach for Ian's broad elbow. It disappeared under a woman's back.

"Owen," Ian grunted.

Then he was gone.

"Help!" Owen shouted. "Maddy! Emerson!" He looked up through a hole in the roof to a steel sky. The giant's eye was nearly full, and the steel light allowed him to see the tengu circling a tower at the top of the palace, nestled against the slate side of the mountain. A wall had broken free, and through it, he could see a flash of green flames.

The passage.

He couldn't save Ian unless he stopped the horde, and the only way to stop the horde was to stop Empress Izanami.

"We have to go up," Owen said, sparing one last glance at the space where Ian had been. "I'll come back. I promise." Dread filled him as he grabbed Emerson's hand and dragged her through the slush of bone dust and water, through the tightly packed horde, toward the back of the room. If they were too late, Dax might have already given the final stone to Izanami.

At the back of the main room was a hall, and they dove through a spider's legs to enter it. In the darkness, the path cleared. Bouncing off crumbling walls, they followed the maze of turns, hands outstretched. The stench of mildew and blood rose in the shivering air. Panic gripped Owen's chest as he tripped over debris he couldn't make out beneath his feet.

"Stairs!" Maddy cried.

Owen cut to the left, following Maddy's voice and Emerson's footsteps. He stumbled on the first step, his shins smacking against the corner of the boards. His hand found the side paneling, and he climbed, hearing Emerson's sharp breaths in front of him.

"Keep going, keep going," Maddy chanted. "We're almost there."

He had no idea how far it would be, or even if they were taking the right stairs, but Maddy's words pushed him on. They climbed what felt like endlessly, feeling their way through the dark and dust, until at last, the stairs flattened, and a light appeared from a room down the hall.

"Do you see Dax or the empress?" Owen asked, but Emerson grabbed his wrist and pressed her own finger to her lips.

Heart pounding, he nodded. They crept forward, the wind punching the walls in fitful bursts. The light ahead grew steadily brighter, its green hue throwing a sickly tint over Emerson and Maddy's damp skin. As they neared the room, the crackle of flames sparked Owen's nerves, and the sound of voices reached their ears.

"You've done well, young yōkai," a woman said, her voice thin and crackling.

A sick feeling wormed through Owen's stomach. Was this the empress? If she'd already been revived, it could only mean that Dax had truly given her the stones. That she could now cross over to their world with her army of failed players, just downstairs.

"You were right to give them the cards," the woman groaned. "It took some time, but they completed the challenges so many others could not."

"Yes, Empress," came a low voice that confirmed Owen's fears.

"Dax," whispered Maddy.

Cold understanding cut through the fog of Owen's memories. The cards had been Dax's. They had come here to play this game because of Dax. He'd seen it all in the hall of mirrors. He'd seen what had happened to Ian.

Ian.

Owen felt a sudden pull to return to the room below to help his friend, but he couldn't. Not until they stopped Dax and Izanami.

He tipped his head to look into the room and gaped at the sight before him.

Dax—skin ashen and eyes like a black sea—stood in front of a stone table where a figure sat. Her feet, draped over the edge, were skeletal and white, her slender ankles covered by a dry knot of skin. The harsh curve of her back made her head droop to the side. The weight of her frail form seemed entirely supported by the black robe whipping around her shoulders, as if her body were the source of the wind circling through the blown-off roof to the pale sky. The fabric rose from her arms, swirling around her head with her long, black hair, a sharp contrast to the wall of green flames behind her.

As Owen watched in horror, Empress Izanami inhaled. Her corpse face lolled back, revealing the open V of her ragged cloak, and the golden light pulsing in the center of her gaping chest. Tendrils of flesh and sinew stretched across it, as if worms were burying the two halves of her stone heart under the earth.

"But there is regret in you," the empress groaned. "I sense it."

Dax's head tilted, like a dog who'd heard a high whistle. "If there is, it is only because I took so long to serve you."

Owen saw the spear flying through the air, planting in Ian's monstrous shoulder. He saw the crazed light in Dax's eyes when he'd said they needed to give the stones to Izanami. Owen was around actors all the time; how had he missed Dax's true intentions?

The empress's leg jutted out straight as a layer of skin rolled over her swelling thigh muscle, covering it. "Your mind was tainted by the engimono's magic. I do wonder how such an ordinary boy came upon such a fascinating artifact in the first place."

Maddy, hunched beside Owen, shot a gaze his way. In a flash, he recalled how Keneō had said his skin clothes were better than any engimono, and how Kuchisake had called out the word in surprise when Dax had stabbed him in the neck with his knife.

Dax had acted strangely after Maddy had given him CPR . . . until Owen had returned that knife.

His fingers dug into the trembling floorboards.

Owen had never seen Dax without it, but as he looked to Dax's hands, he saw no knife. Only a knot of white spine.

The vertebra Owen had gotten with Ian. The final stone.

His temples began to throb as Dax moved silently around the stone table and gently opened the collar of Izanami's robe over her shoulders to expose her back. Owen's gaze shot to the green flames behind them, eating through the wall.

Beyond it, he could see a metal bridge, and the grassy bank of Smale Park.

Home.

His legs weakened; he pitched forward into the beam around the door. They had finished the game, gathered the seven stones. Their exit was here—the final gate that would take them from Meido. They just had to escape before Empress Izanami and her yōkai crossed over.

"He's going to give her the final stone," Emerson hissed. Beside her, Maddy scooped up a broken board from the floor, her knuckles flexing as she squeezed it in her fist.

They had run out of time. Ian, in his current form, would have been a nice distraction, but he wasn't here now. It fell to them.

With a cry, Maddy charged from their hiding place. Emerson tried to hold her back, but she slipped through her hands. With a sickening crunch, the empress's head lurched up, turning to Maddy. Her teeth, revealed from her lipless face, were bared as she swung a bony arm in defense. Before it struck her, Maddy was flung to the side, hitting the ground hard. In a blink, Dax was above her, pinning her to the floor with a surge of power.

The vertebra was no longer in his hand.

"Maddy!" Emerson choked as Dax leaned closer, a push-up over her struggling body. The board she'd grabbed from the floor was pushed away by the wind.

"How could you?" she cried. "I trusted you! *Ian* trusted you." Owen could feel her rage press through the space between them, as sharp as the cutting wind.

"There is no Ian," tutted Empress Izanami. "Not anymore. He ceased to exist when you and your friends abandoned him to my world." With a rippling crack, her spine straightened to a rigid line and she slid off the table. Her black robes and long, silken sleeves snapped through the air as she stepped closer to Maddy and Dax.

Tension coiled in Owen's muscles. The empress had all seven stones, but she still seemed weak, her body knitting itself together. Owen could feel the pressure of time pushing against him on all sides. He needed to stop her, but how? Dax was protecting her— Owen hadn't even seen him move when he'd fended off Maddy's attack.

His gaze followed Izanami's skeletal legs to the floor, where she stepped over a small piece of metal.

A blue pocketknife.

An idea seared through Owen's mind.

Maddy kicked out hard, but Dax straddled her. "We didn't abandon Ian," she spat. "We came here for him."

"So fiercely she defends him," said Izanami. "This mortal she can't even remember. A sad consequence of trying to cheat the game."

Maddy screamed in frustration as Dax grabbed her wrists.

"Distract the empress," Owen told Emerson.

"What are you going to do?" she hissed.

While the empress stared down at Dax and a struggling Maddy, Owen stepped carefully into the room, keeping to the shadows.

"How does one survive this land of death without memory of their purpose for being here?" the empress mused. "The others before you could not. Remove their goal, and remove the strength that came in its wake. But these players are anomalies. Meido takes their memories of this boy, and they only bind together tighter and fight harder. Curious, is it not?"

"Yes, Empress," Dax told her.

Keeping to the wall, Owen slid around the back of the room, heading away from Maddy, Dax, and the decrepit empress, toward the stone table. When it was impossible to go any farther without stepping into the light, he glanced back at the entrance of the room for Emerson, but found her missing.

"It matters little," said Izanami. "Punished or not, you have succeeded, and all the lost players along the way have become my loyal subjects."

"You can't do this," Maddy told her. "Dax, you can't—"

The sleeve of Izanami's gown slapped Maddy into shock. Above her, Dax flinched.

"Do not be sad for her. Grief is for the living." Izanami clicked her wet tongue—a tongue that Owen had held in his hand just hours before. "Love would only have betrayed you, as it betrayed me." Her whipping cloak lifted her frail arm, and she caressed Dax's cheek. "It will pass. Eventually, all echoes fade to silence."

Owen's heart was pounding. With one harsh breath, he leapt from the shadows and raced across the room toward the stone table. To his side he heard a shriek, but he didn't take his eyes off the gleaming metal knife on the floor. A shadow moved in his peripheral vision, a bolt so quick he couldn't dodge out of the way. With one last burst of strength, Owen launched himself forward, his hand outstretched, fingers seeking their last chance at salvation.

He was caught by the long sleeve of Izanami's robe, a snapping lasso that encircled his throat. White stars exploded behind his eyes. His spine popped with the stretch as he was jerked like a rag doll to face the dark empress.

"Ah, the coward," said Izanami as Owen kicked his legs in panic. "Were you running for the passage? Trying to escape before anyone saw?"

Owen's fingers went numb. He couldn't breathe.

"Maybe he was just clearing the path." Emerson kicked at a weakened beam in the wall beside the arch of green flames. The boards snapped around her boot, caving inward. With a spray of splinters, the wall fell, suffocating half the fire.

"No!" howled Izanami, her robe loosening its hold on Owen's throat. "If you put out the passage's flames, you'll never return to your world."

"And neither will you," Emerson told her, giving the wall another kick. Izanami rushed toward her, dropping Owen. He fell to his knees, sputtering, blood rushing back to his limbs. Dizzy, he crawled toward Maddy, swallowing shallow breaths through his crushed throat.

Dax rose, dragging Maddy up with him. He trapped her back against his chest, his forearm pressed to her throat. Owen glanced up at them, his heart pounding too hard.

"You showed honor in the game," Dax told him. "But you lost."

"Not yet," Owen said. Then he wheeled back, and with a flick of the knife, stabbed Dax in the leg.

The blue handle protruded from Dax's thigh, a wet, black circle forming around it. Hissing, Dax reached down to pull it out, and as his hand closed around the grip, he stilled.

Shuddered.

Gasped.

With a grunt, Dax pulled the knife free, squeezing it in a shaking fist. He let go of Maddy, falling to his knees. When he looked up, white rings of fear circled his brown irises.

"Maddy?" he whispered. "Owen?"

Relief rushed through Owen at the familiarity in his voice.

"Dax." Maddy dropped to his side, her hand pressed between his damp shoulder blades.

He trembled as she tied off his wound with the silk belt that had been around her wrist, and grabbed her arm. "You need to go. Get out of here. You, Owen, and Emerson, go through the flames. I'll take care of Izanami."

"We're going together," Owen said. "All of us."

Dax looked at him as if seeing him for the first time. "You don't know what I am."

A scream from the far side of the room made Owen flinch. Izanami was on Emerson, the magic sleeves of her robe slashing her like knives.

"Emerson!" Maddy screamed. But before she or Owen could run to Emerson's aid, a crash came from the entrance of the room. Owen glanced back, expecting to find spiders, or the horde of split faces. Instead, he faced Ian, red, scarred, and heaving breath.

Izanami took one look at him and screamed. Spinning from Emerson, she flung herself toward the remaining arch of green fire. Before she could cross over, Ian hit her like a rocket and slammed her to the ground. She flung him off with a slash of her sleeves, knocking him into the stone table so hard it cracked.

"Ian!" Owen charged toward him.

A black spot swooped down from the open roof, and in a rush Owen remembered the tengu. He could see the gray above them in the growing dawn—a thousand swirling birds waiting for their empress to lead them through the flames.

A roar from behind drew his eyes back to the room's entrance. The horde burst through the open doorway. So many red-slashed faces, he couldn't count.

"Get out of here!" Dax shouted again, then hurled his body drunkenly toward the door. Like a bowling ball, he took out the first line, knocking those directly behind them backward down the stairs. It stunted the group's momentum only for a moment, and soon they were crawling over one another to get into the room.

As Owen watched, Dax threw himself into the wide beam supporting the entry. Already loose from the quakes, it groaned under his attack, splinters flying into the air.

Maddy joined him, and together they hit it again.

The beam broke with a crack and fell sideways, crushing two people crawling across the threshold. The ceiling beam toppled without the support. A thunderous roar filled their ears as it crashed down, taking the connecting beams with it.

Dax shoved Maddy backward out of the way as planks fell like dominos. Splinters and gravel exploded from a cloud of dust.

The room lurched hard to the side, the floor tilting beneath Owen's feet.

It wouldn't be long before the palace was completely destroyed.

Owen staggered toward the table. He blinked, his vision still dim from Izanami's choke hold. As he reached the fight, he registered Emerson on her hands and knees beside the stone slab, and Ian guarding her body with his own.

Then the razor-sharp sleeve of Izanami's robe sliced through the air and stabbed Ian through the heart from behind.

For a moment, time seemed to stall, all of Owen's awareness focused on the black point emerging from Ian's chest and his choking gasp of surprise. Ian fell with a crash, the floor denting beneath his massive body.

"No!" Owen scrambled over the broken table, sliding to his knees at Ian's side. His vision wavered under the welling tears in his eyes, the monstrous red face below shimmering to dirt-streaked skin, a narrow nose, and blue eyes before returning to the knotted scars that had taken over.

Dax leapt over the table in one bound, throwing himself at Izanami before she could cut through the fiery gate. Faster than humanly possible, they fought—swinging fists and twisting robes. Dax was thrown against the floor hard enough for his bones to break, but he leapt back to his feet and charged again. Maddy grabbed Emerson's arm, dragging her to safety, and they crawled to Ian's side.

"It's okay," Owen said quickly, as the light of the full, open eye sliced through the army of tengu. It felt weighted, like a bright fist pinning Ian down.

Dawn had come at last.

Owen placed his hands over the gaping wound on Ian's chest. Black blood flowed from it, traveling in streams between the twisted scars of his body. "It's just a scratch. Couple Band-Aids and you'll be good as new." His voice shook.

Maddy's eyes filled with tears as Ian's quick breaths began to slow. Their friend looked up at the sky, his eyes clouding over.

"No," Emerson whispered.

The last of Owen's control shattered when Ian's head slumped into his lap.

Owen shook him, but he didn't move. "Ian? Come on, Ian."

"He's gone," Emerson said from somewhere far away.

"He's not gone," Owen said, the words punishing him in a way this game never could. It was as if his insides were being wrung out, twisted, and bent until he could feel himself breaking apart. When he looked down at himself, he expected to find blood. How could something hurt this bad and not bleed? But he was still in one piece.

He didn't remember rising to his feet, but suddenly he was there, moving as if by magnetism toward the empress and Dax. Behind him he heard Maddy yell, but he couldn't tell what she was saying. He felt Emerson's hand slide through his, but it didn't stop him.

The empress had done this. She had killed Ian. She thought he was a coward, but she was wrong.

Owen had nothing left to lose.

He circled the stone table. As Dax threw the empress to the ground, Owen leapt on top of her, kneeling on one arm with its wild thrashing sleeve while Dax took down the other. Maddy and Emerson grabbed Izanami's legs, holding her while she bucked and roared.

"Her heart!" Dax shouted, pressing Izanami's face to the side as her jaw clicked and snapped with each vicious bite. The lines of her mouth and jaw were smoother, younger than they'd been minutes before, but warped with a sneer. Her eyes had narrowed, the dark gaze hateful as she glared at him.

"I will destroy everything you love," she hissed.

"You already have," Owen said.

Then he buried his hand in her half-open chest.

The slick flesh pulsed around his wrist. Muscle and sinew wrapped like string around the cold stones that made up her heart. He closed his hand around the slippery metal, feeling it pulsing in his fist.

Steeling himself, he yanked it free.

With a scream, Izanami withered. Her flesh dried. Her blood boiled, then burned to black ash. Skin sucked to bone as her teeth and tongue came free. Soon, she was no more than a pile of pieces in a shroud of black cloak.

The heart still beat in his fist, its metal hue shining through the black blood. He stared at it in horror, the reality of what he'd done catching up with him in a powerful thrust.

On numb legs, he turned back to Ian, the ground still shaking beneath his feet. He didn't know what he was doing as he knelt beside his friend. He barely registered the presence of the others. Tears were streaming from his eyes as he placed the heart on Ian's chest, wishing he could give him more. Wishing he'd been here sooner.

Wishing a thousand words he could never say.

"I know him," said Emerson in a soft voice. "I remember." The mist had lifted from her memories—Owen could see it in the pain reflected in her glassy eyes.

"We're all here, Ian," Maddy said quietly, tears dripping from her chin. "The Foxtail Five, all back together."

Owen dropped his forehead to Ian's shoulder, pain stabbing through him. The world was falling apart but he didn't care. He didn't want Ian to be alone.

"Owen," Emerson said. "Owen, look!"

Owen didn't pull back until she shook his arm, and when he did, he didn't know what to make of the sight before him.

A tendril of Ian's scarred skin had crossed over the heart on Ian's chest to bind it in place. As he watched, the skin pulled tighter, dragging the heart into the depth of the wound Izanami had made.

"It's beating," Maddy said, then flinched as a crash came from the broken door behind them. The horde was breaking through, or maybe the palace was finally collapsing, Owen didn't know.

The heart glowed and thumped faster as more thin ropes of muscle inched over the stone to bind it down. Ian's ribs began to crack as the heart was swallowed into his chest.

"What's happening?" Owen asked, looking to Dax, but Dax didn't know. The knife was still open in his hand, painted with his own black blood.

Ian's arm twitched.

"Ian?" Owen grabbed his hand, squeezing it tightly. Maddy reached for his throat to find his pulse.

"He's breathing," she said.

"We have to get out of here," Emerson said. "We have to go!"

She pointed to the far wall, where what remained of the passage flames was rapidly shrinking.

Confidence surged through Owen. "Get up," he ordered, his voice raw. "Hurry! Get up!" The flames were now down to the size of the tunnel mouth they'd once crept through.

Emerson rose in a shot, Maddy behind her. Owen reached for Ian, not bothering to be gentle as Dax helped hoist his massive, shuddering body up and carry him behind the stone slab toward the fire. At the flames, Emerson hesitated.

"Go with her," Dax told Maddy. "I'm right behind you."

Maddy met his gaze, then stepped closer and kissed him. "I'll see you soon."

"Not soon enough," Dax told her with a smile.

Hand in hand, Emerson and Maddy stepped through the fire off the ledge of the room. The air rippled, like a pebble dropped in a pond. Then Emerson and Maddy were gone, and the night beyond was still again.

"It worked," Owen said. He looked over the edge, but there was nothing but the base of the mountain below them.

"Come on, Ian," Owen said, bracing against Ian's weight while Dax supported his other side. The gate of fire was closing, a tight fit with Ian's size. They would have to squeeze through sideways.

Even with Dax's newfound strength, Owen's legs threatened to buckle under his friend's weight. A thought flashed through his mind of what others would think when they saw Ian like that, but he pushed it away. They had to get home, then they could worry about that.

"Owen," Dax said. There was something wrong with him. A tightness around the corners of his mouth that filled Owen with unease. The gate was shrinking, their time running short.

"What is it?" Owen asked.

Dax met his gaze over Ian's slumping head.

"Do me a favor?" he asked.

Owen nodded.

"Tell Maddy I'm sorry."

"Tell her yourself."

Dax nodded, but Owen could see the truth in the flex of his jaw.

"You're not coming back." He shook his head, even as he said the words. They were going back together. It didn't matter what Dax had done. He'd made up for it now.

The horde broke into the room, pressing toward them, but Dax didn't look. Sadness filled his eyes as he slid out from beneath Ian's red arm.

"He was right to choose you," Dax said, glancing to their friend. "And I was wrong when I said you weren't brave. I was wrong about a lot of things."

A vise closed around Owen's lungs. "Dax—"

"They're lucky to have you in their corner. I was lucky, too. Luckier than that damn knife ever made me, anyway." A small smile lifted the corner of his mouth. It broke something in Owen. He could feel soft things for Ian, for Maddy and Emerson, but not Dax. Dax had always been thick-skinned and untouchable. He annoyed Owen on good days, and made him furious on bad. His arrogance was a pillar, and their five-point tent was collapsing.

"Wait—"

"I'll never forget."

Owen stumbled as Dax pushed them through the gate. Green fire consumed his vision as he fell, tumbling through space with no sense of gravity. He tried desperately to cling to Ian's body, but in the end, he was pulled out of Owen's hands.

Then everything went dark.

IAN

It began with a whisper, the breeze speaking to the earth. It called to the smallest remains—a footprint, untouched for four years in a cave. A thread from a T-shirt saved by a mother in her nightstand drawer. A hair from a comb a father couldn't throw away. They drew together, pulled by magnets of memory. Echoes of laughter. A game of tag in the park. Holding hands in a dark tunnel.

His body was remade in the dark, the layers of scarred skin shed, the horns turned to ash. Under a canopy of stone, his skull was re-formed, his legs stretched straight. There was no pain until his nerves refired, then there was only pain—flames from the roots of his hair to his toes. It burned endlessly, then halted suddenly, and he gasped, his lungs brittle and untested. He wiggled his fingers. Bent his knees. Curled his spine.

Returned.

When he opened his eyes, Owen was there.

Owen helped him up, helped him walk out of the cave to the river. The cold water stung his skin as Owen washed him with a hundred apologies. He cleaned off the mud and the filth, the bits of leaves and twigs. Ian's head fell forward in exhaustion as Owen carefully dried him, and when he blinked, Maddy and Emerson were there with clothes and food. He couldn't eat. He only stared at the water, drifting in and out of consciousness, as Owen called his mom.

"Mrs. Spencer," Ian heard him say. "It's Owen. I'm at the river. I think you need to get down here. It's about Ian."

Ten minutes later, she arrived, still in her pajamas. Not even wearing shoes. Her face was older, her hair peppered with gray.

She moved slowly, the tentative gait of a scared animal. He didn't know why she was scared of him. He didn't like it.

"Mom," he whispered, his voice crackling.

"Ian?"

She touched his cheek. Ran her fingers over his long, ratty hair. Then she held him, and they both cried.

———•·•———

A month later, Ian stepped into The Bean Coffeehouse. It was his first time out since he'd come back, and his chest tingled with nerves as the bell rang over the door.

"Ian!" Emerson waved to him from a corner booth, and he hurried toward her, still unused to the fitted clothes that were popular now.

It had been a strange month. Since coming home, he'd stayed exclusively at his house. His confused parents had eventually settled on the conclusion that he'd been abducted and had finally escaped after four years. Dazed and disoriented, he'd called Owen for help, who'd messaged Maddy and Emerson on his way to the river. The police had come and asked everyone questions. The press had lain in wait outside his house for three weeks. His dad had brought a therapist in to talk to him about what he'd gone through, but Ian always gave the same answer. He didn't remember.

Which was true. Mostly.

He remembered being in the tunnel the first time with his friends. He remembered the walls quaking, and the urge to run. But after that, there were only flashes.

They were worse than nightmares.

Emerson jumped from her seat, wrapping her arms around him. They'd seen each other a few days ago, and his mom had let her call as much as she wanted. Owen and Maddy too.

When they'd told him what had happened, he hadn't believed it.

Awkwardly, he hugged her back, smiling a little as her short hair tickled his neck. He went still when Owen rose from the other side of the booth.

"Hey." Owen's eyes gleamed behind his new wire-rimmed glasses. They looked good on him.

Pretty much everything looked good on him.

He thought Owen might try to hug him too, so he opened his arms, but Owen went for a handshake. He tried to switch at the last minute, but so did Owen, and he ended up crushed against the other boy's chest, his arms pinned at his sides.

"Definitely not weird," said Emerson.

Owen heaved out a happy sigh.

Ian scratched the back of his neck and laughed.

They sat. Owen had already ordered three drinks for Ian, two which had way too much coffee, and a tea that tasted like Christmas smelled.

"So how are you?" Owen asked.

Ian gave a one-shouldered shrug. "Okay. A little overwhelmed." His therapist had told him to say that when he felt too many things at once. He tilted his head outside, to where his dad was sitting in his truck parked at the curb, pretending to read his phone. "My parents are pretty paranoid."

"I wonder why," Emerson said. "It isn't every day your kid comes back from the dead."

He winced.

Emerson did too.

"Are you . . . remembering anything?" Owen asked. Ian noticed he wasn't drinking the coffee in his mug, but tapping a wooden stirrer repeatedly against his knuckles.

He'd had a dream last night that he'd attacked Dax with his teeth and razor-sharp fingernails—but he didn't want to bring that up.

Dax was gone, they said. Stuck in the other place. *Meido.*

"Not really." He pulled at his hair. It was shorter than he was used to.

"Lucky you," Emerson said.

Was it? Based on how everyone was acting, he knew he should have been grateful to not remember, but he wished he had something more to draw from. It was like he'd gone to sleep and woken up twenty years older, not just four.

"You think your folks will let you come to my place this week-end?" Owen asked.

"Maybe." He was pretty sure not. He couldn't eat a sandwich without his parents hovering over him. "Where's Maddy? I thought she was coming."

Emerson scowled. "She's not answering my texts. Something must have come up."

Ian didn't miss the dip in her voice, or the way her smile seemed forced after that. He may not have had all the details of what had gone on in Meido, but he knew that whenever Dax was mentioned, Maddy went quiet.

"She'll be all right," Owen said, answering the concern spiking between all three of them.

After that Emerson launched into a description of the movie she was seeing Tuesday with her parents, and before a beat of silence could pass, Owen took over, talking about how he'd been replaced by an understudy in some play he'd been acting in. Ian smiled and drank the tea, but it curdled in his stomach. He couldn't imagine Owen on a stage, or Emerson not in school.

He'd been looking forward to this visit all week. Why was it so hard?

He stood suddenly, smoothing down his shirt. "Sorry. I . . . uh, forgot to wash my hands." He flashed his hands in front of him, realizing this excuse was as ridiculous as they obviously thought.

He didn't wait for them to counter him. He rushed toward the bathroom, his breathing harsh as he jerked open the door to the men's room and strode to the sink.

Alone, he gripped the porcelain edges, telling himself to get it together. Turning on the water, he splashed some on his face, counting his breaths backward from fifty the way he'd practiced in therapy. His heart was pounding unevenly, too hot in his chest, and he scratched at it, feeling the itch of a wound that would not heal.

The knock at the door made him jump, and on a gasp, the pain receded, sucked into a vacuum behind his ribs.

"Ian? You all right?"

Wiping his face on his sleeve, Ian stepped back from the sink. Owen stuck his head through the crack in the door, worry drawing a line between his brows.

"Yes," Ian said quickly. "I'll be out in a minute."

A beat passed, and the door closed softly. He rubbed his chest. How could he explain that his heartbeat sounded wrong in his ears? That it felt wrong in his body, like it wasn't his own.

Ian looked at the mirror, at his pale skin and damp brow. A face he barely recognized now. As he stared at his lake-blue eyes, a cold voice whispered in his head.

Finally.

Finally, we are home.

He took a steadying breath, then straightened, his lips curling into a vengeful smile.

He was exactly where he belonged, at last.

MADDY

Tricounty Wellness Center was in upstate New York, in a small town called Middlefield. The facility was tucked in the woods off a farm road, a yellow, two-story Victorian home with a greenhouse in the front and a red barn peeking out from the field behind the porch. The wooden stairs creaked as Maddy climbed them, welcoming her toward a worn gray sign on the door: HEALTHY HEARTS, PEACEFUL MINDS.

Turning the handle, Maddy made her way into a warm room, greeted by soft voices down the hall. A man in jeans and a tucked-in golf shirt was seated at a desk against the far wall, squinting at the screen of a laptop.

He looked up and smiled. "Can I help you?"

"Hi." She checked his name badge. "Raul. I called earlier about visiting my aunt."

The practiced lie slipped off her tongue.

"Ah," he said. "Maddy, right?"

He turned the laptop toward her, opening a check-in screen. "Vera will be glad to see you. She doesn't get many visitors."

She clicked her way through the forms, then flashed her ID.

"I wish I could come more often. It's hard to get away, with school."

Raul led her down a hall lined with artwork, past a dining room where a dozen people sat around a table, engaged in what looked to be group therapy. They all glanced over as Maddy and Raul passed. She looked down quickly, hiding her face. Her thumb rubbed gently over the scar on the inside of her right wrist.

By now her parents would have figured out she wasn't at an away meet for swim team. From there, it was just a matter of time before they realized she hadn't returned to the swim team at all, or that the family vacation she'd emailed the school about from her mother's account was just an excuse for a road trip.

She felt sorry for lying to them, but if they were disappointed with her, that was their choice. There were bigger terrors out there than her mom and dad's anger.

At the end of a hallway, they turned into a wide, sunlit room with an unlit fireplace. A few residents dressed in street clothes played board games on a coffee table between two couches—checkers and Connect 4. A TV over the mantle was on; a man was sacked out on a blue velvet armchair in front of it.

Raul and Maddy stopped in front of the window, where a woman with dark hair sat in a chair, staring out toward the barn behind the house. Leaning against the wall beside her was an acoustic guitar.

"Here she is," said Raul. "Ms. Vera, you have a visitor!"

His enthusiasm slid off the woman like she was coated in Teflon.

"Maybe she'll play a song for you," Raul said, winking at Maddy. "She's very good."

Maddy looked at the woman near the guitar, her throat tying in knots. She knew this person. She'd seen her in the arena in Meido, tengu overhead, stuck in a wall of thorns while her body decomposed. No wonder she was watching Dax kill the tengu. She was his mother.

How had that happened? How had she been here and there at the same time?

Raul's smile dipped. "Some days are better than others."

After a moment, he patted Vera's shoulder and turned to go.

"Hi, Vera," Maddy said, her stomach twisting as she remembered the teeth falling from Vera's mouth as she'd eaten the fear card.

Maddy pulled up a chair, but the woman didn't even seem to notice her. Her lips were moving slowly, and when Maddy leaned forward, she heard the whispered words she repeated again and again.

"My fault, my fault, my fault."

Tentatively, Maddy reached for her hands, fisted in her lap.

She'd been envisioning this moment for a week. Since the day she'd found the article about the fire that had burned down an apartment complex in Cincinnati, a block from Ian's house.

The survivor, a Colorado native, claimed her ten-year-old son had been attacked by his father, an evil ghost who'd wanted to take him to hell. In the struggle, a candle had been knocked over. The mother had been charged with criminal neglect and third-degree murder, but deemed not competent to stand trial by the state.

She'd been sent to a long-term care facility in upstate New York called Tricounty Wellness Center.

The boy had died of smoke inhalation.

His identification had been sealed due to his age, but a visit to the county clerk's office and a few greased palms had revealed his name.

Dax Perkins.

"I know where your son is," Maddy whispered.

The woman stopped mumbling. Her back straightened. When she turned, there was a clarity in her eyes that hadn't been there before.

"I'm going to find him," Maddy said. "And I'm going to bring him back."

FROM THE AUTHOR

I have always been fascinated by tales of the underworld from any culture, but the tale of Yomi no kuni (hell) and the trials of Japanese Buddhist Meido (a purgatory of sorts) always spoke to me. While sometimes horrifying, I always conceptualized these tales as an adventure story. A hero's quest. Someone needs to get from point A to point B without getting their eyes pecked out by giant birds, or eaten by a river full of snakes, or failing an ancient lie detector test, all the while getting chased by demons. It's the ultimate obstacle course, a challenge with little likelihood of success. If you make it to the end, you've earned the right to pass through the torii.

For those who are well versed in Japanese mythology, I hope you accept my tale as just that—an interpretation, pulling themes from the Japanese Buddhist underworld, Meido, and the Shinto creation story, where the first great lovers, Izanami and Izanagi, were separated by death. Izanami's Yomi no kuni, the dark land where Izanami decomposed after being killed giving birth to fire (where Izanagi later locked her for all eternity), is very different from Meido. There, souls must go through various trials, where they must cross dangerous bridges, meet judges like Keneō, and run from tengu toward the torii that lead to hell, heaven, or a chance at reincarnation.

Maybe because I am mixed myself, it gave me great joy to combine these two places, these different worlds from the same place, and to add some of my favorite legends—an oni, the tengu, Shinigami (a grim reaper who escorts the dead to the afterlife), and Kuchisake-onna (just Kuchisake in my story), who cruises around asking children if they think she's beautiful, only to reveal that her mouth is slit from ear to ear. Aka Manto is, to me, the creepiest of the Japanese ghosts, a spirit who asks the fateful question, "Red or blue," aka, "How would you like to die?" (red being bloody, blue being oxygen-less). Calling Aka Manto in a closed, dark bathroom is something I still, even as an adult, absolutely refuse to do.

So there it is. Welcome to my blended underworld. Enjoy yourself, but don't stay too long, or you might forget why you came.

Kristen

ACKNOWLEDGMENTS

I am so grateful for the people who made this scary story come to life. As always, to my agent, Joanna, for her support and unwavering belief in me. To my editor, Ali, who has been so thoughtful and enthusiastic as we've worked through revisions—honestly, this book is yours as much as it is mine, Ali, and I'm so glad you love it. To Saraciea, my publicist, and Isa, Andrew, Valeria, and Dianna, who have worked so hard in-house to help this book reach readers. I'm thankful for everyone at Tor Teen who has been there for me from one story to the next.

Thank you to the bookly friends I have made—the media specialists and teachers who share their passion every day in schools and libraries, the booksellers who read and recommend my books, the readers who message me with !!! and ??? and HOW COULD YOU??? (your tears feed my muse, please keep it up), the Bookstagram army, and the community of writers who always strive to make our books better and more meaningful.

Thank you to my very thorough and incredibly wise sensitivity readers.

Thank you to Matthew Meyer for his love of ghosts, Japanese folklore, and all things spooky. Matthew—thank you for walking me through Meido and for your amazing illustrations. I've spent a lot of time on yokai.com for inspiration!

Thank you to Dr. Noriko Fujioka-Ito for proofing my Japanese.

Thank you to A. R. Capetta for helping me figure out how to put this story back together once I'd torn it apart. Somewhere there's a bathroom ghost just for you, my friend! (It's really sweet, don't worry.)

Thank you to my friends—writer, mom, and Jazzercise—who

have been there for me through dropped plot threads, stressed parenting moments, and just one more set of push-ups (I swear, Pat!). Katie, who is always on call when I need her. My Scone Camp friends—Cory, August, and Jess, you are SO POWERFUL. Lish and Chelsea—our Zooms kept me going this year. I am surrounded by the best people. I hope you know how special you are to me.

And finally, my family. Mom and Dad, thank you for giving me the stories of my foundation. Steve and Elizabeth, and Lisa and Lindsay, thank you for all your love and support. Deanna, I don't know what I'd do without you. Lindsay E., I love you, sister.

To my husband, Jason, a special thanks, for always terrifying me with scary stories and your love of horror movies (but also just for being my favorite person ever).

And for Ren. Being a mom is scarier than anything I could write. But it's also the best, and I wouldn't trade it for this world or any other.